Never Had
a
Dream Come True

by

Jennifer Wenn

The Royal Family, Book Two

Never Had a Dream Come True

Cover Art by *Tamra Westberry*

The Wild Rose Press, Inc.
PO Box 708
Adams Basin, NY 14410-0708
Visit us at www.thewildrosepress.com

Publishing History
First English Tea Rose Edition, 2014
Print ISBN 978-1-62830-175-5
Digital ISBN 978-1-62830-176-2

The Royal Family, Book Two
Published in the United States of America

Rake walked slowly to her side and pulled out the book she had just placed on the shelf. "Promise me you won't go to Gretna Green with Thomas or any other man."

"You can't ask me to promise you that. I don't know what lies in my future, and such a promise is impossible to make."

"Then promise me you won't go to Gretna Green without telling me, so I have a chance to stop you."

She laughed outright. He was hilariously outrageous sometimes, this Lord Richard Darling.

"You want me to tell you if I'm about to elope, so you can stop me?"

"Yes. I want you to promise to inform me beforehand, so I have a chance to interfere."

"If I ever do elope, my reputation would be destroyed immediately, and the only thing to save me then would be a marriage. Do you really think I would then want you to interfere and make sure a marriage never takes place?"

"I might marry you myself, to save you."

She laughed again. "Then I promise to never elope to Gretna Green, if only to save you from a fate worse than death—marriage."

Rake chuckled as he ambled toward the door. "With the right woman, marriage would not be a complete waste."

Praise for Jennifer Wenn

"This was a fantastic book! The plot, the characters, the love, loss, pain, and just everything about life that we know is out there is blended into the pages almost seamlessly as though they were born there. I have no idea what more I can say about this book? Why are you still sitting here! Go and get it, you will not be disappointed!"

~Valkyrie Fatality, Rockin' & Reviewing (5 Stars)

"I enjoyed the characters and their interactions. Fanny's family is fantastic and it was fun to see how a family of all men deals with the only girl in the family line. I loved the basic plot...a fantastic novel, and I would definitely re-read it."

~Victoria Lane, The Romance Reviews

~*~

NEVER HAD A DREAM COME TRUE
is a sequel to
A FAMILY AFFAIR,
also available from The Wild Rose Press, Inc.
Both are included in **The Royal Family** series.

Dedication

Molly, Max, Wilmer and Emma ~
You are my dream come true

Chapter One

August 1813

"Having a nice swim, are we?"

Lady Penelope de Vere closed her eyes in horror as she heard the too-familiar voice.

Unfortunately, surprise made her forget her current floating position in the lake at Chester Park. As she stiffened in response, she sank like a stone.

Sputtering, she reappeared from the lukewarm water, silently hoping her imagination was playing tricks on her. *Please, dear Lord, don't let Rake be there when I open my eyes,* she prayed, but in vain.

Lord Richard Darling leaned, relaxed, against the trunk of a willow by the shore. With his arms crossed over his broad chest and his normal amused grin in place, he looked just as handsome and rakish as ever.

She had never felt more mortified, but, too proud to let him know, she only bowed her head slightly in greeting while ignoring the water that ran from her hair across the corner of her eye.

"My lord."

"My lady."

His amusement was even more apparent as he returned the somewhat misplaced greeting with a highly arched eyebrow. His grin deepened, letting her know without words how hilarious he found her.

"I hope all's well with you?"

She murmured a polite answer, not able to come up with something witty and intelligent. All she wanted was for him to go away and leave her alone, but to her chagrin it seemed he had no such intention.

"And how are your parents?"

So, he was going to have some fun as she was in this awkward position? She straightened her back, as much as the water treading allowed her, and gave him the small polite smile she saved for persons she couldn't wait to get rid of. "They are fine, thank you."

"And your sister fares well?"

"Yes, thank you. Charmaine and our parents are still in London but will be returning soon."

"It must be hard being the youngest and having to stay behind while your family is off to London for the Season."

"Not really." She shrugged, and just managed to save herself from ending up under the surface again. "I would have been much more miserable caught all alone in our townhouse than I am here in the countryside, enjoying life under the guardianship of your parents."

Unconsciously he glanced toward the magnificent castle hovering above them with all its towers and pinnacles. His eyes lost their usual arrogance for a short second and the love he felt for his home and his parents was evident.

Penny caught herself from sighing in awe. He was such a handsome man. His dark brown hair framed his strong face lovingly. He was tall and broad shouldered, opposite of the gracious and slender wisp that was the height of fashion these days.

Not that his unfashionable looks made him any less

popular among the opposite sex. He was a devoted libertine, infamous for his affairs with more women than anyone could count.

But strangely enough that didn't matter in the eyes of the loving mothers of society. Even though he was the seventh and youngest son of the Duke of Berkeley and not once had hinted that he wanted to change his lecherous lifestyle, he still was one of the most eligible bachelors of society.

"I cannot thank your parents enough for inviting me to stay here with them and Francesca. They have made sure I had the most wonderful time."

He nodded absentmindedly, still gazing at the castle. "They are the best."

Love filled her heart as she thought about his parents. They were indeed the best; she would never disagree with him about that.

Her own parents were not the most affectionate, and she had more than once wished they would grant her just a little of the love the duke and duchess showered upon their loved ones.

It was saddening to think Rake's parents offered her more love than her own did.

Lord and Lady Nester had not been able to hide their relief when the duchess asked if Penny could stay with them at Chester Park during the Season.

To them it was the perfect solution.

They didn't want their underaged daughter with them in London needing to be entertained somehow when all they wanted was to show off their gem, the beautiful Charmaine, and thrive in her popularity as the incomparable queen of the *ton*.

"We were told you all were going to arrive

tomorrow." Penny changed the subject shyly, and he woke from his thoughts.

"Ah yes." His usual arrogant face was firmly in place again. "It was the plan, but then I had some friends who were passing here, and so I took the chance of getting here earlier. I haven't seen my parents for a couple of months now, and selfishly I wanted them to myself for a few hours. As soon as all my brothers return, there is hardly any chance for a private talk, you know."

"Your parents will love having you all to themselves, if only for a mere day."

"Well, not *all* to themselves, I presume." He grinned. "You, Fanny, and Charles are also crowding Chester Park."

She looked up at the enormous castle that contained hundreds of rooms and shook her head mentally. "Crowding?"

When she met his smoky grey eyes again, they were laughing at her, and she blushed, mortified over her own stupidity and that she offered it to him so easily for his teasing.

"We'll try to keep ourselves out of your way," she murmured, and couldn't stop a small shiver.

The water felt much colder under the willow than out in the sun, even though it was August and summer still ruled. She glanced longingly at the blanket which she had left in the sunlit grass. The mere thought of covering herself with its dry warmth made her shiver even more.

If only Rake hadn't been there.

She knew she looked a mess, with her hair wet and tangled and her chemise completely soaked. It shouldn't bother her, as this was only Rake, her best friend's uncle, whom she had known for her whole life, but it did. And all because her silly heart had decided many years ago that it was madly in love with him, and she knew by experience there was nothing she could do about it.

She took a deep breath and squared her shoulders for strength. This was not the time to let her awkwardness toward him get her sick. She swam closer to the shore until her feet touched the sandy bottom, and before she could change her mind she started to make her way out of the water.

Not until she had passed the muddy part of the shore and regained her balance and posture did she look up at him. To her surprise he had lost his mirth and instead was frowning at her, as if something bothered him immensely.

"Do you mind?" she asked, with a gesture toward her blanket at his feet, but he only blinked at her, as if his thoughts were miles away.

"I would like to change my clothes without an audience," she advised, and finally she caught his attention. He lifted his head and met her eyes, and this time it was she who unwillingly frowned.

Something was different.

She had never seen him look at her like this. His eyes were all dark and smoldering, and something warm started to build up inside her in response.

"I don't mind at all." A lazy grin grew upon his handsome face. "Please don't let my humble person stop you from getting warm and dry."

She frowned at him again, not wanting to change into her dress in front of him. The mere thought of him watching her squirm out of the wet chemise while hiding behind the blanket made her groan.

"Was that an agreement?"

She decided wisely enough to ignore him, and instead she crossed her arms over her chest, bracing herself against his constant teasing. "Could you please just go away, so I can change my clothes in private?"

"No."

"No?"

He took a step closer to her, forcing her to bend her head backwards to be able to look into his eyes. "No," he breathed, and something in his voice made her heart skip a beat.

She had never met this Rake before.

Being his niece's best friend since she was a little girl had made her as interesting to him as a piece of furniture. If he hadn't any use for her, like fetching him his book or getting him a scone, he mostly ignored her.

She, on the other hand, had stayed as close to him as she possibly could, just in case he would talk to her. Fetching a book was a small price to pay if the man of your dreams noticed your existence for two whole seconds.

But even then he had never looked at her like he did now. It was like *she* was the scone he wanted to eat.

The cold damp chemise made her shiver, and again his eyes darted downwards. "Bloody hell," he muttered, and her frown deepened.

What on earth was making him groan like this? She followed his gaze and gasped as she realized the source of his interest. The damp cloth didn't hide anything. Her breasts were just as visible as if she had been standing naked in front of him.

She immediately lifted her arms higher, concealing her bosom from his eyes.

"That's too bad." He grimaced disappointed.

"Take your eyes off my person," she ordered, outraged, and when he looked up into her eyes the raw need in his dark gaze made her blush intensely.

"Why?" he asked, with a pout worthy of a small child.

"Why?" she gasped again.

"I must admit I like it when you gasp."

"W-what?" she stuttered, not knowing how to handle this strange Rake.

He gave her a slow smile which made her forget to breathe. "Your gasps make you even more enchanting, as your cheeks turn such a pretty pink out of embarrassment."

She did not know what to say. Or more importantly, she did not know what to think. Was she dreaming? Had Rake, the secret love of her life, just called her enchanting?

Her treacherous heart rejoiced, but this was not the time to celebrate. With a whimper, she reached down, scooped up the blanket from the ground, and held it in front of her.

"G-go away from here." She was too embarrassed to care about how impolitely she addressed him. All she wanted was for him to disappear and let her collect the scattered pieces of herself again.

"Can't say I want to," he drawled softly. He lifted his hand and let a finger lightly trace the edge of the blanket covering her chest.

"Oh, my God."

His smoldering gaze burnt her as he leaned even

closer to her, until his lips almost touched her ear.

"You may call me Rake," he whispered softly.

His teasing woke her up from her stupor. With another gasp she stumbled backwards until she had put enough distance between the two of them.

"Coward," he whispered softly, and she glared at him in a desperate attempt to intimidate him, but it only gained her another slow smile and a beckoning with his finger asking her to come closer again.

"No, thank you," she said icily. "I would prefer for you to remove yourself from this area now. Please."

"Are you sure?" he grinned, and she nodded most haughtily.

"Yes I am."

"I don't mind you changing your clothes in front of me, as I have already seen your entire beautiful person."

She blushed again but didn't answer his rakish teasing; instead she nodded toward the lake.

"It seems you have missed that Fanny is in the lake, too. As you can see, she is closing in on us, and as she is dressed just as I am…"

She didn't finish the sentence, but he got her meaning anyway, and he visibly blanched at the thought of seeing his niece practically naked. His eyes darted to the lake, where Francesca swam with her usual strong strokes toward them.

"Tell Fanny I'll be waiting for her in the library so she can tell me how much she has missed me."

He gave the very efficient blanket a disappointed look before he turned and walked toward the castle.

Before she could stop herself, she called out after him, "Coward."

He stopped mid stride and looked back toward her over his shoulder with one of his perfect black eyebrows arched.

She offered him her best look of feigned innocence which obviously didn't fool him for a second.

"So, you are trying to play my game?" It wasn't hard to see he was quite amused. She could tell by the way his left eyebrow arched even more upwards.

He took a step back toward her, and she gasped, horrified. She gave a quick glance at Francesca, who now had reached the shore, and he hesitated.

He obviously didn't want to see his niece with as little clothing as Penny, and with one last lingering look toward her, which she ignored blushingly, he continued on his way toward the castle.

"Was that Rake?"

Francesca's voice, filled with joy, cut through Penny's thoughts, and she gave her friend a nod and a reassuring smile. Her friend squealed with delight and hastened to dry herself. After diving into her dress, she rushed off toward the castle, where her uncle had promised to await her.

With shivering fingers Penny put her own dress back on, ignoring the still damp chemise. Slowly she walked toward Chester Park, her head filled with irrational thoughts, none of which made any sense.

Her deep sigh echoed as she walked through the portal leading into the grand courtyard. For as long as she could remember, she had lived for the day Rake would finally see her as the woman she had become. Every night she had dreamt about how he would come to her vowing to die if she didn't give in and make him the luckiest man ever by marrying him.

And today he *had* seen her. He had told her exactly how attractive he found her.

And all she wanted to do was cry.

Why did he do this to her? Why?

His timing couldn't be worse, as she finally had decided she couldn't waste her life and happiness on a dream that would never come true. Francesca had nagged her about this for years, and in the end Penny had to give in. She too realized Rake would never be hers. At least not as she wanted him—desperately in love with her.

And that was the sole reason why yesterday she had accepted Thomas Bedford's wish to court her.

She sighed, defeated.

For the first time in months she longed for her family. If they only could come home, so she could leave Chester Park. Leave Rake.

She desperately needed to escape and save her poor heart from being shredded by him. He was, after all, a well-known scoundrel and a devoted libertine. But more importantly, she knew he had never been able to resist a challenge, and stupidly she had presented him with one by calling him a coward.

He was the man of her dreams and the sole possessor of her heart. If he gently demanded her, how would she ever be able to resist him?

Chapter Two

Lady Francesca Darling slept soundly in her bed, even though it was five o'clock and too late for an afternoon nap. She didn't stir when Penny pulled the heavy curtains from the large windows to let the warm August sun in.

For a moment Penny stood still, watching her friend. Francesca slept safely, without noticing she had an intruder in her bedroom.

Such trust amazed her.

But then, if you were surrounded by a large family who adored you beyond reason, there was not much to worry about, she thought with a tender smile.

She climbed into the bed and stretched out beside her friend, nudging her now and then to wake her up. But Francesca wasn't so easy to wake up when she took a nap, and in the end Penny had no choice. She pinched Francesca. Hard.

With a loud groan, Francesca woke up and put a hand on the pinched part of her arm. She winced before opening her eyes to face her gruesome attacker.

"You!" she said with contempt. "I should have known it. No one but the evil and heartless Lady Penelope de Vere would wake up a sleeping beauty by almost wrenching her arm off."

Penny laughed and ignored her friend's obvious desire to falling asleep again. Instead she grabbed one of the pillows and hit Francesca in the face with it.

"Ouch," her friend muttered from beneath the pillow before she stretched like a cat, yawning until her jaws creaked.

This wasn't the first time Penny had the doubtful pleasure of waking her friend, as Francesca had a thing for sleeping. If she could find time to spend in her bed, she would use it.

"It's a beautiful afternoon out there, and here you lie in your bed, wasting it completely."

Francesca muttered something inaudible, apparently not as fascinated with the beauty of the day as her best friend was.

"What time is it?" she mumbled, before putting the pillow back over her head.

"Almost five," Penny enlightened her cheerfully, happily ignoring the outraged gasp from her friend somewhere under the pillow.

"Five?"

"Yes, five."

Francesca growled at Penny, who again ignored her friend's irritation. She snatched the second pillow away too, and put it with the other in a neat pile at the floor. Then she covered them with the thick bedspread, stolen without mercy from her friend.

When Francesca's maid Nell joined them a bit later, her mistress was already dressed and enduring Penny's rather harsh tugs through her hair. "What are you doing, Miss Penelope?" Nell rescued the brush from Penny's incapable hands. "You know you are to stay away from Miss Francesca's hair!"

"I just wanted to help."

Nell's frown intensified. "I told you to let Miss

Francesca's hair be, didn't I? Last time you handled that brush, you succeeded in tangling her hair so much it took me a whole afternoon to undo your handiwork."

Francesca, now more awake, ignored her irritated maid and looked at her friend in the mirror with a concerned frown of her own. "Why are you waking me up this early, by the way? Has something happened?"

Penny shook her head, her lovely violet eyes filled with laughter. "Just because I dragged you out of bed before seven doesn't mean something bad has happened. Maybe I just wanted your company."

"Is this about Uncle Rake?" Francesca asked, giving a resigned sigh and rolling her eyes at her maid via the mirror.

"No." Penny sat down on the bed and tried to look as though nothing could be farther from the truth. But her friend knew her too well.

"Of course it's about Uncle Rake." Francesca sighed again. Defeated. "It always is."

"I have a suitor." Penny felt a desperate need to change the subject. For the first time, she did not want to talk about Rake. And especially not about what he had said that morning.

She had spent the afternoon in her bedroom, pondering how to tell Francesca about the encounter. But in the end she had decided not to tell her at all. She wasn't really sure what actually had happened between her and Rake.

All she knew was that he finally had seen her. The mere thought of how he had looked upon her made her blush again.

"Do you now?"

Francesca's obvious disinterest was quite telling.

Penny hid a smile. Her guess was that her friend was a bit tired of hearing about Rake.

"Yes, I do."

"And how on earth did he propose this time?"

Penny didn't care about her friend's indifference. She was too used to it, after all, since she had been in love with Rake for so many years and had told Francesca all about it repeatedly.

"There was no proposal of marriage."

Francesca mumbled something inaudible as she reached for a scone from the tray Nell had so kindly brought with her.

"Yesterday, with your grandparents' blessing, I accepted Thomas Bedford's wish to court me."

"That's nice."

Penny shook her head, smiling. Francesca wasn't listening to her at all, and for the tiniest moment Penny thought about not enlightening her friend.

But as Thomas now was quite a large part of her immediate future, she wanted Francesca to know more, preferably before dinner, when Penny would have to face Rake again.

"Thomas Bedford."

Penny's announcement broke through Francesca's scone-eating indifference. "Who?"

"The man I agreed could court me."

"What?"

"I see I have your attention now."

Penny grasped her skirt nervously, twisting the delicate fabric while ignoring Nell's pointed looks.

"What *are* you talking about?" Francesca's voice was high-pitched with surprise. "What have you done?"

"I have told a very decent man I will accept his

courtship of me, and your grandparents have given us their approval."

Francesca looked ready to burst with madness. Her eyes glanced around as if not knowing what to focus on and she stood up and sat down again repeatedly. Nell, more sensitive to situations than her harsh looks would indicate, silently left the room and closed the door behind her.

Several minutes went by before Francesca regained her wits enough to hold herself still. "What *are* you talking about? When did this happen? And Thomas Bedford? Boring Saint Thomas?"

Penny knew better than to try to answer Francesca before she had thought it all through. Her friend had never been a good listener until she had her own thoughts named and categorized correctly.

Francesca threw her hands out in despair. "How could you do this to me? How could you do this to yourself? Next year we are off to London for our debutante Season. We have looked forward to it for ages, and you plan to get married before that? How can you do this to us?"

"I'm not marrying him, and I still plan to go to London next year. I've only told him that he can officially court me. Your grandparents made it most clear to him that there would be no talk of engagement or marriage before I have done my first Season."

Francesca's eyes narrowed as she gave Penny a look that made it quite clear she did not believe a word of what her friend was telling her. "As if my grandparents would agree to this! They would never."

"But they did."

Francesca was looking a bit unsure. "B-but how

long have they known about this? How long have *you* known about this?" She sat down beside Penny and grabbed her hands. "Why didn't you tell me?"

Penny could sense the hurt behind the last question and wished she had a good answer. "It just happened. The day before yesterday, during the assembly down at The Devil's Folly, we sat next to each other and started to talk. He's such a nice man and so easy to chat with. He loves books too, and we had the most interesting discussion about the latest one he had read. You know how insecure I get around other people, and especially men. But with him…"

Penny stood up again and started to walk to and fro. "It was like talking to you. Although you with a brain."

"But why didn't I notice? And why didn't you tell me?" Francesca ignored Penny's gentle insult and instead looked like a sad, neglected little puppy.

"Well, you had so much fun with your beaux that night, and when we sat in the carriage on our way home you had so much to tell me about, that I rather forgot to mention him. And then yesterday he came to visit when you were out riding, to leave me a list of his favorite books, as he'd promised me the evening before."

"But how could it ever move from a list to an almost-proposal?"

Penny laughed. "Your grandparents invited him to stay for tea, and after a while he just blurted out his question. The duke immediately said no, of course."

"Of course he did." Francesca rolled her eyes again, knowing all too well how protective her grandfather was.

"But the duchess thought it was a very good idea

indeed. She said she could see that Mr. Bedford and I had much in common and would make a very good match. Then the three of them turned toward me, wanting to know if I accepted his courtship."

"Lord, it sounds so dull."

Francesca was obviously starting to accept what she was being told, despite her groaning and eye-rolling.

"My first thought was to decline, as my heart does belong to Rake. But then I started to think about what you have told me all along—he will never marry me. Why should I throw my chances away, just because I never will be able to have the man of my dreams? And as I met Mr. Bedford's kind, intelligent eyes, I knew in my heart that I could be happy and satisfied with him. I could have a good life with him. It wasn't as if I promised him anything by accepting, and I have every right to tell him no, in the end, if he ever does propose to me. But why shouldn't I get to know him better?"

"What did he say when you agreed?"

"Not much. He thanked me graciously and asked if he could come and visit me tomorrow."

"How passionate," Francesca snorted, and Penny put her hand on her friend's.

"I don't want someone sweeping me off my feet passionately. Not any more. I want love. I want to be cherished and needed. And most of all I want to be wanted. Don't you think I'm worth some happiness in my life?"

"Of course I do." Francesca sighed. "But it feel so strange to hear this, when all you have been talking about until now has been Uncle Rake this and Uncle Rake that. You as well as I know that he equals passion."

"But why spend the rest of my life yearning for passion, when I can bathe in a sea of love? I have thought about this a lot lately, and I want a home and children of my own. My heart cries with joy upon the thought of Rake being the husband and father, but I have finally come to the same conclusion you did a long time ago—my own happiness is more important than sharing my life with him."

Francesca gave her an odd look. "I hate to admit this, but hearing you repeat my words so clearly makes me realize how wrong I've been. Now they don't make much sense to me at all. You are seventeen years old, for goodness' sake. You are on the verge of adulthood. Why throw away Uncle Rake before your time in the sun even begins?"

"Fanny, I'm not throwing Rake away." Penny laughed, and Francesca too had to giggle over her own choice of words. They fell backwards upon the bed and all the tension disappeared as they laughed almost hysterically.

When they finally calmed down, they stayed on the bed, side by side, as they had done so many times before. A comfortable silence ruled as they lay there, content with each other's company.

Penny took a deep breath as she stared up at the painted stars in the ceiling. She had lived seventeen long quiet years, in which nothing special or out of the ordinary ever had happened. But now, during two short days, her whole future had changed.

She closed her eyes, and immediately the beloved image of Rake popped up in her mind's eye.

But this time it was different.

This time it wasn't her imagined version of him looking upon her with soft eyes, shining with love. No, this time it was the memory of his hot smoldering gaze from earlier in the day.

She couldn't stop a shiver of delight—and, oddly enough, fright—from going through her body.

What would happen now?

What would Rake do?

He was as unpredictable as a thunderstorm. You could never tell what he would say or how he would react.

Would he let her be?

No, not the Rake she knew. The infamous libertine would never let this be. She had seen him lust for other women, and she had recognized the gleam in his eyes when he looked upon her.

He wanted *her*.

Another shiver ran through her body, and this time Francesca noticed and turned on her side to face Penny.

"What is it? You look terrified."

Penny gave her frowning friend a wobbly smile that didn't seem to calm her as it was meant to.

"It scares me, growing up and becoming an adult. My life has been so easy up until now, a cozy mixture of books, lazy days, and you. But now, from out of nowhere, I am supposed to make decisions that will not only affect the rest of my life but also the lives of everyone surrounding me. What if I make a bad choice? What if I will come to regret the path in life I take and end up like my mother—defeated, bitter, and unhappy?"

Francesca sat up in bed and gave her friend a hard stare. "You will never turn into your mother, and do you know why? Because I will never let you marry an indifferent man like your father, not without a fight. So maybe Boring Saint Thomas isn't the most dashing of men, but you are right—he is perfect for you. Everything I find dull with him fits you, even though I hate to admit it. He is..." She hesitated slightly, searching for the right words. "He is somewhat handsome and does have the kindest heart of all the men in the county. Just like you, he likes to read and would probably not mind you walking around daydreaming, as you tend to do. As a matter of fact, he'll probably walk beside you, with his head stuck in the clouds too."

"Now you make *me* sound dull." Penny giggled, but Francesca didn't smile back. Instead, she sat up and forced Penny to do the same by grabbing her hands.

"Promise me you will never settle for someone, just to get married, without talking to me first."

"Fanny…"

"Promise me!"

Francesca's eyes filled with tears, and Penny felt a lump fill her throat as she nodded in response. "I promise I will never marry anyone without your consent," she whispered hoarsely, and then she groaned as Francesca gave her a hug worthy of a bear.

"Well then, that's settled." Her friend beamed, all evidence of her tears dried away, and Penny smiled lovingly. Francesca was just as unpredictable as her uncle but the best friend one ever could have.

"Why don't we go down to dinner so you can stare dreamingly at Uncle Rake now, as he has returned from London?"

"Fanny!"

"Oh, come on. Just because you almost have promised your hand to another man doesn't mean you can't still enjoy the gorgeousness of the man of your dreams."

Penny sighed, shaking her head as she followed her outspoken friend out the door. Where would this evening end?

Chapter Three

Dinner at Chester Park was quite a loud affair even though most of the Darling family were still in London. Penny had known them her whole life, but it still amazed her how much noise they could make.

Her own family endured their meals together in silence. The ladies tended to rush from the table with relief as soon as her father had read his paper and his daily letters.

But not this family.

No, they could sit for hours, eating and arguing about something which would engage every last family member.

Penny had more than once sat at the table listening to them discuss things like how to prune a rose, or which road was the bumpiest between London and Oxford. There was nothing that couldn't end up as a discussion topic when it came to the Darlings, and they all thrived in the chaos they called dinner.

During the social Season, the list of attending family members was short, but tomorrow the others would return from London and every chair at the huge table would be filled. This evening only six chairs were occupied.

Hannibal Darling, the Duke of Berkeley, was a large man with bushy white hair and a booming voice. He loved his seven sons and their offspring more than anything and was constantly making sure they were aware of it—to their frustration, as he tended to be a bit too interfering. But as they all loved him most sincerely in return, none of them had the heart to tell him to stay out of their affairs.

Hannibal rarely left Chester Park, as he loathed the social life of the *ton* in London. Instead, he and his second wife, Anna, stayed behind and took care of the family's country estate while the rest of the crowd socialized with their friends.

The duchess was more than twenty years younger than her husband and had met him when she and some friends were visiting the duke's oldest son, George—Francesca's father—one summer long ago. She was a happy, content woman who loved her husband and all their sons dearly. Lady Anna, as Penny affectionately called her, had never made any difference between Hannibal's three sons from his first marriage and their own four. She was always there with a soft hug whenever it was needed.

Francesca's good-hearted Uncle Charles was the parish vicar, an easygoing man with a heart as large as Berkshire. He had more than once saved the two adventurous young ladies from disasters and the disgrace of having to admit their folly to their parents.

For Penny, these four persons—including Francesca—were more her family than her own blood relatives ever would be.

Her own father had never cared about her. Lord Nester was too awed by his older child, the beautiful Charmaine, to be able to see the one just a year younger.

Not that Penny minded much.

Jeremiah de Vere wasn't a better father even to Charmaine, who had more than once hinted she much more would have preferred him being indifferent toward her too.

Lady Nester loved her younger daughter dearly but was too much under her husband's thumb to have the nerve—or the strength—to show Penny more love than a sorrowful smile now and then.

And Charmaine was Charmaine—beautiful, spoiled, and completely self-absorbed.

Penny knew her sister loved her and would never, ever, betray a secret. However, she seldom had time to listen to her younger sister's thoughts, as she was almost always surrounded by their parents or in the company of her maid.

Penny rarely complained. With a freedom few others of her standing had, she spent her solitude with her books and her daydreams.

The only thing her father liked about her was her closeness to the Darling family. As he was a man who collected social contacts like others collected butterflies, he urged her to spend as much time with Francesca as she possibly could so he could brag about the tight bond between the families.

And then there was Rake.

With an amused grin he sat in the sixth occupied chair at the dinner table, telling his family all about his months in London.

He wasn't the most beautiful of men, Penny had to admit, but his charisma was breathtaking, and wherever he walked he left crushed hearts behind him. Women had a tendency to fall head over heels for him, and not one of them realized—until it was too late—that his heart wasn't in the flirtation.

The duchess had once told her youngest son that he was a snake who mesmerized his poor victims before he ate them. Rake had only laughed and shrugged the criticism off, but Penny knew his mother had told the truth.

He was a snake.

And this time she was the mouse he wanted to mesmerize. Every time she looked his way she met his smoldering gaze, and it took all the strength she could muster to force her eyes off him at once. Otherwise she knew she wouldn't be able to stop herself from jumping over the dining room table and into his waiting arms.

He was staring so heatedly at her that even his mother noticed, and the duchess's probing gaze had moved from Rake to Penny and then back to Rake again many times during the meal.

Francesca—bless her heart—was as insensitive as ever and chatted away with her uncle without noticing the underlying currents that passed over the table.

"But what did Lord Alvanley say when he noticed that his favorite cane was missing?"

"Oh, he whined about it until your cousin Drake organized a search throughout our hosts' home, much to their chagrin."

"Did he find it?"

Rake grinned devilishly. "Of course he did. It was exactly where Drake put it in the first place. And the hosts were devastated at how the stolen painting just happened be hanging on the wall where the cane was."

Francesca clapped her hands with excitement and Penny smiled over her friend's obvious pleasure at her uncle's amusing tales.

The duke snorted. "I can't believe what has happened to our class nowadays. Nobility used to mean pride and honor, but today's noblemen and women don't care anymore. They steal and lie and don't give a bloody bit about anything but the façade."

"The world isn't just black or white. You can't put everyone in the same room. This lord and his lady did the unthinkable—they stole from their friends—but it doesn't mean everyone else of our acquaintance does the same. I know for certain our family doesn't."

The duke gave his wife a look which would have made grown men weep, but the duchess only gave her husband a sweet smile and raised her glass in a quiet salute. She knew better than to put more wood on her husband's fire.

The duke could be a bit stubborn when he was upset over something, and they had all learnt the hard way it was better to keep quiet than to continue with an argument they never could win.

"So, Richard, did you meet anyone special this Season?" The duchess gave her son another sweet smile as he groaned over the question.

"Mother, really, isn't it about time to give up about me getting married and just let me be? For years you have been nagging me about finding the right one, and I can't help but wonder when you will realize I haven't the slightest wish to marry."

"Dearest, you are but twenty-seven years of age. There is no way I'll put you on the shelf and let you *be*, as you so nicely put it. I'm your mother, and it is my duty to try to make you as happy as you possibly can become."

Rake snorted, clearly not believing his ears. "And

you think marriage is the perfect solution to make me happy? Please!"

"I think the perfect woman can."

"There are too many perfect women out there for me to settle with only one."

This time it was the duchess's turn to snort. "But one is all you need, as long as she is your perfect match."

"There is no such thing as a perfect match or a perfect woman. I know what I'm talking about, as I have been socializing with too many other men's perfect matches and perfect women."

"Richard!"

"Yes, Mother?"

The duchess threw her hands out in despair, a quite common thing for her to do when it came to her youngest son. "Oh, I give up. If you don't want to be happy, fine. I can't force you into anything against your will. All I ask you to do is to keep your mind and your heart open, because one day the right girl will appear in front of you, and I would hate to see you miss out on your own eternal happiness."

"I'll keep my eyes open," Rake drawled, sending Penny another hot gaze—which she unfortunately didn't miss, as she had been staring dreamily at him during his discussion with his mother.

Of course his look reminded her of their encounter of the morning and exactly what he had seen. She blushed, and his soft chuckle told her he noticed her discomfort.

"What do you say, Charles?" Rake nodded toward his brother. "You are not married. Are you happy? Or are you slowly dissolving in a pool of loneliness?"

"Richard!"

Rake ignored his mother's outraged gasp and instead gave his brother an amused grin that was returned in full.

"Between the people of our church and our heathen family, there is not much time for me to be lonely. So my answer is no, I'm not dissolving at all. Sorry."

The last word was directed toward the duchess, who sank back into her chair and rolled her eyes.

"Don't think you have defeated me, my son. I love you too much to consider giving in to your wish and letting you be. I have my mission, and I'm stubbornly refusing to give it up."

"Heathen family, you say?" The duke glared at his son. "Is this something you usually say when you are amongst others, or is it just with your family you're using that word?"

Charles gave his father a smile, one as wicked as any of Rake's, and the duke shook his head. "This family will be my death," he boomed to his wife before he left the fivesome at the table without another word.

"So, Lady Penelope," Rake purred. "How has it been for you, living under the roof of this heathen family?"

"We are not that heathen," Francesca laughed, unknowingly saving Penny from having to answer Rake's teasing. "I must admit we are not as civilized as most other families out there, but at least we try to behave in public."

"We do?"

"Richard!"

"Mother, you do say that a lot." Rake stood and went to his mother to give her a peck on her forehead.

"But I forgive you. You are, after all, my mother, as you tend to point out every time we meet."

The duchess rose and patted her son lovingly on the cheek before she ushered Penny and Francesca before her out of the dining room, leaving the men to follow the duke to the library and their glass of port. In the duchess's salon, a tray with tea awaited them, and they sank down into the comfortable chairs, sipping on the warm liquor.

Penny sat silent as the duchess and Francesca discussed the upcoming annual August Festival at Chester Park. Teary-eyed, she took in every feature of the two, savoring the picture of them forever in her heart. She would miss them immensely when she returned to Harveyfield the next day.

She would of course see them again, as she had the habit to walk over to Chester Park every day, but it wouldn't be the same. She wouldn't be a part of the household and a part of the family.

Next year she and Francesca would go to London and join the *ton* for their debutante Season. Gone were the innocent childhood days. They would be adults and expected to behave as such, and maybe they both would be engaged or even married by this time next year.

Life as she knew it was over.

Francesca didn't see it quite the same way. She longed for her debutante Season and could hardly wait to join the social swirl she had heard so much about. She was the granddaughter of a well-respected duke and an heiress beyond imagination and would be welcomed with open arms.

For Penny it was different. She was daughter to a penniless earl and younger sister to the outstanding

Charmaine. Conversing with strangers had never been her strength, as she was terribly shy and awkward amongst people she didn't know. She would, as always, end up in a corner of the assembly room, daydreaming, until her parents told her it was time to go home.

The duchess interrupted her sorrowful thoughts. "Are you looking forward to Mr. Bedford's visit tomorrow?"

"I think I am."

Francesca snorted. "You think you are? Either you are or you are not. No one would blame you if you wanted to back out of this courtship now. After all, it is Boring Saint Thomas we're talking about."

"Fanny! That's rude."

"We have known this man our whole lives. We know everything there is to know about him, and you should know, Grandmother, there is not so much to know. He is boring. He reads."

"Francesca Darling, you are not boring because you read. Penny reads, and you don't find her boring, do you?"

"Yes I do, but then, I'm not going to marry her." Francesca gave her friend a wink, and Penny had to bite her lip to not laugh. She couldn't help feeling a bit sorry for the duchess, who was surrounded by a family that loved to tease her to pieces.

"Mr. Thomas Bedford is a good man from a good family. He has eight thousand pounds a year and is the owner of a well-kept home. Any woman who marries him will have a good life with him."

"Good is so boring," Francesca moaned, and this time Penny couldn't hold back her laughter as the duchess gasped, outraged.

"Ah, you two!" The duchess finally chuckled as she caught her granddaughter's game. "You will be the death of me, too, you will, and not only of my dear husband."

She leaned forward and put her hand against Penny's cheek, and the love in her smile was endless.

"Never forget we too are your family. If there is anything you need help with—small or large—don't hesitate to ask for our help."

Penny felt tears run down her cheeks as she nodded and gave the older woman a warm, desperate hug. The duchess opened up one arm for her granddaughter and Francesca too joined the hug. For once her usual mirth was gone, and instead she planted teary-eyed kisses on both her grandmother's and Penny's cheeks.

"Can I join too?"

Rake's amused voice broke through the ladies' sentimental little moment, and they ended the tender closeness with small wobbly smiles.

"Ah, cucumber sandwiches," Charles breathed as he threw himself over the plate, stuffing his mouth full with a couple of the delicious triangles.

The duke gave his third son a disgruntled look as he sat down beside his wife and put his arm around her. Penny had always found the casual way the duke showed his wife his love most endearing, and it was something she wished for herself in the future.

Before, it had always been Rake she had pictured next to her, but this time she tried to put Thomas Bedford in his place. To her surprise, she had no trouble at all replacing the man of her dreams with her suitor. It told her more than anything that she was more than ready to let Rake go.

31

If she could sit here in the same room as Rake and daydream about Thomas Bedford, she had to be walking down the right path in accepting the courtship.

Maybe this was what she had needed all along. Was a kind and goodhearted suitor all it took for her to be able to close her heart to Rake?

She desperately hoped so. She needed him out of her heart so she could have a life of her own. But what if their earlier encounter meant that he was ready to love her? To marry her?

She looked at him, where he leaned casually in the doorway, and she knew nothing had changed. He was still the same. The only difference was that the libertine in him had discovered her. He wouldn't start to love her because of it. He had known her for ages, and if it were love he felt for her, it would have shown itself in many ways already.

Before she had a chance to look away, his eyes met hers and he gave her a lazy grin that made her heart leap with excitement. Slowly he walked over to the sofa where she sat and, without another word, settled beside her. She scooted as close to the arm of the sofa as she could, but unfortunately he caught her game.

With a soft chuckle meant only for her ears he moved slightly, until she was caught between the sofa and the warmth of his body. Nobody seemed to notice how closely they sat together, and when Charles sat down on the other side of Rake Penny knew no one would think anything of it. But she did.

Strange emotions flared through her body and she didn't know what to do. Having him so close to her made her feel warm and breathless, almost exhausted. She had never felt anything like this before, but she guessed this was what Francesca had talked about. Passion.

"Penny dearest, you look a bit flushed, are you sure you are all right?"

The duchess's eyes were filled with concern, and Penny leaped at the chance of escape.

"No, Lady Anna, as a matter of fact I do feel quite worn out. If it is all right with you, I will retire to my room for the night."

"Of course, my dear. You go and have your rest. It's a big day for you tomorrow."

With a grateful smile to her hostess, Penny quickly moved away from Rake and, after giving her hosts a small curtsy, practically flew out the door. She stopped in the hallway for a second, feeling faint and lightheaded.

This was a side of adult life she had never encountered before, and that it was Rake who had woken up the woman inside her scared her immensely, especially considering how easily she had responded to him.

Was this how all women felt when he preyed on them? No wonder they let everything go for a blessed moment in his arms. If the rest of his family hadn't been there, she wouldn't have been able to leave him.

Mesmerized by the snake.

She took a deep breath as her heart started to beat more slowly, and then she made her way through the grand hallway and up the magnificent staircase.

Not once did it occur to her that he would grab this opportunity of solitude and follow her to her bedroom, eager to continue the teasing seduction of her innocent heart.

Chapter Four

"Sneaking away again, are we?"

Penny closed her eyes and grabbed the handle of her bedroom door hard, trying to find some strength.

Bloody Mary.

She opened her eyes again and looked over her shoulder at Rake, who slowly strolled toward her with a wicked grin.

Bloody Mary and Elizabeth.

"I'm not sneaking anywhere. I was simply making my way to my bedroom for a little solitude."

"Why?"

With a last lingering step, he stopped in front of her, so close she could feel his hot breath against her face. He leaned his head to the side as he sent her one of his smoldering gazes.

"B-because I need m-my sleep."

"Do you really?"

She swallowed and nodded.

Again he gave her one of his lazy grins, and this time he leaned even closer to her, until their lips almost touched. Unwillingly she took a step back and bumped into her bedroom door. The grin he gave her as he moved after her could have melted an iceberg.

"W-won't your parents m-miss you?" she stuttered nervously, and he shook his head slowly, not taking his eyes from hers.

"No. They think I had a very private errand to do and won't miss me for quite some time. As for now, I'm all yours."

"Please go away."

"Why should I?" He leaned forward and, as his firm lips touched the crook of her neck, she forgot to breathe. Strange sensations washed through her body, leaving her numb and unable to move. Her knees went weak, and if he hadn't been pressing his body against hers, she would have fallen most disgracefully to the floor.

He put his hands on her shoulders and let them slowly run down her arms until he reached her hands. In one swift movement he lifted her arms and put them around his neck.

Her fingers locked automatically, holding on to him, as his hands this time travelled downwards to end up cuddling her buttocks.

How could he turn her into this puddle of nothing? She had no strength and depended entirely upon him to hold her upright.

His lips moved from her neck up to her ear and she felt him nibble lightly with his strong white teeth.

"Goodness me," she breathed, and he chuckled in response, a hoarse guttural chuckle which made him sound as affected as she.

"Open it," he urged her with a whisper as he gave her cheek a soft kiss, slowly moving closer to her mouth. "Open the bloody door."

Her eyes flew open as her mind started to work again. Open her door? He thought he was going to follow her into her bedroom to…?

All the feelings she had felt under his capable

hands died, and without forewarning she let go of his neck and pressed her hands between them, pushing him hard in the chest and forcing him to stumble backwards.

"Are you out of your mind?" she hissed as he looked back at her with surprise written all over his handsome face. "Have you completely lost your dignity?"

"Penny…"

"Fondling me, your parents' guest, in your own home? What are you thinking?"

He took a step forward again but stopped as she put out a hand. "Don't."

"Why not?"

She scoffed at him, too upset over his outrageously selfish behavior. "I'm a family friend you have known for ages. What on earth has possessed you to behave like this?"

Something flickered through his eyes, and if she hadn't known for a fact that he had no conscience, she would have recognized it as embarrassment. But this was Lord Richard Darling, the most infamous libertine of his time. Why would he be embarrassed over fondling a young woman?

She gave him a last lingering look as she opened her door and put all the contempt she could muster into it. "Could you have been more disrespectful against your parents? I'm under their guardianship, and yet you still harass me. This is too much, even for you."

"Even for me." His voice sounded hollow as he echoed her words, and for a moment she hesitated. She wasn't usually this crude toward others, and although he had handled her in a most disrespectful manner she couldn't help feeling she had overreacted a bit.

But as she opened her mouth to apologize, he gave her a small nod and turned to walk stiffly down the hall, disappearing into the shadows.

She stared into the darkness, not knowing what to do or what to think. Had she behaved wrongly?

No, she hadn't—he had. But why did she feel this exhausted and uncomfortable?

Giving a small sigh, she walked into her bedroom and locked the door tightly behind her, even though she knew without a doubt he wouldn't follow her.

Not again. Not after what she had said.

As she moved around her bedroom packing her few belongings, she replayed the encounter in the hallway over and over again in her head.

What had he thought of her harsh words?

If it had been any other man, she would have been certain of his devastation. But not Rake. He was the kind of man who laughed in the face of rejections, who shrugged insults off without being affected at all.

She sighed again as she threw the last of her dresses into the bag. She was too tired to think about this. As a matter of fact she didn't want to think about it at all.

Tomorrow Thomas Bedford was going to visit her at her parents' house, and right now it was all she wanted to think about. She couldn't stop a small smile of contentment as she thought of her suitor. He was a good man; the duchess was right about that. She knew exactly what to expect from him, and it felt strangely good and uplifting to do so.

Rake, the selfish snake, was as unreadable as a stone. He never gave away his emotions.

But Thomas did.

When he looked into her eyes, his lovely brown eyes were warm and caring. When she talked about a book she had read, he looked at her with genuine interest and asked her questions and invited her to share her insight.

Rake made her shiver, but Thomas made her bloom.

She spent the night tossing and turning in her bed, and as the dawn broke through she gave up the thought of getting some sleep. Instead, she quickly penned a note to her hosts, thanking them for their hospitality, and then one to Francesca, enlightening her about her whereabouts, before she quietly left Chester Park behind her.

The winding road which connected the castle with Harveyfield was breathtakingly beautiful in the early morning hours. A lazy fog had spread its dew on everything it passed: flowers, trees, and bushes. Now the landscape glistened in the sun.

The beauty of nature eased her mind, and when she walked through the small iron gate that led to Harveyfield she felt serene and at ease. Inside, the servants scurried around, desperately cleaning any speck of dust they could find before Lord and Lady Nester arrived.

When Penny walked into her own modest bedroom, she was surprised at the contentment she felt, seeing all her things. It wasn't that she didn't feel at home at Chester Park, but this was *her* room. Every little thing in this room belonged to her and told a spectator all about who she was.

Books lay on every flat space, and small paintings she had made hung everywhere on the walls. The flowers she had collected and dried lay on the tray where she had put them the last time she was here, and she could still smell their delicate scent.

The servants hadn't cared for her room these months she had been away. She could tell by the cloud of dust that rose from her bed when she sat down on it.

Coughing, she opened a window, and to her surprise the family carriage had just stopped in front of the house, and her parents tumbled out from it, followed by her yawning sister. Penny ran down the stairs to greet them.

"Penny, dear child, you are home." Lady Nester opened her arms and Penny walked into her soft, warm embrace. Her mother put a hand against her cheek and looked upon her with tired eyes. "How are you, my dear? How has your time at Chester Park been?"

"Very good, indeed. The duke and the duchess made sure I had a wonderful stay while you were away."

"I do hope you have behaved and not caused me any embarrassment." Lord Nester peeked at her over the pile of letters he was scanning through.

"I have a suitor." Penny squealed to her mother, ignoring her father's remark.

"Oh, so we heard!" Lady Nester clapped her hands together in sheer delight. "Come, my dear, you must tell me everything about it. I was so pleased when I received the duchess's letter saying Mr. Bedford wanted to court you."

"Couldn't even get a proper proposal out of him, could you?" her father snorted as he followed them into the salon and sat down in his newly dusted chair. "Your sister would have secured one already, if this had been her suitor."

Charmaine sat down beside Penny on the sofa and ignored their father's usual rudeness. "I think it is good that he didn't propose to you. Now you two have all the time in the world to get to know each other, to make sure it will be the right choice."

"Charmaine would have had a proposal already," Lord Nester repeated stubbornly, not caring about how he walked all over his younger daughter's feelings.

"No I would not have," Charmaine replied icily to their father. "Thomas Bedford has never been interested in me, and that is one reason why I like him even better for Penny."

The last part came with a wink toward her sister, and Penny knew what she meant. All the men Charmaine met stumbled all over their feet to get closer to her, and many of them stuttered out a proposal of marriage even before being properly introduced.

Charmaine loathed them for it.

Not one of them cared about her. They only wanted her divine beauty at their arm, to show off. But the few who took a good look at her and then dismissed her, those she liked immensely. Rake had been one, and now Penny was told Thomas was another.

It pleased her more than she could say.

Her father, on the other hand, wasn't as pleased. "What? Has Thomas Bedford never proposed to you? We have known him all his life, and he should have asked for your hand at least a couple of times by now."

"But he hasn't, which is good for Penny, isn't it?"

Lord Nester didn't care about answering his daughter's question. Instead, he stood up and pulled the cord to ring for a servant. "I want you"—he pointed at

Charmaine—"to go immediately and get changed into your very best day dress. I'll be damned if I can't get a proposal out of the man before dinner."

"Papa!"

The outrageousness of Lord Nester's words was unbelievable, even for the three ladies who were used to his rudeness.

"What?" His frown deepened at the threesome staring at him with disbelief.

"Jeremiah, don't you think it is Penny who should change into something more suitable, as it is she whom Mr. Bedford is coming to visit? Charmaine is not the one he is interested in."

Lord Nester threw out his hands in despair over such ignorance from his wife. "But he should be. Penny is nothing next to her sister. Nothing. If there is going to be a proposal today, it shall be Mr. Bedford asking for Charmaine's hand, not Penny's."

"But he is Penny's suitor. Why should Charmaine try to take her own sister's suitor away from her? The thought is ridiculous."

Lord Nester gave his wife a look which made his wife pale. Without another word she sat down again, just as the door opened and a maid popped her head inside.

"Yes?"

"Nothing." Lord Nester waved the maid away before sitting down in his chair and returning to his pile of letters.

Penny didn't know whether to laugh or cry.

This was her own father dismissing her as a possible wife and wanting his other daughter to seduce her suitor away from her. He had done and said many stupid things over the years, but this was a winner in every category.

It hurt that he cared so little for her, but she wasn't surprised. A long time ago she had given up on his ever feeling any warmth toward her.

Charmaine gave Penny's hand a squeeze, and her smile was a mixture of embarrassment and compassion. Penny smiled back and rolled her eyes so Charmaine would know she didn't take it too hard. Her sister took a deep breath before regaining her composure, looking just as bored and uncaring as ever.

"The duchess wrote that he was coming for a visit this afternoon." Lady Nester gave her daughters a sorrowful smile. "It will be so nice to meet your young man, Penny. I'm sorry we don't have time to get you some new dresses, now that you are officially being courted, but we will take care of it as soon as possible. You will have to have new dresses anyway, as you are about to make your debut next Season."

"Penny will not get any new dresses." Lord Nester's tone held as little warmth as his words. "Especially not if she has already caught a man who is interested in taking her off my hands. That would be money thrown into the Thames. No, our small funds will again go to new dresses for Charmaine. She is the incomparable queen of the *ton*, and as such she must be correctly clad."

"Lord Nester!"

Again the threesome stared at him, and again he didn't care about their feelings.

"Penny will not get any new dresses, and that is my final word."

"But Father, I don't need any more dresses."

Charmaine tried to rescue the situation. "We should better spend that money on Penny, who never has had any dresses made up just for her. It is not fair to have her wear my old dresses for her debutante Season."

"The decision is mine to make, and this is final."

Lady Nester gave her youngest daughter an apologetic shrug, and Penny swallowed the lump in her throat.

"It's all right, Mother. Charmaine's dresses will do just fine. We are not the same height, but with a few small changes they will fit me just perfectly."

"But they are not your colors…"

"If it looks good on Charmaine, it will do for Penny. All these decisions wear me out. I'm going to my study, where I can be alone."

And without another word Lord Nester left the three ladies and pursued his hunt for solitude.

Charmaine stood up as soon as the door closed behind his back and turned toward Lady Nester.

"Really, Mother? You won't do anything about this? He's taking everything from Penny and handing it to me, and I don't even want it. I refuse! Next year is Penny's debutante Season, and she is the one who should be clad in clothes made especially for her. With her lovely violet eyes and honey-colored hair, she should wear much darker colors than I, with my blond hair and blue eyes."

Lady Nester shook her head sadly. "Dear child, you know there is nothing I can do about it. It is his decision, just as he said. I'm so sorry."

The last words were directed to Penny, who gave her mother a wobbly smile.

It didn't matter. Not really. Thomas Bedford liked

her as she was, clad in Charmaine's old clothes, and there was no one else she wanted to overwhelm by her sheer beauty.

A vision of Rake popped into her head, but she pushed it aside. Not anymore. Rake was done in her life. From now on he would be what he always had been to her, her best friend's uncle.

Charmaine sighed, defeated. She too knew that if Lord Nester's mind was set there was not much that could be done about it. With one last sad look toward Penny, she left the salon, and they could hear her running up the stairs to her room.

As always, Lady Nester immediately followed, as if Charmaine wouldn't last a minute without her mother by her side.

Alone in the salon, Penny looked down on her hands, and tears dropped into her palms. She should be used to this by now, but somehow her father always seemed to find a new way to make her feel unwanted and unloved.

All she'd ever wanted was to be just that, wanted. But neither her mother nor her father had ever given her that. No, they always chose Charmaine, and that hurt more than she would ever let anyone know.

The more she thought about it, the more Mr. Bedford became her savior. Maybe he was the one who was intended to end her loneliness and finally make her feel wanted.

Maybe he was her dream about to come true.

Chapter Five

The rest of the morning Penny spent alone in her room, listening to her parents fussing over Charmaine in the room next to hers. Not once did anyone come to her room to ask if she needed help or company.

When a maid knocked on her door and announced the arrival of Mr. Thomas Bedford, Penny had been ready for hours. Quietly she walked downstairs to find her beau in the salon with her parents and a magnificent-looking Charmaine.

Penny ignored her family and instead gave her suitor her most genuine smile when he stood to greet her, and the smile he returned told her he was as unaffected by Charmaine as ever.

To him it was Penny who mattered, and that thought was unbelievably soothing.

She heard her sister's relieved breath and knew Charmaine had been uncomfortable with the situation too. It was—as ever—the misdirected scheme of their father, who couldn't get over the fact that he had sired such an exquisite daughter.

"Lady Penelope, how nice to meet you again." Mr. Bedford took Penny's hands with warmth, and she was delighted with his direct behavior even though she could hear her father snicker. Mr. Bedford led her to the sofa where he had been sitting and politely made sure she sat comfortably before he joined her.

"Mr. Bedford has just told us about the new books he is adding to his library," Lady Nester said politely, and Penny squealed with delight.

"Oh, please do tell me."

Mr. Bedford, who quite obviously liked Penny's excitement, gave her a kind smile, and his lovely brown eyes warmed her like a nice cup of hot chocolate. "It's just a collection of journals about gardens that I want to visit next spring. There is nothing better than to read everything you can find about a place before you visit it."

"It sounds marvelous. I too have read about the most wonderful places, and I would love to go to some—or all—of them one day."

Mr. Bedford gave her a hopeful smile, full of promises. "Who knows, maybe one day we can go together?"

Penny blushed prettily. His forwardness was unusual but refreshing. It was nice to talk with someone who said what was on his mind.

She could feel more and more that this was the right path for her. Thomas Bedford was everything she needed. So what if he didn't make her shiver with delight? She much preferred the contentment she felt with him at her side.

"Is that a proposal?" Lord Nester interfered in the tender moment.

Mr. Bedford drew back slightly. "No, my lord, I have promised Her Grace that I won't be proposing to Lady Penelope until next year, after her first Season in London. And I am a man who keeps his promises."

Lord Nester sighed, defeated, recognizing the stubbornness in the younger man's voice. Penny was grateful he didn't persist; it had been too embarrassing for her that her father so obviously wanted to get rid of her as soon as possible. Or, rather, he wanted to get rid of the cost of her.

Penny was not money well spent, in her father's eyes.

To save the situation, Lady Nester dragged Mr. Bedford into gossiping about their neighbors, and Penny spent the time watching her maybe-future husband, taking in every little detail of him.

He was a tall and lean man, more slender than muscular, and yet there was a distinct air of strength surrounding him. His hair was light brown, almost golden, and his eyes brown and intelligent. He was a handsome and well-kept man even though his clothes were not of latest fashion.

The duke had told her Mr. Bedford was a man with a good yearly income, which he preferred to spend on his home and the people who helped him maintain it rather than spending it all on his own person. She liked the thought of a man who prioritized the people he was responsible for.

As the visit progressed, she noticed new things about him, like how he touched the side of his forehead when he thought hard on something, and how he sent her small smiles when he thought no one noticed.

Charmaine did—of course—and was mouthing *marry him or I will* every time she thought he didn't notice. He—of course—did notice but hid his amusement politely and didn't mention Charmaine's indiscreet behavior.

She liked the careful way he held the fragile tea cup in his large hands and how he politely nodded with interest when Lady Nester told him something or other that he must have found disgustingly tedious.

He was a man in full control of himself, and he didn't let the surroundings affect him. It was obvious he didn't care for her father—not many did—but he continued to be polite, even though her father now and then let his jovial façade slip and forgot to hide his insults.

But mostly she liked the kindness in his eyes when he looked upon her mother and the warmth in them when he looked upon her.

"Lady Penelope, I wonder if you would grant me the pleasure of your company down to Sandhurst tomorrow to look for books to expand my collection?"

"I would love to go with you," Penny breathed, and they both turned to look at Lord Nester, waiting for him to give his approval.

"Sure, sure," Lord Nester agreed, waving an uninterested hand. "Why not? The little thing needs to get outside now and then, I suppose. Not good to spend all one's time inside reading, you know."

"We should be in need of a chaperone."

Lord Nester looked at the younger man and sighed. "I'll send a maid with Penny. That will do."

Her father's obvious disinterest was quite embarrassing, but for once Penny didn't care. The happy smile Mr. Bedford sent her when her father agreed took away her dismay at the awkwardness of her family and left her giddy with excitement.

She was going book-hunting with Mr. Bedford tomorrow. For once, life was absolutely perfect.

As Mr. Bedford took his leave, she followed him to the front door, where he turned and looked down at her with a smile.

"I do look forward to tomorrow, Lady Penelope. It will be a real treat for me to share the excitement of finding a good book with you."

"Please," Penny breathed, and she could feel her cheeks turning red, "I would be honored if you would call me Penny."

The smile he bestowed on her was radiant with sheer happiness. "Then I must ask you to call me Thomas, in return. It would feel very good if you would oblige me."

"Then I will, Thomas."

As she met his warm eyes, her heart knew the warm sensation of a new love awakening.

He held out his arm, and with a sweet smile she put her hand neatly in the crook of it. Slowly they strolled through the front garden, which drowned in color from all sorts of flowers. At the gate in the low wall which surrounded Harveyfield, they bid adieu, and he climbed up into his carriage where it awaited him outside the wall.

Dreamingly she watched him drive down the road, admiring his straight back until he disappeared around a bend of the road. If she had previously thought she'd done the right thing by accepting his wish to court her, she now knew it was the right thing.

Thomas Bedford was everything she wanted in a man. Everything she needed. So what if she didn't feel the overwhelming shivery sensations that Rake always inspired. This was better.

Rake always made her want to feel more. But Thomas made her feel content. And if she had to choose right now, she much preferred being sated rather than yearning.

"So that's your suitor."

Surprised, as she hadn't heard him approaching, Penny looked up and met Rake's amused grey eyes. More handsome than ever, he sat in the driver's seat of a fashionable carriage, and immediately her silly heart skipped a beat. Thomas and all the cozy feelings he'd given her disappeared in the turmoil Rake created inside her.

"Yes, Mr. Bedford is my suitor."

"Boring Saint Thomas? Don't you think you could do better?"

"I don't need better. I need Thomas."

Rake chuckled, his eyes glistening wickedly at her. "So you admit there is better?"

"No, I don't," she gasped, and his eyes darkened until they once again nailed her down with their smoldering heat. The faint memory of his confession to how much he liked her gasps raced through her mind, and she blushed as she felt her body respond to the sultry promise in his eyes.

"Come. Ride with me."

Rake held out his hand, inviting her to go with him down a road of no regrets.

But she couldn't. Not anymore. A week ago she would have thrown everything away for him with a naïve wish that he would do the honorable thing in the end and marry her. But now she knew better.

Rake promised her heaven for a short time, but then she would live in hell for the rest of her life.

But she didn't yearn for a life in either heaven or hell anymore. She had found that for her it would be enough to have her own place on earth, a modest home and a family of her own.

And, most of all, she wanted Thomas.

"No."

He arched an eyebrow and slowly put his hand back in his lap. "Are you sure?"

"Yes. I don't want this. I don't want you."

He snorted, obviously not believing a word of what she said, and she couldn't blame him. She did have a tendency to react to him like all she wanted was to forget everything in his waiting arms.

But the memory of Thomas and their budding romance came back to her, and so did the wonderful feeling of contentment he brought up in her.

"Yes, you do." Rake gave her another one of those wicked smiles that sent her heart beating faster than she thought possible. But this time she didn't hesitate when she answered him, and she knew he could read the truth in her eyes.

"No, I don't. I want Thomas."

"Why not enjoy the company of both of us, at least for a while?"

The coldness of his words stunned her.

"I can't believe you just said that." Her voice echoed her broken heart. "Do you really think I would give myself to you and then marry Thomas without any remorse?"

"Penny, my love," Rake sighed with a tired grimace. "This constant assumption of yours that I am a cad is starting to get quite old. I *am* a gentleman, no matter what my mother dramatically declares, and I would never..."

To her own surprise she actually harrumphed. Like an old, patronizing matron she stared at him down her nose—as well as she could manage considering he was sitting in his carriage looking down at her—and cleared her throat loudly.

"A gentleman, you say?" she sneered and caught herself just as she was about to put her index finger up and wag it at him. "Would a gentleman tell me to disrespect the man I'm about to marry? Would a gentleman tell me he wants me, although he is well aware of me being more or less betrothed to another man? No, he wouldn't!"

"Then I guess I'm just a man who's looking at the woman he wants, begging her to want him back."

She looked into his dark, intense eyes and wanted nothing but to give in to him. For once he sounded sincere, as if he really meant what he was saying.

Then again, he didn't mention marriage. He only offered her himself for a short moment in time. But she wanted more. Bloody hell, she knew she deserved more.

With one last lingering look upon the face she had adored secretly for most of her life, she said the only thing she could think of.

"Goodbye, Rake."

She gave him a small curtsy, and before he had a chance to react she turned and ran inside her home. Breathlessly she hid behind the front door until she heard his carriage drive away, and not until she was sure he had left was she able to breathe normally again.

"What happened with Rake?" Charmaine came out into the foyer just as Penny was about to rush up to her room to dwell upon what had happened. "You two looked like you were having quite an intense conversation. Has anything happened between the two of you while I've been away?"

"It was so stupid," Penny admitted, not able to stop the telling heat which crept up on her cheeks. "Fanny and I were taking a swim in the lake when Rake happened to come by, and I was dressed in only my wet chemise."

"Oh!" Charmaine's blue eyes grew wider.

"Yes," Penny sighed. "He saw it all."

"Oh, my."

"I know. I was so embarrassed. But what was even more awkward was how easily he changed his attitude toward me from niece's-best-friend to woman-I-want."

"He did?" Charmaine clapped her hands with excitement. "This is indeed incredibly good news. This is what we have been talking about since you first fell in love with him. But what about Mr. Bedford? What is he in all this?"

"Thomas is the only suitor I will consider."

Charmaine stared at Penny in disbelief. "The only suitor you will consider? What about Rake? Isn't this what you have wanted for most of your life? Rake wanting you?"

"You know it is. He is the man of my dreams, but unfortunately he will stay that. You see, Rake may want me badly, but not as his wife. No, he wants me to become his mistress."

"Oh, my!"

Penny nodded. "Do you know what he just asked me outside? He told me to give myself to him before I marry Thomas."

"He said that?"

Penny blushed deepened. "No, not really. But I'm sure that it is what he meant."

Charmaine shook her head slowly. "I can't believe Rake would act like this. It's so selfish and rude, not at all like the person we have always known. He must want you very badly if he has thrown all caution away and haunts you even though you are almost a part of his family."

"Oh, he wants me badly. But not as his wife, and I'm afraid that's all I ever want to be. Thomas offers me my heart's deepest wish. His genuine kindness touches me in a way I never thought possible and makes me feel so full of hope about our future together."

"But he isn't Rake."

"No, but I don't want Rake. I want Thomas, the perfect, sensible choice."

"It sounds perfectly sensibly boring. Are you sure this is what you want? What if Rake suddenly changed his mind and asked you to marry him? Would you change your mind then?"

"No."

Charmaine gave her sister a very doubting look but didn't stress the matter. "It's sad, though. You and Rake make such a perfect couple, and it breaks my heart that your wonderful dream never will come true."

"A dream is just a dream. What I seek now is reality, and I think Thomas will be the perfect man to offer me what I want. And what's even more important—he will offer me what I desperately need."

"Love?"

"Serenity."

Charmaine snorted, showing without words exactly what she thought about such a naïve goal. "Serenity? That's too bland even for you. I too want a man who loves me and a relationship which will make me feel cherished and safe, but I won't throw myself away to the first available man who makes me feel at ease."

This time it was Penny who snorted disrespectfully. "Fanny said just the same thing. I'm not throwing myself away if I accept Thomas's proposal, *if* such ever will be offered me. You have to understand that I'm not you. I'm not the incomparable queen of society, who has more beaux than all the other unmarried ladies of the *ton* together. I don't have as many choices as you do."

"Who said I have many choices?"

Charmaine's voice was unusually small, and Penny frowned as she looked into her sister's vivid blue eyes. The endless sorrow she saw made her feel uneasy, and she couldn't help but wonder why a young girl who was supposed to have everything at her pretty feet seemed as pitiful as a bird caught in a cage.

It wasn't the first time Charmaine had let her ice-queen façade slip when they were alone, but this was the first time she had mentioned being unhappy.

"Charmaine…" Penny didn't know where to start. How did you ask the most perfect woman in the world what was wrong with her? "Is there something you want to share with me? You have seemed so distracted the last couple of years, and I can see there is something bothering you."

"There's nothing bothering me. I'm fine."

And there was the façade back firmly in place. But this time Penny wasn't going to give in so easily.

"There is nothing wrong with you at all?"

"No. I'm perfectly fine."

"Is that so?"

Charmaine's shiny smile was meant to stun with its

loveliness, but Penny was too used to her sister's beauty to be dazed.

"If you are so fine, why did you then decline Lord Dane's proposal?"

Charmaine paled, obviously not at all prepared for the intimate question, and it was clear to Penny she had found the sore spot.

Or at least one of them.

"Last year you were over your head in love with Lord Dane. He was all you ever talked about, and we all could see how much he fancied you, too. But out of nowhere you suddenly turned cold against him, and dismissed him most cruelly. What did he do?"

Charmaine twisted a handkerchief between her stressed fingers, forever destroying the delicate lace. "H-he didn't do anything. I-I just...I grew bored with him. That's all."

"I don't believe you. Lord Dane is anything but boring. He's one of the most handsome men I've met, and had such a lovely kind heart, and he liked you very much. Not your looks, but *you*. And yet you denied him—and yourself—eternal bliss when you denied him your hand."

"He wasn't for me." The sadness in Charmaine's eyes were heart-wrenching. "And furthermore, he showed us all just how much he loved me by marrying that Yorkshire heiress one month after he proposed to me. One month. That's how long his love lasted."

"But you were no heiress and yet he still wanted you. That had to stand for something. A man like Lord Dane would never..."

"There's no reason to talk about this anymore," Charmaine interrupted rudely. "What is done is done and can't be changed. Yes, I loved Lord Dane with all my heart, but I had no other choice in the end. I had to turn him down. It might have broken my heart, but at least yours is still able to find true love."

"What has me finding love to do with you not marrying Lord Dane?" Penny frowned at her sister. Charmaine was acting more and more confusing.

"Oh, nothing. Why should it?" Charmaine's laughter was forced and stiff. "Well, let's leave Lord Dane to his new wife, and let us continue with the more interesting discussion about you choosing between the righteous Mr. Bedford and the infamous Lord Richard Darling."

"I'm not choosing between them," Penny sighed, letting Charmaine's problem be for now. Her sister's unwillingness to talk about it was quite obvious, and this wasn't the moment to pressure her. "I told you, Rake is not an option for me anymore, not even in my dreams. I will instead spend as much time as possible with Thomas to get to know him as well as I possibly can until this time next year."

"Ah, there you are," Lady Nester breathed, relieved, as she joined them in the foyer. "Charmaine, I've been looking all over for you. Could you please come and help me choose what invitations we shall accept?"

With a disappointed sigh, Charmaine followed their mother back to the salon and left Penny staring unseeingly at the closed door, her thoughts whirling inside her head.

Something was bothering her sister, and it hurt that Charmaine wouldn't tell her what it was. No one could look so heartbroken over nothing.

And even more strange was the whole Lord Dane affair. Charmaine had not denied him of her own free will, of that Penny was certain. And the more she thought about it, she couldn't help but think their father was the sole reason why Charmaine still remained unmarried.

Lord Nester loved to brag about how many proposals his oldest daughter had received, and for the first time it dawned on Penny how strange it was that Charmaine could get asked to marry so many times and not even consider it once.

Why?

With one last sigh, Penny followed her mother and sister into the salon, even though her presence hadn't been requested. As always, pain pricked her heart when she thought about how insignificant she was to her parents, and she became even more determined to get away from this house. She needed to be wanted for her own sake. She desperately wanted someone to miss her enough to come searching for her.

It didn't matter that everyone found Thomas boring and uninteresting, not as long as she didn't. For what it was worth, she knew he would miss her.

And that was a good enough reason to consider him as her future husband.

Chapter Six

Sandhurst was showing its most beautiful side as their carriage slowly rocked down the bustling main street. Everywhere mongers called out to them, offering them good merchandise for the best price.

Children ran to and fro, laughing and playing among the strolling adults who peeked at what was offered to them. As it was harvest time, the market was filled to its brim with food, especially fruit and vegetables, each stall looking more inviting than the next.

Thomas halted the carriage outside the bookseller's shop and then helped Penny down to the street. He held out his arm with a warm smile and a lighthearted Penny put her gloved hand in the crook of it. Slowly they made their way through the colorful crowd and escaped into the dark and musty-smelling store.

"Can I help you?"

An old man behind a counter looked up at them as they entered, but when he saw it was Thomas he just waved with his hand toward the shelves farther inside the store. Thomas obviously was a known and well-liked face in this shop.

"Come, let me show you. Mr. Wells keeps all the best books in the back. He says I'm the only one who ever is interested in them, as everyone else prefers the much lighter reading material in the front. I come here a lot, and tend to spend many hours among these fascinating creations all alone, without anyone disturbing me. It is truly a shame that no one else realizes what treasure rests in this modest shop."

Penny turned to the maid who had accompanied her as chaperone and told her to go do the errands her mother had given her. It seemed they were going to spend quite some time in the bookshop, and she didn't want to waste the young maid's time. On light, grateful feet the maid disappeared out through the door, not overly upset at being dismissed.

"Look here," Thomas called out from farther in among the shelves, and Penny followed the sound of his voice until she found him hovering over an ancient-looking book. "This is one of the first books ever printed. Can you see how absolutely perfect it is? The men who did this must have been artists, as it is perfect in every detail."

Penny let her hand glide over the brittle page and she had to agree, the book was beautiful. "It must be worth a fortune."

"Unfortunately not," Thomas sighed. "In these modern times, people are not interested in books, and therefore books as valuable as this are not worth many shillings. But to me they are, and I collect every piece of perfection I can find, as I think they will become extremely valuable one day. A man has to think about his descendants, doesn't he?"

He gave Penny a sheepish grin, and she couldn't help but giggle. Thomas might say it was for the generations to come, but they both knew he bought them for his own sake only. The man loved his books, and she adored him for it.

"I think future generations will be thankful," she agreed with a wink, and he laughed heartily before returning his attention to the shelf of books. Slowly she strolled down the aisle between the shelves until she found the one where Mr. Wells kept the journals about travelling.

What wouldn't she give to be able to travel around the world to visit all these wonderful places she had read about in journals such as these? All her life she had not been farther away than Windsor, and even then she could still see the roof of Chester Park glistening in the sun. With a forlorn sigh, she headed back to where Thomas was searching through piles of unsorted books. Why bother with dreaming about travelling to distant places when she had no money of her own to spend on anything, not even a book.

"Look at this!"

Thomas looked like a young boy who'd just caught his first fish as he handed her a small leather-clad book.

"*Poetry from the Heart.*"

"Such a good book," Thomas breathed. "You really should buy it. I have two copies of it already, and I promise you it will be worth every penny spent."

"I'm sure it is. But I would prefer borrowing yours, when I visit your home."

Thomas froze and Penny blushed, mortified. Had she been too forward now? She must have spent too much time with the Darling family these last months, as she would never have been this direct otherwise.

"I would be honored if you were to visit my home." Thomas gave her his sunny little-boy-smile, which seemed to brighten the whole store. "As a matter of fact, why don't I scribble down an invitation for your family to come and dine with me later this week? I think that would be most suitable, don't you?"

Penny nodded, thankful that he was willing to overlook her brazen way of inviting herself. She wasn't used to socializing with anyone other than the Darlings, and for the first time she couldn't help but wonder how she would be accepted in London by the *ton*. She had a sinking feeling no one would notice her at all, except for comparing her to her sister and finding her uninteresting and ignorable in contrast. Her destiny was to become a wallflower, one of those debutantes who sat on the outskirts of a ballroom, forever watching society from the outside.

Accepted but not wanted.

Not an unusual place for her, she thought wryly.

Thomas interrupted her pitiful state of mind with another excited yelp, and she shook the doomsday feelings off her shoulders. There was no need to stand here feeling miserable over the unalterable. Much better to enjoy this moment of solitude with the man she hoped to marry.

Three hours later they walked out of the dusky shop and put a whole pile of newly bought books and journals into the carriage. The maid, who had been napping on the seat, awoke, and Penny urged her to follow them to the Devil's Folly—the local inn—where they were to have their afternoon tea.

When they entered the inn, Penny was surprised to find it crowded with cheerful gentlemen and ladies enjoying each other's company.

Thomas put his hand against the small of her back and guided her through the crowd until he found a small table in a corner where no one else seemed interested in hiding.

"Here we go." He sounded surprisingly relieved. Penny bit back a smile as she sat down on one of the chairs, carefully choosing the one which gave her the best view of the rest of the inn.

It was a bad habit of hers, wanting to watch other people. Or, considering her future wallflower life, maybe it was one of her best qualities. It was something to amuse herself with during the long hours of a ball. People tended to forget her presence, and she had more times than she could count overheard things which weren't meant for her delicate ears, or seen things she wasn't supposed to have seen.

During her younger years she had worked this quality into perfection when she realized how close she could come to Rake without him noticing. Her ears had turned rather red sometimes, but on the other hand she knew there wasn't much she didn't know about her childhood Prince Charming. Not even his parents had such deep insight into their youngest son's mind as she did.

"I always forget how crowded this place becomes as the social Season in London comes to its end."

She woke up from her past-dwelling thoughts and followed Thomas's gaze toward the socializing peers surrounding them. Fashionable gentlemen flirted discreetly—or not so discreetly—with elegant ladies who pretended to be offended but whose laughing eyes told a different story.

This was the life which awaited Penny in London, and she knew without doubt it wasn't for her. Some people—like Francesca—thrived in settings such as this.

But not Penny.

She needed solitude.

She needed space.

But most of all she didn't need to be thrown at a bunch of strangers, people she was supposed to know and therefore have spirited conversation with.

She, who couldn't even have a normal conversation with her own father without stuttering, was supposed to impress her family's acquaintance with her wit and her humor. Charmaine had mastered the art of talking about nothing with anybody.

But not Penny.

"It is quite strange that they still have this much to talk about, considering they have spent most of the last couple of months together," she mumbled with a forlorn smile, and Thomas gave her a curious look.

"How do you mean?"

"Oh." Penny blushed. She had not been aware of speaking her thoughts aloud. Embarrassed down to her toes, she couldn't help but wonder what he must think of her. She must seem the most dimwitted person alive.

But as she looked up into his face she could see only curiosity and kindness. There was not a trace of the usual frustration she met from her family when she spoke without thinking first.

"It just amazes me that some people thrive while interacting with others. If I had spent over three months in London with the same people, I would have searched at once for a quiet corner when arriving at my country home. Not seeking the first place to meet the same people again, chatting about the same things we have been talking about for months."

Thomas gave her a slow and unreadable smile

without responding to her unusual thoughts, and Penny felt her cheeks growing hotter. She was thoughtlessly talking this courtship to an end before it even started.

"I tend to be a bit partial to solitude, I'm afraid. I enjoy my own company too much sometimes."

Thomas laughed. "I'm so glad to hear this. I too find the social life a bore and much prefer to spend my precious time with my books."

"You do?" Penny lit up, and her earlier embarrassment started to fade.

"I admit I do. That's why I haven't been to London the last couple of years. It's a complete waste of time, in my opinion. You know, most men of my acquaintance think less of me because of my decision to stay put. 'Boring Saint Thomas' they call me, and don't understand how I can choose to spend my time alone in the country when I could use my time chasing as many skirts as possible…"

This time it was Thomas who blushed uncomfortably when it occurred to him how openly he had spoken. Penny couldn't help but feel sorry for him. He wouldn't know she spent most of her waking hours with the Darlings, who tended to talk much more colorfully than he just had done.

It wasn't easy to get to know someone new when etiquette ruled your every move, especially if you were an unmarried lady in search of a husband. You were supposed to hold back every spontaneous thought and hide your amusements as much as possible.

You never know if the perfect man or someone connected to him would happen to be watching, so you must always control your urges and behave as properly as you can. Her mother's words of wisdom echoed in

Penny's head and efficiently removed the amused smile from her face. Her first spontaneous reaction had been to tease him about his blunder, but the remembrance of her mother's words stopped her effectively.

She did find Thomas a most suitable prospect for husband. Maybe she should keep that in mind and behave as she had been brought up to do, instead of throwing every caution aside and behaving as she was used to with the Darlings.

"Oh, look!" Thomas interrupted her thoughts. "There's your family. Do you want me to call them over?"

Penny looked across the large room and found her parents and Charmaine in the midst of the cheerful crowd, greeting their friends.

Her father stood between his ladies, his wife at one arm, his daughter at the other. His booming laughter echoed throughout the room, sounding jovial and kindhearted, as he always appeared among others.

Lady Nester didn't look as happy. Penny could see the pain she tried to hide behind a gentle smile, but no one else seemed to notice, as all were concentrated on one thing—Charmaine.

Her sister looked like a diamond among rocks. Her beauty shone brighter than the sun at midsummer, made even more breathtaking by the little smile she bestowed on an admirer. Everyone surrounding her gawked with a mixture of admiration and envy. No one noticed the strange sorrow hiding deep behind the shiny exterior.

"No, please don't," Penny finally answered Thomas. "They are obviously having a wonderful time with their friends, and I think I would prefer a quiet cup of tea. If you don't mind?"

"No, of course not."

Thomas gave her one of his kind smiles, and with a wave of his hand he caught the attention of one of the serving wenches. Soon two steaming cups of tea were placed in front of them.

"I must admit I'm not used to being surrounded by family. I lost my father in a hunting accident fifteen years ago, and my mother died six years later after catching a cold she never recovered from. As I have no siblings, I have spent most of my time alone this last decade, living life in my own head."

"Haven't you felt lonely, having no one to share your life with?"

Thomas shrugged. "Not really. My house is filled with servants who have known me since I was a little boy, and even though I eat most of my meals in solitude, I tend to use the time to read a good book. My days are usually filled with managing my estate, which is far more time-consuming than for those who employ a supervisor, and most nights I go to bed early. I need my sleep too much to be able to rummage around the countryside, searching for any available party to join."

He was a man to admire, Penny thought, as she watched him butter a scone. His devotion to his estate and the people in his care reminded her much of Hannibal Darling, the Duke of Berkeley, a man she held in high esteem. In her eyes, it was just one more thing which made Thomas the perfect choice of husband.

"But I have a distinct feeling my life is about to change in the year to come."

Penny blushed as the meaning of his words dawned on her. "I hope it will be for the better."

"Oh, definitely better," Thomas said, and the smile he bestowed warmed her all the way down to her toes. "I can't think of anything I would welcome more than this possible change in my life."

She wished they had been alone, as she wanted nothing more than to grab his hand from the table next to hers and hold on to it as hard as she could. She knew the Duchess of Berkeley had only had Penny's best interests in mind when she made Thomas promise to wait until after her first Season, but right now Penny wanted nothing more than to haul him down the aisle of a church and make him hers forever.

"I too find myself in favor of the future," she admitted shyly and then laughed out loud when he made a funny face, looking proud as a peacock.

The serving girl came back to remove their dirty dishes, and while Thomas asked the girl about the well-being of her family, Penny leaned back with a contented sigh and let her gaze roam the crowd on the other side of the room.

She met the eyes of Charmaine, who stood in the midst of a group of too-admiring beaus, and her sister sent her a discreet roll of her eyes, obviously not too impressed by her entourage. Or amused.

For the first time ever, Penny did not feel envious of the attention her sister received. Instead she knew perfect satisfaction with her current position on the fringe, all because of the man who sat beside her.

What a difference a little interest in her person could make.

The laughing crowd's sudden cheering interrupted her thoughts, and as she unconsciously sought the reason for the gaiety, a movement at the far side of the group caught her attention and her eyes met Rake's inscrutable gaze.

Her silly heart skipped a beat as it always did when she laid eyes on his handsome person.

In the midst of a group of colorful friends, he looked fashionably bored and patronizingly amused. A beautiful lady with décolletage deep enough to remove any curiosity was flirting outrageously with him, but he didn't seem to notice.

His whole attention was on Penny, and when she met his eyes he sent her a look which made her blush from the heat of it. His lips curled into a wicked smile as he noticed her response, and his eyes grew even darker and hotter.

He was seducing her from the other side of the room, using only his smoky eyes, and to her horror it was working perfectly. She had to hold on to her chair to keep from walking away from Thomas and throwing herself into Rake's waiting arms.

It scared her how weak she was when it came to Rake. Was this how her life would be in the future? Happiness and contentment with Thomas until she unwittingly met Rake and one lustful look from him would turn her whole world upside down?

As if on cue, Thomas stood and caught her attention as he held out his hand to her. Relieved at the opportunity to ignore Rake, she grabbed Thomas's hand and stood, letting him lead her through the crowd toward the door.

Her mother gave her a sad smile as they passed. Her father never looked at her, his eyes glued to Charmaine in the midst of the crowd.

"Leaving already?" Rake's familiar voice stopped

Thomas's stride, and Penny, who had been looking at her sister, bumped into him.

"Lord Richard." Thomas's voice was clipped, and it was clear he didn't fancy Rake. Not surprising, since the two men's personalities were direct opposites. Where Rake was the easygoing, socializing, and wicked-minded man about town, Thomas was the dutiful, responsible, and kindhearted gentleman.

"And taking my Penny with you as you go, I see."

Thomas tensed, and she squeezed his hand lightly. Rake had a way of finding everyone's sore point and pressing it hard.

"Yes, Penny and I are heading homewards."

Rake raised an amused eyebrow. "You make it sound like you're an old married couple."

Thomas looked down at Penny and gave her a warm smile. Rake, too, noticed the intimate look before his eyes travelled farther and saw their entangled fingers. Something cold and dark filled his grey eyes for a second, and if Penny hadn't known better she would have thought it was jealousy.

But this was Rake. And Rake had no feelings, especially not for her. Oh, he wanted her. But it was his body speaking, not his heart.

"I guess I just look forward to the future." Thomas managed to tear his gaze from Penny and look back at Rake. "Next year at this time I may be standing here in front of you with Penny and have the honor to present her as my wife."

Penny warmed with a blush as Thomas sent her another loving smile, and if it hadn't been for the tall, dark man standing in front of them, she would have been dizzy with outright happiness.

"Something to look forward to, indeed," Rake mumbled as Thomas passed him, dragging Penny with him. She felt Rake grab her free hand for a second, and the wave of heat his touch sent through her body made her shiver. She heard him breathe her name, and it took all her mental strength to rip her hand free and escape from the inn.

Thomas didn't say much as they started the trip back home, but Penny didn't mind. The comfortable silence was a perfect ending to a perfect day.

She sneaked a look at him where he sat silently staring at the road ahead of them, and she found herself wishing the sleeping maid long gone so maybe they could share a kiss. Or two.

"What are you thinking about?" Thomas asked her as he caught her staring at him, and without thinking she opened her mouth and spoke.

"Kissing you."

The world turned quiet and the earth stopped moving as Thomas stared at her in disbelief.

"Oh, my God," she gasped mortified. "I didn't mean to say that out loud. I'm so sorry."

"Y-you were thinking a-about kissing m-me?" Thomas stuttered, and Penny nodded hesitantly, humiliated.

"I'm sorry," she whispered, tears gathering in her eyes. Tears over a relationship destroyed by her dimwitted behavior before it had a chance to start.

"Don't be," he said softly and put a hand under her chin, forcing her to look into his warm, chocolate eyes. "I'm not."

"You're not?"

He shook his head, a tender smile on his face,

before he cast an eye around to make sure they were alone. The chaperoning maid slept soundly in the back of the carriage as Thomas leaned forward and softly placed a chaste kiss upon Penny's shivering lips.

As he lifted his head again she gazed dreamily up into his warm eyes. "Oh."

Thomas laughed. "Was that a pleased 'oh' or a disappointed one?"

"Very much pleased," Penny said breathlessly. "It was a very perfect first kiss. Thank you."

He grabbed her hand and hauled her closer, until her side was pressed tightly against his. "First kiss ever, or first kiss with me?"

She laughed. "First kiss ever, I'm afraid. My life has not been filled with gentlemen yearning to kiss me."

"It is I who should thank you," Thomas admitted as he unknowingly echoed her earlier thoughts. "I don't think I have had such a perfect day for a long time, and I'm so glad I spent it with you."

A perfect beginning on a perfect life filled with perfect days. Life couldn't be more promising than this, Penny thought as they slowly drove down the lovely country road back toward Harveyfield.

Chapter Seven

"Merry Christmas," Francesca howled as she threw herself at Penny and gave her a hug worthy of a bear.

"Merry Christmas to you, too." Penny's reply was somewhat muffled, as her face was hidden deep in Francesca's curly hair.

"I have waited so long for you to come! I thought you never would. I can't believe how slowly the days go by when you long for someone so much as I have longed for you."

Penny laughed and gave Francesca a peck on the cheek. "I have missed you, too, but I have only been gone visiting my relatives in the north for a fortnight."

"So many days and so much pain."

Francesca winked and giggled as she dragged Penny away from the door and helped her remove her coat while the butler Ivanoff silently stood beside, waiting for his young mistress to finish the job.

"Come, they are all waiting for us in the salon. Even Rake, who hasn't been anywhere near here since August, and now we are finally complete."

"Fanny dear," Penny laughed as they walked down the hallway. "I'm not a part of your family, and your family *is* complete without me."

"But I'm not. I need you to be near, dear sister of my heart, and especially when I have excellent news to tell you."

"You do?" Penny stopped midstride. "About what? Please do tell."

"He's back."

"Rake? You just told me that."

Francesca rolled her eyes. "No, not Uncle Rake. I thought you were completely un-in-love with him and head over heels in love with Boring Saint Thomas."

"Oh, I am."

"In love with Thomas? Or not in love with Uncle Rake?"

This time it was Penny's turn to roll her eyes, and Francesca giggled in response. "No, I meant *my* man is back. Devlin Ross has reappeared in society."

Penny gasped with delight. "Really, Fanny? This is excellent news, indeed. When did he return?"

"He came back to his father's funeral, and according to Rake, who as you know happens to be a very good friend of the new Duke of Hereford, he will be staying for the next Season."

"But this is amazing. The man of your dreams, who has been abroad for so many years, just happens to return when it's time for your debutante Season. It's like…like…"

"A fairytale come true."

Penny bit back a smile as Francesca hummed dreamily. Happiness for her best friend overwhelmed her. This had been Francesca's dream since she was just a little girl, and being so in love herself, Penny couldn't think of anything that could make her even happier.

"Maybe we could have a double wedding next year?" she teased.

"Lord, I hope not," Francesca sighed. "A double wedding would mean you are going through with marrying Mr. Bedford."

Penny sighed, defeated. She had hoped Francesca would be on her side regarding Thomas, but to her surprise her friend—who had spent years trying to get Penny out of love with Rake—had turned and was now in favor of Rake and completely against Thomas.

"But it's a life I want."

"No, it is not. It's a life you have persuaded yourself into wanting. But the truth is that you still want my uncle, and nothing you say or do will ever change that."

"Fanny…"

"You just have to make him realize marrying you is the best thing for him. You two are made for each other, and you'd better admit it before it's too late and you are caught in Mr. Bedford's web forever."

"Web? Really, Fanny."

Francesca stopped with her hand on the door handle to the salon without opening the door. "He's not the same anymore."

"Who? Hereford?"

"No, Uncle Rake. He's unusually still and thoughtful. Even Uncle Jamie remarked about it, and he is Uncle Rake's twin brother and should know what he's talking about."

"It saddens me to hear about it, but it has nothing to do with me. I haven't even seen him since August, when I met him in Sandhurst while shopping with Thomas. And then he was his usual witty self and teased Thomas just as wickedly as he always does. Later I missed your family's August festival, as mother was sick, and then he left for London. It's not me, Fanny."

"He asked for you."

"Rake?" Penny cursed silently as her heart skipped a beat. Why couldn't she stop reacting to him like this?

"Yes, at the August festival. He spent most of the evening staring at the barn door and didn't dance one dance, which, as you are well aware, is highly unusual when it comes to Uncle Rake, as he never misses a chance to flirt with the ladies. Not until the party was almost over did he come over to me and ask why you hadn't come. When I told you cancelled because of your mother's sickness, he walked right out of the barn, and the next day he left for London without another word."

This was news to Penny, and for a second a flare of hope burst through her body. But just as quickly she mentally subdued the feeling. It was not for her anymore. She had made her decision and she had chosen a life with Thomas. She knew now that her feelings for Rake probably never would go away; the way her body reacted to him told her as much.

But she could live with it. She just had to make sure Thomas never learnt about it, as she could only guess it would hurt him more than he deserved.

But more importantly, she had to make sure Rake never found out. If he knew exactly how large her unwanted weakness for him was, he would never end his efforts to turn her into his mistress.

Rake would get over the attraction he felt sooner or later, and then everything would be fine again. Everything would be back to normal.

She would forever put a lid on her feelings and concentrate on being perfectly, sensibly happy and content with Thomas.

"You don't have to sacrifice Uncle Rake to become happy. I'm not stupid, you know. I know you are only trying to belong to someone. You want to be wanted. I understand that. But you are already a part of something. You are already a part of this family. Marrying Thomas would take you away from us."

Tears filled Francesca's eyes, the same grey eyes Rake had, and Penny swallowed hard to keep her own tears away.

"It's not so easy," she whispered. "I only want to be happy, and that I would never be with Rake."

"Oh, come on!" Francesca's sudden burst of anger surprised Penny. "Now you are lying to yourself. Why wouldn't he make you happy? He is the man of your dreams. He is the man you have talked about since you were a wee child. Of course marrying Uncle Rake would make you happy. The only problem is that you would probably be too happy for your own good."

"Fanny, you know what he is like. After a couple of months of marital bliss he would get bored and be on the hunt again. Flirting with anyone with a skirt and having a new mistress every week. How should I ever be able to live with the knowledge that I'm not enough?"

Francesca opened her mouth and then closed it again. Of course she knew what her uncle was like and couldn't argue with her friend's harsh words. Rake would get bored sooner or later, and then the happiness would go away and leave only bitterness and loneliness.

"You always have me. I'll never leave you."

Penny couldn't stop a giggle. "You are going to marry your handsome duke and move to his home, and I will see you only once or twice a year. Marrying

Thomas would mean no difference to that, but at least I wouldn't be abandoned between visits."

Francesca snorted, but Penny could see the smile she tried to hide.

"Just promise me one thing, Penny," Francesca said as she pressed the door handle. "Don't go to London with your mind set on Mr. Bedford. Leave your options open. Even if Uncle Rake isn't the one, you might meet someone else who is."

"Fanny…"

"Promise me!"

Penny sighed, knowing her friend would never let it be until she did as asked. "I promise."

"Penny!"

The Duchess of Berkeley came forward to greet Penny with a warm hug before she leaned back and gave her the usual look-over. "You look absolutely fabulous, my dear. I'm so thrilled Mr. Bedford's courtship suits you so well. But I'm even more thrilled you will be staying with us for Christmas. I can't tell you how happy I was to receive your letter about your family leaving Harveyfield for the holidays."

"She's been dancing around for days," the duke boomed behind his wife, and he gave Penny a quick peck on the forehead before he sat down again with his cup of tea.

"Come, we'll sit here." Francesca tugged Penny's arm and dragged her to the table where her parents sat. The Marquis and Marchioness of Newbury greeted her warmly and had a footman bring another cup for the newcomer. After obligatory questions about her family—which no one really was interested in, as no one liked them—they resumed their conversation about the upcoming Season, now only a few months away.

Penny sipped her tea, enjoying the lively talk around her. The Darlings had never been able to talk about anything without turning it into a heated discussion, and this occasion was no different. Soon Francesca's two brothers, Sinclair and Sebastian, joined the foursome at the table to have their say regarding the dos and don'ts of the Season.

Penny looked out into the large salon filled to its brim with members of the Darling family. All the seven sons of the duke and duchess were there with their families, and everyone was looking forward to the upcoming festivities. They were such a colorful family, and thrived in each other's company.

Rake sat on a sofa in the middle of the room, laughing with his twin brother James and the other set of twins, William and Edward. She let her eyes linger on his person for a few seconds, memorizing him forever in her heart.

He was the essence of a nobleman in his fashionable clothes, his shiny Hessians, and his perfectly combed hair. Even when he laughed he looked arrogant and haughty, but the wickedness in his smile and the amused twinkle in his eyes gave away the true Rake.

He was a libertine and a scoundrel but also, unfortunately, a very loveable one, and the crushed hearts he left behind him told the tale.

Before she had a chance to look away, he turned his head and met her eyes. For the shortest of time his face was filled with unreadable emotions, but soon he hid them all behind his usual mask and winked at her, looking pleased to have caught her staring at him.

She gave him a small smile before again turning her back to him, pretending to listen to her company at the table.

This had to end. She had to avoid him from now on. It was too obvious she had no strength by herself to withstand him, and even after passionately declaring her love for Thomas to Francesca she had been caught ogling Rake.

During the next several days she succeeded better than she would have thought possible in avoiding Rake.

Not that he tried to find her alone.

He seemed to have forgotten all about his earlier infatuation with her and instead spent his time with his brothers and nephews, playing games and going out visiting the neighbors—preferably the female ones.

Not until her last day at the castle did she find herself alone with him, when he happened to come upon her where she sat reading alone in the library.

When he noticed her, he hesitated for a second before greeting her politely and coming to where she sat curled up in the windowsill of one of the large bay windows overlooking the lake.

"Avoiding Fanny?"

Penny couldn't hold back a giggle. Her friend had been a bit overzealous in the last several days, entertaining Penny until she was ready to kill for some time of her own.

Fortunately the marchioness was a very perceptive woman and had taken her daughter visiting to give Penny some peace and quiet.

"I'm just reading."

"Then I am disturbing you and will soon leave you and give you your solitude back. Father asked me to fetch him an atlas so I can show him where I have been for the last months."

"Oh?"

He chuckled at her badly hidden interest. "I guess you too are curious about my whereabouts over the last couple of months."

"Not as much as envious of your opportunity to see the world. I'm afraid I have to read my way out of England, whereas you are free to go wherever you like."

"You make your life seem quite sad."

"Not sad, only restricted." She shrugged. "I'm a mere woman, and as such I have no say over my own life. I might nurture a wish to travel and see all those wonderful places I have read about in other people's journals, but in the end I have to submit to what my father and later my husband's wishes are."

"Then I guess you will have to find a husband who shares your interest in travelling."

"It's not so easy."

"Or you can live your life by your own head, doing whatever you want without the restriction of a man."

He gave her a wicked smile, and she knew he again was telling her to become his mistress, and she shook her head with a dejected sigh.

"You never give up, do you?"

"When it comes to you? Never."

"I will never become your mistress."

"I know."

She looked at him in surprise. "You do? So why do you persist in asking me?"

He leaned closer to her, until she could feel his warm breath against her face. "Because my body wants yours, and I know yours wants mine, too. Both our bodies would already have been satisfied beyond our imaginations if your head weren't so stubborn about getting married to your boring suitor."

She was speechless. The scoundrel knew she would never give in, and yet he still continued with his persuasion.

Her body wanted his…How did he know? She had never done or said anything that told him so.

And yet somehow he knew…

"Gretna Green?" His hoarse voice broke through her errant thoughts, and she followed his gaze to the book she had been reading.

"Eh, yes. It's an amusing journal from a couple who went to Scotland to get married. They describe the small border city most enticingly, and I feel I must put it on my list of places to see."

"I thought you were supposed to wait with marriage until after next Season? Or does your beau lust for your luscious body as much as I do?"

"Thomas doesn't lust for me," Penny gasped, outraged. "He's a gentleman and a man of honor. He would never behave toward me as you do."

"Oh, he wouldn't, would he?" Rake leaned even closer, forcing her to unwillingly press herself backwards against the cold glass of the window. "Then why was he kissing you in the middle of the road last summer?"

"What?" Penny breathed, and Rake snorted angrily, for once not hiding his true feelings behind his arrogant libertine mask.

"I followed you when you left the Devil's Folly, to make sure your honorable gentleman took you home as he was supposed to."

"You did what?"

"Do you deny it? Your gentleman took advantage of you in the middle of the road, and he can thank his lucky star that he didn't push for more, as I would have knocked him senseless if he had tried."

"You would have what?"

"I would have saved your honor."

Oh, my God. Penny closed her eyes, horrified. What was happening here? Was this really Rake, on some strange crusade in pursuit of saving her virtue? For what? For himself, so he could take it instead?

"You can thank me now."

She opened her eyes again and looked at Rake. He now had his mask back on and his actions in full control. He lifted an eyebrow as he waited for the gratitude he thought she would bestow on him.

"Thank you?" she asked. "For what?"

Rake sneered. "For saving your virtue."

"You didn't save my virtue."

"No, not literally. But I would have, if he had continued with his rat-like behavior."

"He wasn't behaving in a rat-like manner. He was only giving me what I asked for."

"You asked to be ravished?"

"No." Penny sighed. This conversation was beyond strange. "I asked him to kiss me."

For the first time ever, Rake was speechless. He stood silently staring at her in disbelief.

"I wanted to know how it felt to kiss him, and Thomas kindly obliged me."

"Y-you asked *him* to kiss you?"

This time it was Penny who sneered. "Well, he is

courting me, and I am very much considering marriage to him, if he ever will do me the honor of proposing to me. It felt right."

"You could have asked me."

"You? Why would I want to kiss a mouth that has kissed every other woman available to whom you are not related?"

Rake froze and stared at her with his inscrutable eyes, and she took the opportunity to slip away from him and the window. Slowly he took a step to the side and let her pass, and she scurried over to the shelf where she had found her book and put it back in its place.

"Penny."

She looked back at him over her shoulder and found him still at the window.

"It is astonishingly clear in what low esteem you hold me, but I still want you to promise me two things."

"And what would that be?"

"Promise me you won't go to London and consider yourself already engaged to be married. Thomas is not the only man in the world, and I think you should at least consider the men you meet."

Rake's wish was an echo of Francesca's earlier words, and Penny nodded solemnly.

"I will not consider myself engaged while in London. And the other promise?"

Rake walked slowly to her side and pulled out the book she had just placed on the shelf. "Promise me you won't go to Gretna Green with Thomas or any other man."

"You can't ask me to promise you that. I don't know what lies in my future, and such a promise is impossible to make."

"Then promise me you won't go to Gretna Green without telling me, so I have a chance to stop you."

She laughed outright. He was hilariously outrageous sometimes, this Lord Richard Darling.

"You want me to tell you if I'm about to elope, so you can stop me?"

"Yes. I want you to promise to inform me beforehand, so I have a chance to interfere."

"If I ever do elope, my reputation would be destroyed immediately, and the only thing to save me then would be a marriage. Do you really think I would then want you to interfere and make sure a marriage never takes place?"

"I might marry you myself, to save you."

She laughed again. "Then I promise to never elope to Gretna Green, if only to save you from a fate worse than death—marriage."

Rake chuckled as he ambled toward the door. "With the right woman, marriage would not be a complete waste."

"That's not what you told your mother."

He stopped midstride and looked back at her with an amused grin. "So you remember what I said, do you? Honestly, Penny, do you really think I would let my mother know if I were considering marriage to someone? She would never leave me alone. Better to lure her into giving up on my ever finding a wife and then surprise her with a wedding to plan. But don't tell her this, for goodness' sake. She would go wild if she knew."

"Oh, I won't tell a living soul." Penny shook her head at him. "No one would believe me."

"I'm still the libertine to you, eh?"

"A very much confirmed bachelor, I would rather say."

"You remember what you promised me?"

"Yes, I do. Both of them."

"Good girl." And with that he disappeared through the door, leaving her alone again to enjoy her solitude. But the cozy feeling was long gone, so she thoughtfully climbed the stairs to the guest room which had been her home for nearly a week.

With her head full of daydreams, she folded the few dresses she owned and put them in her bag. Tomorrow after breakfast she was heading home to Harveyfield again. She would have preferred to stay at Chester Park, but her father had sent a letter in which he more or less ordered her to join them again.

Thomas had invited her whole family to join him at his home for a couple of days, and coming almost from out of nowhere this was something her father deemed important. Maybe it had something to do with the party Thomas had promised to hold in Penny's honor, but she honestly didn't know or care.

All that mattered to her was meeting Thomas again and stepping into the wonderful bubble of contentment he always created for her. She needed it now more than ever, after the strange conversation with Rake.

She knew he had only been teasing her about getting married, but she still had felt an ugly prick of jealousy tear through her heart at the mere thought of his being in love and wanting to get married. She knew now better than ever she needed to get as far away from him as possible.

Francesca had confided he was about to leave for a

trip to visit a couple of his friends and wasn't due back until the beginning of March. This suited Penny. She would have a chance to spend time with Thomas without the constant reminder of her weakness for Rake.

She would be leaving, with her family, for London at the end of March. The Easton Ball, the unofficial start of the Season, was to be held at the beginning of April, the ball where Penny would be launched as one of the year's debutantes.

A debutante in her sister's old gowns.

Her father had put his foot down and told his wife not to spend one penny on Penny. All the money they didn't have would go to Charmaine's new dresses, and Penny was to alter Charmaine's old ones to fit her own smaller frame. So what if they weren't her colors and were originally made for a larger, more curvaceous body. She wasn't going to London to find a husband.

She didn't care about the promises she had made to Francesca and Rake. In her head she was already engaged to Thomas, and she wasn't about to lead any other man on. They didn't understand how good she and Thomas were for each other.

They fit perfectly together.

A match made in a perfectly sensible heaven.

Chapter Eight

It was a disaster from beginning to end.

From the moment Penny walked into the Easton Ball, people took one look at her and compared her with her sister—and with a snicker they ruled her out. Completely.

Charmaine was so angry she was seething, and only Penny's sincere assurance that she really didn't care had stopped the older sister from lashing out at the rude members of the *ton*.

Her father had left the ladies alone almost immediately after they entered Easton House, heading for the card tables in the next room. Her mother watched his retiring back with a mixture of worry and pain. Lady Nester's life was filled with worries, and the one giving her the most heartache was the love her husband held for gambling away their meager income. It took three minutes for Charmaine's dance card to be filled, and then she disappeared into the midst of the dancing couples. Penny led her mother to the wall where all the older ladies sat and fetched her some lemonade before she sat down next to her.

Not one man stepped forward and asked Penny for her dance card, but she didn't care. She wasn't there to find a husband. She was only there out of love and respect for the Duke and Duchess of Berkeley.

They had meant well when they asked Thomas to

let her have her first Season, and even though she personally would have preferred to stay behind and marry him instead, she had decided to endure these months of partying with the *ton*.

Soon it all would be over and she could go home again. Home to Thomas.

He wouldn't be joining them in London during the Season, as he had problems with a nasty sickness going through his people, rendering them sick and even, in some cases, dying. She had told him he must take care of them, that she didn't care if he couldn't be in London, and she *had* meant it with all her heart.

But now she wished he were there to show them all that someone wanted her. Someone needed her.

"Why aren't you dancing?"

She looked up into Rake's grey eyes and blushed as, for the first time, she saw him in his finest clothes. Lord, what a magnificent man he was. Elegant and fashionable, he stood before her, dashing as ever, and her fickle heart rejoiced over the beauty of him.

"She keeps her old mother company." Lady Nester tried to save her, but Penny didn't care about hiding the truth. Not from Rake.

"Actually, no one asked me. I don't mind, though, as I was born with two left feet. I was simply not made for the dance floor."

Rake frowned at her, not too happy with what he heard. "What do you mean? Why has no one asked you for a dance? Your dance card must be filled, such a pretty girl."

Before she could stop him, he had grabbed her dance card and opened it. Something dark entered his eyes as he saw the empty pages. Penny knew from

Charmaine that a girl was supposed to have at least half of those thin lines filled with gentlemen's names if she was to be even half a success. To have not one name was a complete disgrace, and it was clear Rake knew this too.

Without another word he left them, still carrying her dance card, and when he returned a little later, every male member of the Darling family had signed his name on at least one line, almost filling every dance.

"You didn't have to—"

"Of course I had to. You are my girl, and there is no way I'll let you become a wallflower, if I can help it."

Penny's mother tensed beside her as Rake called her his girl, but she didn't say anything. Instead, Lady Nester turned her head away, pretending to be too occupied to hear.

"I'm not your girl," Penny hissed, but Rake ignored her indignant outburst. Instead, he held out his hand, and she looked at it suspiciously.

He chuckled, amused, as he bent and took her hand and pulled her to her feet. "This is my dance, if I'm not mistaken."

Oh, God, no.

Penny could do nothing but follow him out onto the dance floor as a new dance was about to begin, but her whole being screamed with distress.

She really, really didn't want to dance with him. She hadn't lied when she told him about her two left feet, and this was a disaster in progress.

In the middle of the crowd he stopped, and seconds later the dance started. After stumbling a lot in the beginning, trying to remember the steps she had been taught, Penny lost some of her nervousness and would have almost enjoyed herself if it hadn't been for the glowing looks her dance partner kept sending her.

Rake, who hadn't a decent bone in his body, used his time well, and every time their hands met he let his fingers caress hers, until she was boiling with unwanted excitement. She had no walls when it came to him, and her whole body screamed for his touch.

As the dance ended, she tried to sneak away, but he caught her after a few steps and led her in the opposite direction from her mother. He didn't stop until they were standing outside on the dark terrace.

Alone but still in full view of the ballroom, they stood silent for a few moments. She stubbornly stared at the dancers, pretending not to notice Rake watching her. She could feel the heat from his body even though he stood an arm's length away from her.

"You look absolutely divine tonight." His smooth voice sent shivers down her spine, and when she turned to look at him, she saw his eyes were dark and smoldering, and again her heart skipped a beat.

"You tease me." She would not acknowledge the compliment he offered her.

"No, I do not. You are lovelier than ever. I have never seen your hair fastened that way. It makes your neck seem endless, and I can hardly restrain myself from kissing the enchanting spot behind your delicious ear."

She gasped, embarrassed, and his eyes grew more intense.

"I want you." His whisper caressed her ear, and she closed her eyes to keep herself from walking into his embrace and willingly letting him ruin her forever.

"There you are!"

Like a knight in shining armor, Lord Newbury appeared in the doorway and offered Penny his arm. "I believe this is my dance coming up."

"Oh."

Without looking at him, Penny gave Rake a small curtsy and then let the earl lead the way into the ballroom.

The rest of the evening was filled mostly with dancing with the Darling men, and with a couple of others who had seen her popularity and signed their names on her dance card to get to know who she was.

She sat out a few dances with her mother, watching the dancers gracefully moving around on the ballroom floor. She watched Francesca, who had a marvelous time on this her first ball and seemed absolutely dazed in the arms of the most handsome man Penny ever had seen—Devlin Ross, the Duke of Hereford.

But most of all she watched Rake interact with his acquaintances—and especially with the ladies. It hurt her more than she wanted to admit, watching him flirt with other women and seeing how eagerly they responded.

Rake would never have any problem with loneliness; there were just too many willing ladies, ladies who probably would travel to the end of the world if he asked them to. A part of her—a very primal part of her—was more jealous than she'd ever thought possible. But she repressed that jealousy. Whatever he once had meant to her he no longer was, and she must make her silly heart understand that.

But still, she couldn't stop looking at him. Now and then he would look back at her and give her an amused wink to let her know he caught her staring. Strangely enough, she didn't mind him noticing, as long as she could continue to watch…and feel sad over dreams never to come true.

Mentally she tried to put herself beside him with her hand in the crook of his arm, listening to him proudly presenting her to his friends as his wife. But something was terribly wrong with the picture, as she couldn't help feeling misplaced and uncomfortable.

This was not her world, this was Rake's, and he radiantly ruled it. It was obvious how right her choice of Thomas as a future husband had been. This was not for her. She was as unwanted here as at home.

She simply didn't fit in.

In the carriage on the way home, Charmaine was quiet—as usual—and her father kept ranting about how much money he had lost—as usual. Her mother closed her eyes and pretended to sleep, but Penny could see how the deep lines of worry in her face grew deeper by the minute.

Lady Nester hadn't had an easy life.

She was a simple but kindhearted soul caught in the hands of a selfish man. Lord Nester had long ago crushed the little spirit his wife once had, and Penny could remember her only as this empty, shivering shell of a woman. She knew her mother loved her dearly, but not the way she loved Charmaine. Lady Nester always chose her older daughter before the younger, and Penny had a long time ago stopped crying over being neglected.

When they arrived at their townhouse, Lord Nester immediately disappeared into his study to—in his own words—gain some strength, and the ladies went upstairs to their bedrooms.

"I'm so sorry you must wear my old dresses," Charmaine said, hesitating outside her bedroom door. "I wish I had some money myself to spend on you, to make you look your best. You are so beautiful, Penny dear, and it's sad no one can see it when you wear colors that drain your complexion."

"It's all right, Charmaine." Penny gave her a loving smile. "It's not your fault. And besides, I'm so proud of being your sister. It's been a delight to watch how popular you are. You deserve it, with your beauty and your wit and charm. If I could spend every night of the Season watching you, I would be perfectly satisfied."

Lady Nester interrupted the tender moment. "I hear your father coming upstairs, so why don't we all go into our bedrooms—quickly."

Lady Nester and Charmaine disappeared into her sister's bedroom, closing the door firmly behind them. With a disappointed sigh, Penny sneaked into her own room and closed the door.

Alone as always, she sat down on the bed with a thud. She closed her eyes and listened to the muffled voices of her mother and sister on the other side of the wall, and her heart cried, abandoned, *I want more than this.*

She let her gaze slowly travel throughout the room, taking in every aspect. It was a nice, neutral room with only a few books disturbing its utter perfection.

She gave the books a sympathetic smile.

Poor books.

There they lay, filled with impossible dreams of a perfect life and a beautiful but false promise of a love everlasting.

"Love conquers all," the books squealed happily in chorus, and Penny snorted.

"Love conquers nothing. I have loved Rake for years and never won anything by it. Finally I have realized I have loved him too much for my dreams to ever come true. And when I realized this, I met a new kind of love. A quiet, sensible love between good friends."

"Not a true love," the books squealed. "Not an everlasting love."

"I don't want an everlasting love. I want an everlasting relationship," she patiently lectured the books. "I want someone who will miss me when I'm not there, someone who wants me to stand by his side the rest of his life."

"Not a true love. Not an everlasting love," the books squealed again, and Penny frowned at them, not pleased with how they kept chanting about love.

"Once I believed you about true love, but reality has shown me such love doesn't exist. True love is only a fairytale, and you, dear books, are full of them."

The books gasped, horrified over such disbelief. "Everybody wants true love."

"I don't. Not anymore."

This time it was the books who frowned at her, not pleased at how lightly she brushed away everything they had told her for the last decade. "You will be lonely without your true love."

Penny snorted angrily. "No, I will not. I'm desperately lonely as it is, so there is no way a husband who isn't the true love of my life will intensify my unwilling solitude."

"If he doesn't love you, he won't miss you."

Penny snorted again, but this time without any heat, and the books quickly grasped the opportunity to persuade her to join their side again.

"Your true love wants you."

"I know," she admitted. "But he doesn't want me in a way that will render me any happiness. He will only make me feel more abandoned."

"Thomas left you."

Oh. Those cheeky books, they knew exactly what cord to pull. "Thomas definitely didn't leave me. He had things to do."

"He left you."

"He did not."

"So if he didn't leave you, why are you feeling so lonely?"

Penny closed her eyes against the triumphant books. For the first time she admitted to herself how disappointed she felt over Thomas's reluctance to leave the countryside for her. His presence would have made it so much easier for her to ignore her feelings for Rake and the strange power he held over her.

"He had more important things to do."

"More important than you? What on earth can be more important than the woman you love?"

"His people were sick," Penny almost growled.

"Ah."

"What do you mean with that?"

"Oh, nothing."

"I admire him for his devotion."

"His devotion to others or his devotion to you?"

"We are not engaged, so he has no obligation to be devoted to me. I'm merely a girl he's been courting and to whom he might propose this summer."

"What if you meet someone else?"

"If I ever am away from the other wallflowers long enough to meet someone else, it's up to me if I want to accept a proposal. Neither Thomas nor I have promised each other anything."

"He must trust your feelings for him very much, then, if he feels secure enough to leave you alone among all the eligible bachelors of the *ton*."

"He knows my wish is to be with him. I have told him as much."

"But you haven't told him about your long-lasting feelings for Rake, have you? If you had, he wouldn't be so sure of your returning to him still unmarried and his to claim."

"My feelings for Rake are not relevant when it comes to Thomas. I'm done with that part of my life."

"Of course you are."

Bloody cheeky books. They knew her too well.

Of course she wasn't finished with that part of her life. How could she be? Her feelings for Rake consumed her whenever they met. She knew the only way to get rid of them was to stay out of his way, to get as far away from him as she could. And the easiest way to do so was to marry someone who wasn't a part of Rake's crowd and who wasn't interested in Rake's choice of lifestyle.

Thomas.

"What I feel for Thomas is light and uncomplicated. With him I am at ease. Fanny—who has more opinions about my life than anyone could think possible—calls it friendship instead of love, and she insists it proves how indifferent I am. She also insists it proves my heart isn't in it. But I disagree, because the feelings I have for Rake are nothing like the true love you have talked about, either. Those feelings turn my whole being inside out, and instead of being content I mostly feel insecure and confused."

"At least you feel something."

With an angry growl, she collected the books and put them in a drawer and closed it firmly. She had enough with her own mind questioning her. She didn't need a couple of well-read books trying to undermine her decision too.

The only thing she knew for sure was that she wanted peace and quiet in her life. If it meant marrying Thomas—so be it. Maybe he never would love her like she deserved to be loved, but so what?

She just wanted to belong to someone.

Chapter Nine

The next evening Penny knocked softly on Charmaine's door, praying desperately for her sister to still be awake even though it was the middle of the night.

Minutes long as hours passed before the key moved in the lock and the door opened quietly. To Penny's relief it was Charmaine's beautiful face which appeared in the doorway, not that of her nasty maid.

"I need to speak with you," Penny whispered, and Charmaine's eyes narrowed as she took in her sister's pale face and tear-filled eyes. She nodded quietly before she slipped out into the hallway and closed the door behind her. Not until they were safely inside Penny's bedroom did Charmaine open her mouth.

"What is it, Penny? You look devastated. What happened? Is it Father? Has he done something to you?" Charmaine grabbed Penny's hand and together they sat side by side on the bed.

"W-what? Father? No, he hasn't done anything. It's me. I did something incredibly thoughtless, and I don't know what to do."

"Nothing you have done can be that bad, Penny."

"What was I thinking about? Or rather, why wasn't I thinking? But it was as if my worst nightmare was coming true, and I just lost my wits."

"Penny, please. Now you scare me. Please tell me

what happened."

Penny looked into Charmaine's compassionate eyes and her whole body shook as deep sobs tore through her. Her sister dragged her into her arms and Penny closed her eyes and let the sisterly love overflow her as she wept until all her tears were gone and only a sniffle now and then was heard.

"I'm so sorry," she whispered as she finally sat back up, and Charmaine gave her a small smile filled with love as she dried Penny's wet cheeks with a handkerchief.

"Do you feel better?"

Penny nodded. Strangely enough, she did feel much better. Finally giving in to her mortified feelings had taken the worst away and left her only mildly shaken instead of completely devastated.

"Do you want something? Water?"

Penny shook her head.

"Then," Charmaine said with a voice which told she wouldn't accept any excuses, "I want you to tell me what this is all about."

Penny took a deep breath. "When we were at the Green Park picnic today, Fanny and Rake took me aside to talk to me. They said they had something urgent to tell me, and that it was about you."

Charmaine looked just as astonished as Penny had felt. "About me? Whatever could it be that Fanny and Rake could tell you about me?"

"I thought the same until Rake started to act strangely. You know how sophisticated he always acts, a true fashionable gentleman from head to toe."

"Oh, I know. Rake is the essence of a gentleman and always acts with arrogance."

"But this time he wasn't as blasé, and he almost seemed nervous. He was walking to and fro in front of me and Fanny until I thought he would ruin the lawn under his feet. And then it dawned on me…"

"What?"

"Do you remember what my fears were when you went off to your first Season in London?"

Charmaine snorted. "Yes, I do. You were so sure he would fall madly in love with me and marry me before you had a chance to make him fall for you. Such a silly fear, as Rake has known me for his whole life and never cared about me at all. Why would he suddenly have feelings for me?"

"Well it didn't feel silly then," Penny said a bit indignant. "And to my utter mortification, it didn't feel silly earlier today either."

Charmaine sighed, knowing her sister too well. "Please don't tell me you've said something about it to Rake."

"I-I might have…"

"Penny!"

Penny stood up, too upset to be still. "I know, Charmaine, but he caught me off guard. I've been having such trouble ignoring him in my heart the last couple of days, and when he said he wanted to tell me something about you I lost control."

"What did you say?"

Penny blushed, still feeling embarrassed over her own actions. "Something like 'Oh, my God, you are going to marry Charmaine.' "

"That wasn't too bad," Charmaine frowned.

"No, it wasn't. But then Fanny started to soothe my feelings and pointed out how I by now should be well aware that you meant nothing to him."

"Oh."

"And then I asked him with tears in my eyes— 'You are not?' "

"Oh."

Penny sighed. "He's too intelligent to not understand what it all was based upon. A woman who's in love with him."

"What did he say?"

"Nothing." Penny sniffed. "Not a word. He just stared blankly at me before he turned and left."

"He did? Rake, the wicked libertine, didn't even say something absolutely unheard of?"

"No. He just opened and closed his mouth a couple of times before he left, as if he didn't know what to say. Lord, I feel so stupid. Fanny thinks I'm overreacting, that Rake is completely naïve when it comes to feelings, but she doesn't know the whole truth about him and me."

"You never told her about the lake?" Charmaine seemed extremely pleased about being the only one Penny had confided in.

"No, at first I didn't know how to, and later it just felt too much to tell. And now she's too caught up in the Season and her budding romance with the Duke of Hereford."

Charmaine froze, and Penny closed her eyes, horrified. When would she ever learn to keep her mouth shut? Without another thought she blurted out what had started it all, what Fanny and Rake had wanted to tell her about Charmaine.

"Are you sure about this?" Charmaine's voice was cold and clipped.

"About Fanny and the duke?"

"Yes."

"Fanny admitted as much."

Charmaine laughed, obviously relieved. "Fanny can't be sure of this, as the Season hardly has had time to begin, and she just met the man."

"But Fanny told me the duke had acknowledged the attraction to Rake, who is a close friend of his."

"H-he did?"

"Yes. And he wouldn't have admitted to Rake something like this if he hadn't meant it. Rake is Fanny's uncle and close family, after all."

"Oh."

The devastation in Charmaine's beautiful eyes was obvious, and Penny dropped to her knees in front of her sister and grabbed her cold hands.

"What Fanny and Rake wanted to tell me was that Fanny had overheard you telling your friends the duke was courting you. And having the inside information about the duke's feelings, they knew what you said was a blatant lie. They wanted you to have a chance to set things straight before the truth came out."

Charmaine sat like a Roman statue, her face pale from shock.

"Please, Charmaine, why were you lying to your friends? What on earth possessed you to say something you know isn't the truth?"

Charmaine took a deep shaky breath before she released her hands from Penny's grip and stood up.

"I'm not the liar here," she said coldly as she crossed the room to the door.

"What? Charmaine, I just told you how you were overheard telling your friends an outright lie!"

"And you believe your friend over me?"

"No, Charmaine, I don't. But Fanny wouldn't make something like this up, and especially not involve Rake in it if it weren't true."

"So you do believe her."

"How can I not?"

"Believe me when I tell you there is nothing true about what Francesca told you, and I want you to know you have hurt me immensely with your complete distrust in me and my actions."

"Charmaine…"

"No, don't. It's too late. Now I know how you feel about me."

Penny looked into Charmaine's face and knew without any doubt she was lying. As the door quietly closed behind her sister, she sat alone on the floor of the bedroom, too tired to be able to think straight.

She needed to rest.

Tomorrow was a new day, and hopefully she would be able to see things more clearly after a good night's sleep. With tired hands she undressed and lay down on the bed, falling asleep as soon as her head touched the pillow.

****

It was unusually quiet in the Darling townhouse when Butler showed Penny into a beautiful salon.

"Are you sure you want to wait, Miss Penny? The Duke of Hereford never mentioned when he would bring Miss Fanny back from their ride in the park."

"Oh, it's all right, Butler. I don't mind waiting." Penny gave the kindhearted butler a warm smile, and he nodded solemnly.

"I'll bring you a tray of tea, then, for you to enjoy

while you're waiting."

Penny thanked the man and as he left she removed her bonnet and settled herself on the comfortable sofa.

Even though she had slept like a baby for the rest of the night after confronting Charmaine, it still felt as if her head had been screwed on backwards. She was tired and worn from all the emotions flaring through her in the last months—and especially the last days.

She didn't know what to think anymore, and what was worse, she didn't know *how* to think.

Had she done the right thing yesterday when she questioned Charmaine? She didn't know. This morning her sister had refused to look at her over the breakfast table and had left as soon as she possibly could, avoiding a confrontation.

Penny didn't know how she should handle things with Charmaine. Obviously they both knew she lied, but how could Penny ever prove it?

Something was definitely wrong with Charmaine, and now it seemed Penny had lost the closeness they had shared, at least for now.

Butler interrupted her thoughts as he entered with a large tray filled with delicious sandwiches as well as the tea things, and she thanked him with all her heart.

With a small smile he went away again, leaving the door open behind him. She took a large bite of a cucumber sandwich and closed her eyes at the marvelous taste.

"Thinking about me?"

Penny's eyes flew open and she only just caught herself from choking on the sandwich as she met the amused grey eyes of Rake. He had paused just inside the door, but now without another word he quietly closed it, making perfectly sure they were all alone in the salon.

"My maid…" Penny started, but Rake only shrugged.

"We don't need her, do we?"

Penny didn't know what to say or do. She wasn't ready for this, facing Rake. Not after what she had blurted out yesterday. But she could sense his determination and knew there was no escape. She could only pray for someone to walk through the door and interrupt their moment alone.

Slowly, without taking his eyes from her, he walked across the room and sat down next to her on the sofa. She could hardly breathe as his leg happened to touch her skirts, and she moved slightly to the side, away from him.

His soft chuckle caressed her ears, and before she had a chance to do anything his hand gently held her chin and turned her to look at him.

He leaned forward until she could see the light speckles in his grey eyes, and she shivered as he gave her a small victorious smile. "So you don't want me to marry your sister?"

"N-no," she stuttered, and he leaned closer and let his lips touch her soft cheek. A whimper eluded her as his hand left her chin and caressed her cheekbone until it landed on a spot under her ear—the very one he had admired at the Easton Ball.

"I can't help but wonder why you would mind me marrying your sister." His lips caressed her other cheekbone until they landed under her other ear.

"She's too good for you," Penny whispered, caught in the web of pleasure he slowly was building around her.

"Is she?" Rake's hand left the spot under her ear and travelled slowly down her arm until he could fold his arm around her waist and pull her closer to him.

"Please," she begged. She had no willpower when it came to Rake, and now she was completely in his hands.

"Or am I too good to marry her?"

"W-what?" Penny stared blankly up into his eyes, and he grinned wickedly.

"If I didn't know better, I would think that you, Lady Penelope de Vere, have feelings for me."

"I hate you," she whispered, but he only chuckled in response.

"No, you don't. We both know you don't, so there is no need for you to deny it."

Though she hadn't thought it possible, he pulled her even closer, and this time he didn't dawdle. Without any warning his lips touched hers and he was kissing her with a passion which overwhelmed her.

As his tongue made love with hers she started to feel faint and had to grab his shoulders to stop the earth from spinning. The sensations he woke in her body and in her soul were perfect, and with a sigh she gave in and kissed him back with all the love in her heart.

The kiss seemed endless. When he finally lifted his head, she was dizzy with love and passionate feelings she didn't know how to handle. He looked down at her with his inscrutable eyes and gave her a slow, triumphant smile.

"And you say you don't want me."

She frowned at him, as something in his words didn't seem quite right. But before she had a chance to collect her thoughts he kissed her again, and she lost all her ability to think. This kiss wasn't as long as the one before, but Penny still felt like he had taken her to heaven and back.

"Kissing you is just as important to me as breathing," he whispered into her ear. "I don't think I can live without you in my arms. You belong here. You belong with me."

His wonderful words went straight to her heart, and she felt tears fill her eyes. Could it be? Was Rake about to finally give in and ask her to marry him? Had the knowledge of her love for him changed his plan of life and made him realize what was important?

"Promise me you immediately will tell Boring Saint Thomas you don't need him anymore."

"Rake…"

He grabbed her chin and gave her a look filled with fire. "Promise me."

With a small tender laughter she gave in. "I promise."

He grinned as he leaned back and pointed to the tray of tea. "You can serve me now, woman. If you are going to spend all your time with me, you'd better learn how to treat your master well."

"Oh, really?"

"You have to learn how to please your man, and serving him tea is a good start. We have plenty of time to teach you everything else later on."

The sultry promise in his eyes made her blush, but for once she didn't feel too upset about his brazenness. His words about the rest of their lives touched her heart, and she was too happy to care that he was being patronizing.

"You have to tell me one thing, though," he said after she had served him his cup. "Where do you want to live?"

"Where?" She frowned at him, confused over his choice of words. "Do you mean at Chester Park or Berkeley House?"

"Heavens, no," he chuckled, amused. "That will never do. No, I'm thinking more of where you want our little love nest to be. I really don't think my family will appreciate us under the same roof with them. Better to have a place of our own, where it will be only you and me and a very comfortable bed."

Pain such as she had never felt before seared through her heart and ripped it into thousands of pieces. All the joy and happiness she had felt a minute ago vanished as the meaning of his words hit her.

He didn't want her as a wife. He wanted her as his mistress. A kept lady in a hidden house.

"For how long?" she whispered, her voice full of sadness, but he didn't notice her distress as he continued his light plans for the future.

"Well, at least for the first couple of months, I think. Then we might get tired of each other and need the company of others. But I highly doubt that, because you make my body sing, and I don't think I will ever grow tired of you."

"And then?"

Rake drew back slightly as he started to sense something was wrong. "Penny, what's the matter? You don't seem as happy as I thought you would be over the prospect of having a house of your own."

"I can't believe you're doing this to me," she said hoarsely, as her emotions became too much for her.

Rake moved closer to her, his grey eyes filled with concern. "Penny, for heaven's sake, tell me what's wrong."

"You," she cried, no longer hiding her tears. "You are what is wrong. You can't stop, can you? You keep telling me how much you want me, and every time I listen to you against my own better judgment you end up hurting me more than I thought was possible."

She couldn't stand sitting next to him any more and dashed to the fireplace, where a crackling fire spread its warmth.

"Penny, I don't understand…"

"Of course you don't," she interrupted coldly. "You never understand, do you? You live your happy bachelor life, breaking hearts wherever you go, and you never think twice about it. But I never thought you would do it to me."

"I have never wanted to break your heart," he snapped. He was starting to get upset with her, and that suited her just fine. An angry Rake was easier to handle than a confused and oddly vulnerable Rake.

"And yet you just did."

"How? By telling you I want you? You are probably the only woman in London who would be heartbroken about that!"

"Maybe so. But I'm not brought up to be happy over being asked to become a kept lady."

"A kept what?" Rake frowned at her.

"May I ask how many other houses you have throughout London with women eagerly waiting for you to spend some time with them in their comfortable beds?"

Rake chuckled as the meaning of her words hit

him. "Penny, my darling, you are completely misunderstanding me. I'm not asking you to become one of my mistresses. I simply was…"

"One of?" Penny gasped outraged. "One of? How many mistresses do you have?"

"Penny," Rake begged. "This is not relevant…"

"Of course it's relevant. If you want me to become your mistress, I think you at least could be honest enough to tell me how many ladies you visit every month."

"What if I tell you I haven't been able to think about anyone else but you since that wonderful moment when I saw you at the lake and finally woke up to realize that you are all I ever wanted?"

"Oh, come on, Rake. I know everything about you. I spent my childhood learning as much about you as I possibly could. You have never once said no to a lady, and you have never once let a no from a lady stand in the way for the challenge she then becomes. You have not once stopped long enough to even consider marrying anyone—or marrying at all—as you are the most confirmed bachelor of your time. Your words, not mine."

He stood silently, staring at her with dead eyes. She felt her heart respond to the pain she could sense from him, but she hardened herself. He had to learn he couldn't treat her—or any other woman—the thoughtless way he did.

"I can't believe this," Rake whispered hoarsely. "I thought you wanted me."

"No, I don't want you. I want a life. I want love and respect. I want a home of my own to fill with children and laughter. I want happiness."

"What if I want the same?"

"We both know you don't." She ignored his broken voice. "It was quite revealing to watch you at the Easton Ball interacting with your friends. That is your place—to flirt, dance, and socialize. It's not me."

"All I want is you."

"And all I want is Thomas."

Rake took a deep shaky breath before he strode to her and grabbed her hands hard. "Please, Penny, you must listen to me. It's not Thomas you want, it's the life you imagine you will have with him. I can give you what you want, if you just let me."

She looked up into his handsome face, tears streaming down her cheeks as her eyes took in every beloved part of him. "I have loved you with all my heart for eighteen years. Every day and every night I have dreamt about the day you would finally see me and ask me to become your wife. But never once did I dream about you asking me coldly to become one of your mistresses for as long as you wanted to have me."

"Your dream can still come true."

"No, it won't. Because you will never love me the way I want you to. The way I deserve to be loved. Maybe Thomas never will, either, but at least I go into a marriage with him without silly dreams for more. If he wants me, he can have me. I have dreamt about belonging to someone all my life, and if he wants me— it's enough. It's all I need."

With an anguished groan, Rake released her hands and hit his fist hard on the stone mantel of the fireplace. "I can't believe how stubborn you are. Here I stand in front of you, begging you to let me give you everything you ever dreamt about, and yet you still say you want to give yourself to anyone else who claims they want you?"

"I've never wanted to become your mistress."

"And I have never asked you to."

This time it was Penny who groaned, outraged.

"Yes, you did. You told me you wanted me, and then you asked me where I would like my house located."

"For being such an intelligent young woman, you are the most stupid person I have ever met."

And with those last harsh words, Rake barged out of the salon, leaving Penny in a sad heap of raw emotions.

When Francesca a few minutes later entered the salon, Penny couldn't hide her devastation and burst into tears. Her friend hugged her closely until Penny's tears were dried, and she managed to offer a wobbly smile. With great relief Penny told her friend all about Rake, from the meeting at the lake to the scene just minutes before, in the very same salon.

It soothed Penny's feeling to watch Francesca's outrage over her uncle's behavior.

"The bastard," Francesca growled through her teeth. "The sick, awful, horrible moron."

Penny couldn't help but smile through her tears, as Fanny looked ready to kill.

"That evil, selfish…man!"

"I do so agree with you." Penny sniffed. It felt good, having someone take her side.

For a little while Rake had made her doubt her understanding, as he had seemed more touched by her anger than he would have if he hadn't cared. But Francesca's reactions were the same as her own, and even though this was only her side of the story she still felt she had done the right thing.

"*Your dream can still come true.*"

Rake's words echoed through her mind, but she closed her ears and her heart.

"He can't do this. Not to me, and definitely not to you. You are my friend, and this is the worst insult he ever could give either of us."

Francesca seethed with anger, and it took Penny quite some time to get her to calm down and promise not to do anything about it. Penny didn't want to be a thorn between Francesca and her uncle. Just because he behaved like a snake toward her didn't mean he didn't love and cherish his niece.

Reluctantly Francesca agreed. She too knew there was more than Rake's behavior toward Penny at stake here, and she loved her uncle too much to destroy their relationship.

"But there is one thing I want to know before I do anything."

"What?"

"Do you still want him? As a husband?"

Penny didn't know how to answer the question. Saying no would be telling an outright lie. Of course she still nursed a silly hope of him declaring his undying love for her and ending it with an impassioned marry-me-or-I'll-die plea.

But saying yes wouldn't be true either.

"I don't know, Fanny, really I don't. If you had asked me an hour ago, I would probably have told you a loud yes, but now I hesitate. He hurt me, and he insulted me in the worst way a man can, as he trampled all my dignity and honor. In a few words he belittled me into nothing."

Francesca hugged her close, and Penny felt new tears fill her eyes. The love her friend bestowed on her was endless.

"I know, dearest, I know." Francesca smiled sadly. "Just one thing—promise me that if you change your mind, please do tell me, and I will make sure not to rest until he understands how stupid he is."

In the carriage on her way home, Penny couldn't help but feel something had gone terribly wrong this day. Rake had been more honest to her than she ever had seen him before, and he had not tried to hide behind his usual arrogant mask.

Had anything of what he'd said been true?

Was he right when he said she was the one jumping to conclusions? His anger and his pain had seemed honest, but then how could she know? She had believed in true love, and look where it had taken her.

As the carriage halted in front of the Nester townhouse, she came to a decision. She would endure the rest of the Season and try to stay as far away from Rake as she could.

Her tired head and confused heart needed peace, and she would find it only by marrying Thomas. He was a good friend. She didn't burn for him, but he would never hurt her, either.

And so what, if she would now and then dream about Rake? That dream would never come true anyway.

Chapter Ten

"I don't want to go."

Charmaine threw down her napkin with anger, but even she didn't dare leave the breakfast table before their father had finished the daily paper.

"We will go, as this is quite an honor for our family." Lord Nester didn't lift his head to look upon his seething daughter. Instead, he took another sip of tea and turned a page, ignoring her outburst.

"But everyone will be at Almack's tonight. It is the first ball at the assembly rooms this Season. How can we not be going?"

"If a friend invites you to dinner, you don't decline. And Lord Bolton is an old friend of mine whom I respect a great deal and don't want to insult."

"We have never heard about this Lord Bolton before, so what kind of friend is he?"

Lord Nester lifted his head and gave his older daughter an irritated look that made his wife pale.

"There, there," she soothed quickly. "If your father has decided this is best for us, we will of course honor his wish."

"Mother," Charmaine whined, but Penny could see that her sister too caught their mother's subtle warning.

"You will like him," Lord Nester said, and it sounded more like an order than information. "Lord Bolton is the richest man in Essex, where I grew up, and we were very good friends when we were children. Adult life has kept us apart, and that's why I was so delighted when I received his invitation."

"But, Father…" Penny frowned as something nagged her. "I thought you—as all other Earls of Nester—grew up at Harveyfield?"

"I wasn't born the heir," her father admitted curtly. "But when an accident took my predecessor's life, I was by that time the next in line and inherited the title and the small holdings. Not much to celebrate, though. Harveyfield is such a meager house, and the title has neither land nor wealth. I had a better life before I became the Earl of Nester."

"But who is your heir?" Charmaine asked, not able to pretend disinterest.

Lord Nester shrugged. "Some distant cousin. I don't know his name and have certainly never met him. I'm not going to be around when he takes over the place, so I really don't care."

"But what will happen with us if you should die?"

"Penny, stop asking all these questions. They make my head hurt. It's too early in the morning."

Angrily the earl threw down the paper on the table, bumping over the teapot as he did so. As its hot contents spread over the table, he stomped out of the room without a backward glance, and they could hear his footsteps echoing down the hall to his study.

After ringing for the maid to clean up the mess on the table and helping to put things to rights again, Lady Nester sank back into her chair as the last vestiges of the upset were carried out. She gave her daughters a firm look. "You two have to learn to stop in time when it comes to your father. You know he has a problem with his temper, and I thought you knew better by now."

"But, Mama…" Charmaine had trouble letting the subject of the dinner party go. "I want to go to Almack's. All my beaux will be there, and if I'm not there they might find someone else to court."

"Your father informed me that he has admired Lord Bolton since they were children, and to him this is one of the best things to ever happen to him. Please humor him. Let him have this evening, and then we can go on with our lives again. I don't know why we have received this dinner invitation, but I can guess it has something to do with Lord Bolton's third wife, who just passed away. She was quite young, I understand."

"Oh, lord," Charmaine breathed. "Do you think he wants to marry one of us?"

"Your father, who is quite proud of you, has probably been telling his friend all about his exceptional daughters, and now Lord Bolton wants to see for himself."

Penny rolled her eyes but kept silent. Her father hadn't told Lord Bolton about his two exceptional daughters. He had told him about his one exceptional daughter—Charmaine.

"But what if he wants one of us?"

"Your father will never marry you off to some old man, no matter how rich he is. As I understand it, Lord Bolton is not only one of the richest men in Essex, he is also one of the most tight-fisted. Your father won't gain anything by such a marriage, and therefore there won't be one."

"But what if he offers father money?"

Lady Nester gave her daughter a patronizing smile.

"Even then he won't let either of you two go. Charmaine, you know he has bigger plans for you, and when it comes to you, Penny, he promised the Duchess of Berkeley to keep you for Thomas Bedford, and he is too impressed by her to dare to go against her."

"But, Mama…"

"Charmaine, no. This is enough. Now let us all go to our rooms and choose what to wear tonight. Humor your father and try to look your very best."

And with those last words their mother left the table and proceeded through the door.

Charmaine gave Penny a can-you-believe-how-stupid-they-are-look before she remembered she wasn't talking to her younger sister and followed their mother upstairs.

Penny too went up to her room and the rest of the day she spent on her bed reading. Not until she heard her father call for the carriage did she change her dress and quickly put some pins in her honey-colored hair.

Why bother with more? No one ever was interested in her, and after what she'd heard about Lord Bolton she knew he was interested in one thing and one thing alone—Charmaine.

As soon as they arrived at their host's magnificent townhouse he proved her right. Lord Bolton took one look at Charmaine and practically drooled. His eyes never left her, and his not so subtle admiration made Lord Nester most irritated, although he didn't say anything but merely twiddled his fingers in a way Penny had come to recognize as a sign of his agitation.

Lord Bolton was of the same age as her father, but he looked more than twenty years older. He had to use a walking stick when he moved around, and she guessed he suffered from gout or some other painful sickness like it.

Dinner was a horrible event, with Lord Bolton ignoring everyone but Charmaine while she tried to move as far away from him as possible. Penny sank deeper and deeper into her chair, silently hoping their father soon would grow tired of their host's unfriendly behavior and whisk his family home again.

After dinner, Lord Nester ushered his three ladies out of the dining room so he and Lord Bolton could have their port alone, and a mean-looking butler led them to another luxurious salon.

Not until they had finished three cups of tea did the door fly open, and Lord Nester barged in.

"We are leaving immediately. Please get your coats and wait for me in the carriage."

Charmaine squealed with delight and rushed out from the room, closely followed by her just-as-delighted mother. As Penny was about to leave also, her father closed the door, then turned and looked at her coldly.

"I need to talk to you in private, Penny. Please sit down."

Filled with sudden dread, Penny returned to the sofa. Something in her father's cold stance made her shiver with fear, and she tangled her fingers together to stop her hands from shaking.

"You are not going home with us today." Lord Nester paced in front of the door, looking more like a guard on duty than a father talking to his daughter. "Lord Bolton is in desperate need of an heir and has decided he wants Charmaine for a wife. I hope you understand that I will never let anyone like him get his hands on your sister."

Faint with relief, Penny nodded. This was not about her, this was about her sister. Her father needed her help, and she would of course do anything to save her sister from having to marry someone as horrible as Lord Bolton.

"Lord Bolton was not pleased when I told him this, and to my surprise he…he started to threaten me and said he would have you and me and your mother locked in while he had his way with Charmaine and thus he would secure her as his wife."

"Oh, Father," Penny breathed, shocked.

"Luckily enough, I happened to remember something from our childhood, something I know he wouldn't want to become common knowledge. So, as he still wouldn't give up his plans, I made him a bargain he couldn't refuse. I know how much he loves young girls, and I instead offered to let him take you off my hands. In that way we can save Charmaine's virtue and future. To my great surprise and gratefulness, Lord Bolton liked this bargain, and in response I have promised to never mention again what he did to that young girl in our youth."

Penny stared open-mouthed at her father, not believing her ears. Was he about to give her away to save Charmaine? She was his daughter too. She must have misunderstood him completely.

"Father, you can't be serious. You can't leave me here. I don't want to marry Lord Bolton. I'm promised to Thomas Bedford, as you are well aware."

"Who said anything about marriage?" Lord Nester sneered as he leaned over her, forcing her to press backwards into the sofa. "You are to stay and let Lord

Bolton have his way with you in any way he pleases. Then, when he is finished with you, you can write me a letter. I will send a carriage for you, which will take you to that small estate I have in Wales, where you will spend the rest of your life. You will never hear from us again, and you must promise never to contact us in any way."

"B-but this is unheard of," Penny stuttered, blindly trying to find something to say which would break through her father's insanity. "I'm your daughter too. You can't just leave me here. I know you don't love me as much as you love Charmaine, but you must feel something for me. Please don't leave me."

The last sentence was only a sob, but her father didn't even blink. Instead he laughed—a hateful sound which scared her immensely.

"I will tell you two things, little Penelope de Vere. First, I have never loved you and have merely been putting up with you all these years as a possible source of income once you've grown up."

His words were like knives, and Penny's already bleeding heart was wounded over and over again. To sense his indifference was one thing, but to hear him admit it was devastating.

"And secondly, I'm not your father by blood. Nor am I Charmaine's. Ah, that is a surprised little face. Something you didn't know, eh? Your real father had an unexplained accident which killed him and left his wife alone with a small baby and another on the way. When I inherited the title, as soon as you, a mere girl, were born, I did what any decent man would do. I asked her to marry me. She was quite beautiful back then, you know. Your sister is nothing to what your mother once was. She reluctantly accepted, too caught up with having lost a husband, and having a toddler and an infant to take care of. I also made her promise never to tell you two who your real father was. A baby's neck is so fragile, you know."

The threat in his words was sickening, and Penny cried for her mother, who in her worst day of sorrow had been assaulted by this insane man. This explained so much, not just her father's obsession with Charmaine but also her mother's overbearing desperation when it came to her oldest daughter's protection.

His triumphant laughter echoing through the grand room, her father turned his back to her and started for the door, and with one last attempt to save her life, Penny ran after him and grabbed his arm to force him to acknowledge her.

"Father, please don't leave me here. Take me with you. Please…"

"Let go of me, you selfish girl. Can't you think of anyone but yourself? Think of your sister and her virtue. Do you really want her to lose her innocence in the hands of a man like Lord Bolton?"

"N-no, of course I don't," Penny cried. "But I don't want…"

Without forewarning Lord Nester growled and shook his arm free, at the same time shoving her backwards. Helplessly she flew across the room, hitting the side of her head against something hard. The last thing she saw before everything went black was her father disappearing through the doorway.

****

It was the pounding headache which woke her, and she threw herself to one side as her dinner came back up. She lay motionless until the retching eased, and then she opened her eyes.

The room she was in was dark. Only a small source of light originated from somewhere behind her, for which she was thankful, as her head hurt when her eyes met even the dim light.

Slowly she sat up, groaning. Her head felt ready to split in two. When the pain had faded enough for her to be able to open her eyes, she found herself on the largest bed she had ever seen. Despite the shadows, she could see that the room was filled with luxurious decorations.

For a moment she sat there bewildered, staring at all the lovely things. But then reality hit her, and with it the memory of her father's words.

He had given her away to save Charmaine.

And hadn't he admitted to not being her father? Her head seemed to work more slowly than ever, and it took her quite a while to remember it all. But as soon as she did, tears flowed down her cheeks.

The bastard. The lying bastard.

She put her hand against the side of her head where the pain was worst, and winced as her palm came away covered with almost-dried blood. The bastard had shoved her away and not even bothered to check whether she was still alive.

His brutal heartlessness stunned her.

This was the man she had for eighteen years thought of as her father. The man who had known her almost since the day she was born. And still she didn't matter to him. To him she was nothing.

Angrily she wiped the tears off her face.

She had to stop this. He wasn't worth it. With

fierce determination she stood, wincing a little at the searing pain through her head.

First she tried the door handle, but as she had suspected it was locked firmly. Then she went to the windows to see if she could open them, but they too were locked tightly, and there was no one on the outside whose attention she could try to get, as the windows faced the top of the trees in the park beyond the lawn.

As she moved around the bed, she found another door almost hidden in the decorative wall paintings. Eagerly she opened it, only to find herself in a closet full of women's clothing.

As she turned back to the bedroom with a disappointed sob, she found it wasn't empty any longer. Three men stood inside the now open door—Lord Bolton and two men she guessed were his footmen.

"My, my, Lady Penelope. If one didn't know better, one would think you were trying to escape from me."

The footmen snickered over Lord Bolton's joke, and Penny took a shaky breath. *Don't show him your fear,* she thought, over and over again. *Don't show him your fear.*

When she didn't respond to his joke, Lord Bolton frowned, disappointed, and with a crooked finger he urged her to come to him.

"No."

"Oh." It scared her more than anything to see how pleased he seemed at her refusal.

"Maybe you'll need a little push," he continued. "My men are used to handling little girls like you, and I have to admit I do enjoy watching them. Their hands are not too gentle, and you will soon be aware of how easily you bruise…"

He didn't continue, but she caught the meaning and paled. What had her father gotten her into? Was this the man she was supposed to do anything for?

"Unfortunately, I have a late-night appointment which I can't miss, so you will have to wait for my return later tonight. Please try to sleep. It will be more fun for both of us if you have your full strength back."

And with another snicker the three men left the room, and she heard them lock the door. She sank down onto the bed, wringing her hands desperately. What could she do? Falling asleep wasn't an option, as she had no inclination to be handled un-gently by anyone and especially not by Lord Bolton and his men.

She took a few deep breaths and squared her shoulders. If she was going to be saved, she would have to make it happen by herself. No one but her family knew of her whereabouts, and she knew none of them would come back for her. Not that her mother and sister wouldn't want to, but her father's selfishness would never let them.

After thoroughly going over the large bedroom, she knew there was no way out of there other than the one door which Lord Bolton had locked, but she went into the closet in one last desperate hunt for salvation. Clothes covered all four walls, and she prayed that they also covered an escape for her that her keepers had forgotten about.

Not until she searched the fourth wall did she find a small door hidden behind golden dresses, and she almost fainted with relief. Holding her breath, she moved the tiny latch. To her utmost joy, the door opened and she tumbled into another large room, but this one was empty and clearly not in use. Carefully she rearranged the dresses so they covered the small doorway again. She closed the door firmly and wished she had a key so she could lock it.

She ran across the large floor and tried the door to the hallway, but to her disappointment it too was locked. Tears pricked her eyes again as she looked around the empty room. There was no other door and no other escape...

The windows caught her attention, and with one last desperate, hopeful prayer she went to the first one and tried to open it. With a lot of creaking, the window did as it was asked, and Penny almost yelled with relief as the cold, rain-filled air of the April night washed her face.

As she looked down the stone wall, she sent a silent thank you to Francesca who, as the wanton little girl she had been, had forced Penny to climb everywhere and learn to face her fear of heights.

This wouldn't be too hard, she thought. She was just one story up, and the building was made out of stone in such a decorative way it closely resembled a stair for her. She might have to do a little jump in the middle, but then it wouldn't be too far down to the ground. And if she broke a leg she could always drag herself over to the park and hide among the bushes.

Filled with a confidence born of desperation, she started her journey down the stone wall. It was a bit slippery because of the rain, but she managed to stay steady, and as her feet finally touched the pavement she fell to the ground exhausted.

She let herself have a few minutes to get some

strength back and then quickly ran through the streets in what she thought was the direction of Berkeley Square.

Soon she stood outside her family's townhouse, drenched from the pouring rain. She stood still, staring up at the dark windows, as it dawned on her that she couldn't go home.

Her father would probably just send her back to Lord Bolton, and next time there would be no way for her to escape. The snickering footmen would make sure of that.

She turned and looked across the square toward the Darling townhouse, and she knew in her heart she had only one place she could go now—to Francesca.

A carriage came rushing down the street, and she hid in the shadows of the front door portal. As soon as the street was empty again, she rushed across the square. The rain pelted down much more heavily now, and as she reached the Darling townhouse, her dress was completely soaked and she was shivering with cold.

For a moment she hesitated outside the front door, but decided against knocking. It wasn't as if she didn't trust the Darling servants, but she was too worn out to face them, and there was also the risk of having to face Rake.

Instead she went around to the narrow alley leading to the stables and the private garden. All the doors at the back of the house were locked, but to her delight a ladder stood raised against the building almost where Francesca's room was situated.

Penny took a deep breath and told herself it was nothing. If she could climb down the stone wall of Lord Bolton's house, she should be able to climb a ladder.

Ignoring the creaking, she slowly moved upwards until she stood on the small ledge below the windows of the second story. It took her only five shaky steps along the ledge to get to the first of Francesca's windows, and with a tearful sigh of relief she knocked lightly on the glass.

It took four times and a knock hard enough to nearly shatter the glass before a sleepy-eyed Francesca peeped through the covering curtains. If she hadn't been shivering so badly, Penny would have laughed out loud at the look on Francesca's face.

Exhausted, she stood still, watching Francesca's desperate attempts to open the window, but it wouldn't budge. Her hands pulled and pulled at the handle, but nothing happened. The window was stuck, and Penny couldn't stop the helpless tears streaming down her face with the rain.

So close, yet so far away.

All she wanted was to come inside to Francesca and safe haven. Too much had happened to her over the last hours, and she needed to renew her strength to be able to handle it all. She needed peace. She needed to sleep.

With determination written all over her pretty face, Francesca ran over to the fireplace and collected a poker. She motioned to Penny to push as she pried the window with her tool, and on the second joint attempt they succeeded. With a terrible crash the window flew open and knocked Francesca backwards, while Penny tumbled into the room in a big wet heap.

Before either of them had a chance to speak, the door to Francesca's room burst open and the Earl of Newbury came storming through the doorway like an avenging Greek god, closely followed by most of the Darling family members.

They all stopped dead as they saw the soaked Penny on the floor beneath the open window.

"Penelope de Vere, what on earth are you doing here?" Lord Newbury hollered, with more anger than she had ever seen from him before, as he marched past her and closed the window with a bang. "Are you out of your bloody mind? This is the second floor you have entered. *The second!* What, of all stupid things in the world, could make you do such a bloody, idiotic thing?"

Lady Newbury, who wasn't as hotheaded as her husband, put a soothing hand on his arm before she gave Penny a look full of compassion.

"How are you, my dear?" Her voice was full of motherly care, and Penny felt a lump build in her throat. New tears filled her eyes and with a sob she threw herself into Lady Newbury's waiting arms.

"There, there," Lady Newbury whispered into her wet hair, and it felt too good, almost too safe.

"I'm sorry," Penny whispered through her tears, and Lady Newbury leaned back and caressed her cheek.

"Don't be."

"The second floor!" Lord Newbury puffed behind his wife, and Penny almost giggled as Lady Newbury rolled her eyes and sighed.

"You men, get out of here. This is for women only."

"What? No, we too want to know…"

Lady Newbury, who usually seemed the most soft and graciously feminine woman there was, gave the men a hard stare that made them all take an unwilling step back. She didn't have to repeat her demand, as the men left the bedroom, although under mumbled protest, as they all knew better than to challenge her.

Only one man remained inside the room—Rake.

He was clad in his breeches only, and his lean torso glistened in the mild candlelight. For once, his hair wasn't combed perfectly, and his face looked more menacing than Penny had ever seen it. If she hadn't known better, she would have thought him a pirate, not a distinguished gentleman of the *ton*.

"You too, get out." Lady Newbury's voice was hard, and her whole being screamed she wasn't going to discuss the matter.

Not that he cared. "No."

Rake's dark eyes never left Penny's face, and she started to sob again. There was nothing in the world she wanted more than to throw herself into his arms and let him be the secure retreat she desperately needed in her time of distress. But he had been more than clear the day before, when he told her he wanted her as mistress only.

He offered her only passion, not comfort.

"Please," she whispered to Lady Newbury, "Make him go away."

"*Now*, Rake." Lady Newbury chided as she let Penny go and stood to face her disobedient brother-in-law.

"I said no, I'm not leaving her."

Rake's voice shivered with rage as he took a step forward toward his sister-in-law.

But Lady Newbury had never let any of the Darling men patronize her, and with more force than anyone could have imagined possible from her smaller body, she shoved Rake hard in the chest. With a surprised look, he tumbled backwards, out through the door, and before he had a chance to regain his stance, Lady Newbury shut the door and locked it tightly.

"Now, let's get you out of those wet clothes."

A few minutes later Penny was dressed in one of Francesca's thickest nightgowns and sat curled up under a thick blanket in the armchair next to the roaring fire. Slowly the stiffness in her limbs started to ease, and she closed her eyes with a contented sigh.

She heard Lady Newbury ring for Nell, who then immediately was sent for a tray with tea and something to eat. Not until a gentle hand caressed her hair did Penny open her eyes again.

"Here, please have some tea. You need to get the chill out."

Numb, Penny took the teacup. As she nibbled on a warm scone, the older woman sat down next to her and looked at her sternly.

"First I want to tell you how climbing up to Fanny's bedroom was, as my husband said, incredibly idiotic and extremely dangerous. I want you to promise me to never, ever, do something like it again."

"Yes, my lady," Penny whispered, knowing Lady Newbury had every right to be upset with her. She had after all not only put her own life at stake, she had—although unwillingly—terrified both her friend and her friend's family.

"That said," Lady Newbury continued, "I urge you to tell us what you have been through. Penny dearest, you have a bruise on the side of your face which didn't happen by accident."

It was too much too soon.

"Please," Penny whispered. "Don't make me tell you. I don't want to think about it anymore. Can't we just forget about it?"

"Penelope de Vere, I thought you knew me better than this. Of course I won't let this be. You know I love you dearly, as you have always been more a sister, not merely a friend, to Fanny, and I promise you, my dear, I will not let you leave this house until I know what happened to you."

"Mama, please," Francesca begged. "You have to let Penny rest. Anyone can see she has gone through quite an ordeal, and I don't think this is the time to force her to tell you anything."

Ignoring her daughter's outburst, Lady Newbury continued, "I will give you the choice of telling me alone, if you prefer. But I tell you this: if you don't tell me, you will have to answer to both me and my husband first thing tomorrow morning."

"Mama!"

"Fanny, don't you see your friend has been handled quite roughly by someone? I can't ignore that, and I am surprised that you insist that I do."

"It's all right," Penny whispered to Francesca, knowing quite well Lady Newbury was right. She would have to tell them sooner or later. By choosing their home as her refuge, she had put them in an awkward position. They were not her legal guardians and had no right to let her stay without her parents' consent, or to hide her from them.

"Could I speak to you alone tomorrow morning? I don't think I can face…it…now. I-I need to sleep. Please?"

"You can come to my private rooms when you feel

you are ready. I will send my husband away, if it feels easier for you to speak only to me."

"Thank you."

Lady Newbury put her arms around Penny and gave her a soft, motherly hug, meant to strengthen her gently.

"I'm so sorry," Penny sobbed as soon as the door closed behind Lady Newbury. "I had nowhere else to go."

"You know you are always welcome to come to me wherever I am." Francesca smiled reassuringly. "And considering your disheveled person, I am most grateful you did come here. Although I would prefer you used the front door next time."

The gentle, friendly bantering felt amazingly good, and Penny couldn't help but giggle. It was a strange strangled sound, but still a giggle.

"I'm sorry I wasn't able to attend Almack's this evening as we had planned."

"I missed you dearly—for a while," Francesca said with a secretive smile which caught Penny's attention.

"Oh, dear, what happened?"

"Devlin kissed me!" Francesca squealed, unable to hide the extraordinary feelings filling her heart and soul.

"What? That's… That's… What was it like?" Penny knew what Francesca's game was, and she was thankful for it. Talking about something else calmed her and gave her thoughts a chance to settle down again.

"It was divine," Francesca sighed, with a dreamy smile. "Heaven on earth."

The memory of the kiss she and Rake had shared in

this very house echoed through Penny's heart, and she closed her eyes for a second as she remembered the sweetness of the moment.

"Heaven on earth," she whispered, repeating Francesca's words.

"Exactly," her friend continued with a giddy laugh. "It was simply perfect. Ah, I'm so happy I don't know what to do or say. I find myself wandering around squealing with joy now and then. My family thinks I'm crazy, but I don't care. I'm happy!"

Penny smiled and smiled as Francesca told her every little detail of the secret meeting which had ended with this perfect kiss and a joint promise of marriage, and even though she couldn't be happier for her friend she couldn't stop the envy which slowly overtook the giddiness.

It wasn't that she envied Francesca her man or the love they shared. It was the easiness of her friend's life which made her feel small and petty. She too wanted to have such a happy life without heartaches at every bend of the road.

But Penny's life wasn't as grand and easy as her friend's. She didn't have a family who would do anything for her. No, her family obviously preferred to do anything *to* her.

As if she sensed her friend's change of emotions, Francesca got down on her knees in front of Penny and took her cold hands in her warm ones.

"Please Penny, tell me."

Penny looked into Francesca's grey eyes, so much like Rake's but without the wickedness, and saw only love and concern. She swallowed and closed her eyes.

Why not? Why not tell Francesca and get it off her

chest? It wouldn't be easier to talk about it tomorrow.

Images of what had happened earlier flared before her eyes, and before she had a chance to change her mind she started to speak and didn't finish until she had told her friend everything that had happened, from the beginning to the end.

The whole ugly truth.

And in the end it was her friend's outrage that made her able to relax and her tears that let her fall asleep. Just the knowledge that she wasn't alone was enough for Penny to be able to let go of the horrifying experience, if only for a few precious hours.

Tomorrow she would tell Lady Newbury, and then maybe they could talk about the future, or Penny's lack of one.

All her dreams about love and a family of her own were gone. What was left was a scandalously unmarried woman, a pariah to any man seeking a wife.

In one short moment her father had not only destroyed all her chances of a good life, he had also made sure to scar her heart forever by taking away the only thing she had lived for.

A dream that now would never come true.

Chapter Eleven

"You are worrying me, my dear."

Penny looked up from her reading and met the concerned eyes of Anna Darling, the Duchess of Berkeley. With a defeated sigh she put the book in her lap. She had known this conversation would take place sooner or later, with no possibility of escape.

"Please don't worry. I'm fine."

"No, you are not. Anyone who looks at you can see how you are slowly withering away, and I simply cannot stand idle any longer."

"Lady Anna…"

The older woman held up one hand. "It's September, Penny. *September*! You have been moping around like a family ghost for the last five months, and I won't have it further. Enough is enough. You have to start living again. You have to learn to embrace life again."

The duchess's harsh words cut through Penny like knives. "I have been through quite an ordeal, as I thought you were well aware, and I think it earns me the right to expect a little more consideration than this."

"Oh, you think so, do you?" The duchess snapped the book from Penny's lap and threw it across the great library of Chester Park. It landed with a thud on the other side of the room. "Well, consider your days of consideration over. A new era has just begun, and it has no place for a young girl who can't get over the past."

Penny gasped at her hostess's unusual harshness. She had never met this Anna Darling before. She had not thought the petite, gentle duchess could behave this obnoxiously.

"I know you have been through something so awful it would have knocked even the strongest person to the floor. But it happened in April, and everyone has moved on since then. Everyone but you."

"How can I move on?" Penny blinked away the tears of indignation threatening to fill her eyes. "My own father destroyed my life and my every chance for happiness. How can I move on? There is nowhere for me to move to! When this comes out in the open, I will be a social pariah, and not one sane man will consider me as a possible wife, at least not one of my own class."

"But it won't come out. No one will ever know. I won't tell anyone and neither will His Grace. Besides us, it is only Fanny and her parents who know exactly what really happened, even though Richard at first relentlessly tried to threaten us into telling him—the scoundrel."

Penny ignored the remark about Rake. "But there's my family, and Lord Bolton and his two footmen. Believe me, sooner or later someone will talk."

The duchess snorted disrespectfully. "Your family will never say a word. It would not only destroy your reputation but theirs, too. I promise you, they are much too eager to keep their standing among their peers. As to Lord Bolton, he also has too much to lose to let the truth be known. His footmen must know more than anyone else how evil he is and what would happen to them if they should ever mention this to a living soul."

Penny looked down at her hands. She knew the duchess was right, but it didn't mean anything to her. So what if the truth never came out? She knew.

She would always have the horrifying memories of the evening at Lord Bolton's house, and she couldn't pretend they weren't there. Every night she dreamt about Lord Bolton and the insanity which oozed from him, and every night she woke up soaking wet with perspiration, screaming with fear.

How could she ever marry someone without telling that person about what had happened to her? How else could she explain her nightmares? And any man who heard the story wouldn't see her as a possible wife, as she had, after all, been without chaperone in a bachelor's house. And not only in the house—she had been in a bedroom with him.

There was no way around it.

All her dreams of love and a home of her own were gone. All she had left was the Darling family, and she knew she would sooner or later have to leave them too. She couldn't spend the rest of her life living upon them as some sort of poor leeching relative. She would have to find a way to support herself, and the only question was how.

As if she knew what was going on in Penny's head, the duchess sat down beside her and tenderly put a supportive arm around her shoulders. "You know you are welcome to stay with us for the rest of your life. We would love to have you. It's just that we adore you too much to see you waste yourself and the happiness you deserve. You are such a lovely girl and worth so much more than spending your life alone."

"I know," Penny whispered. "But love is not for me anymore. No man will ever want me when he learns what happened to me that night."

"But nothing happened."

"It could have."

The duchess sighed. Penny's words were true. "But what about Richard? He will marry you if you just open up to him."

A strange mix of laughter and sobbing eluded Penny. "No, he won't."

"Sweetheart, I know my son, and I have watched him since you all arrived for Fanny's wedding in August. He wants you badly and suffers because you insist on holding him at arm's length."

"I know he wants me."

"You know?"

"He told me as much."

The duchess gasped happily. "He did? But this is marvelous news. Oh, Penny, I can hardly believe this. I had hope for him to finally come around and leave this stubbornness about staying a bachelor. But this... this...This is fantastic!"

Penny didn't know whether to laugh or cry. The duchess's obvious happiness over the possibility of Penny marrying her son was like balm on her shredded heart, and she really wished she wouldn't have to tell the kind lady the truth.

But she had to. Rake would never marry her, and it wasn't fair to let the duchess believe he would.

"He is still the same, I'm afraid. He is the most confirmed bachelor of his time, as he claims."

The duchess frowned. "But you said he had told you he wanted you?"

"Yes, Lady Anna, he did. He asked me to become his mistress."

The duchess's immediate anger reminded Penny strongly of the wrath Rake had shown the night she had crashed into the Darling townhouse.

"Are you sure he asked you to become his mistress?" The duchess's teeth clenched.

Penny nodded, knowing it was better to spill it all out immediately. "Yes, I am. He even asked me in which part of London I would prefer my house to be situated, the house in which the bed would be quite large and well used."

The duchess sat back and let go of Penny. "I can't believe this. Not Richard. I'm not ignorant of his behavior just because I'm his mother, and I know he has always been a libertine…But this?"

"I'm sorry," Penny whispered, and the duchess gave her a half-smile.

"Don't be, my dear. You did the right thing by telling me. Otherwise I would have been pestering both of you with constant nagging about marriage. I don't know how to handle this, though. Richard is my son and I love him dearly, but this is unforgivable. You are a part of our family, so how could he even think about anything but marriage with you?"

"Lady Anna, please, can't you just let it be, for now? I just wanted you to know Rake is not a path I can choose. You know how much I care for him, and I have thought about this a lot. The only thing I know for certain is that I will never give in to his request, as I would rather live a whole life without him than live a half life with him."

The duchess nodded. "You are stronger than I am,

Penny, that's for sure. All right. I won't mention this, but I am glad you told me. It forces me to rethink my plans."

"I don't know if I like the sound of that," Penny muttered, knowing too well how the duchess loved to interfere when she had her heart into something.

The duchess gave her a sour look, but ignored the comment. "So what about Mr. Bedford? He's been here a couple of times, asking about you and quite upset over your refusal to see him. I think the man rather thought you would be his wife by now."

"I know. I should talk to him and tell him the courtship is over, but I just can't…"

The duchess clapped her hands. "Then we will invite him over so you two can have a little chat and get things out in the air."

Penny shook her head, knowing there was no way to stop the duchess from inviting Thomas. She both dreaded and longed to meet him. He was such a good man, and it wasn't kind of her to hold him to his word when there were other women out there who gladly would marry him any day.

"I received a letter from your mother this morning," the duchess said, effectively catching Penny's attention.

"You did? What did it say?"

"She officially agreed to your staying with us as my companion for an indefinite time, and she also said she would spread the word among their acquaintance so you wouldn't have to answer to them by yourself."

A tear slid down Penny's cheek as thoughts about her mother clouded her eyes. Not being able to meet her mother and sister during these last five months had been awful. Her father had most efficiently removed her from their inner circle and made it clear she was not welcome back to it again.

Sick with longing for the two closest women in her life, she had forced herself to accompany the newlywed Francesca to one assembly while still in London, in desperate hope to maybe have a chance to speak to either of them.

But for once her father never left her mother's side, and she had not been able to come any closer to her sister. Charmaine had been a bit more resourceful and managed to give Francesca a letter for Penny.

It had not been long, only a few hastily scribbled sentences about how much Charmaine missed her and to inform her of how sick their mother had become since they lost Penny. Charmaine feared their mother hadn't so much time left on this earth, but their father still refused to let Penny anywhere near their house.

Penny had been devastated for days, and now, a week later, she again felt tears gather in her eyes at the mere thought of losing her mother and not being able to tell her goodbye.

"My heart goes out to your poor mother, who has no part of this. Your father is the evil one, forcing the rest of you apart because of his selfishness. It still amazes me how a father can act like this against his own child."

The duchess shook her head and Penny bit her lip. The only thing she had never told anyone about the night at Lord Bolton's house was her father's astonishing declaration that he was not her real father, or Charmaine's. She could hardly believe it herself, and in the end she had decided it wasn't important for the

Darlings to know.

"So how does it feel now when Fanny has left with her new husband? It was quite a dramatic time in London before she finally succeeded with her mission to abolish his stubborn plan of not being a part of their marriage."

"I should say!" Penny laughed, relieved over the much lighter subject which didn't involve her own person. "Poor man, he never stood a chance. Fanny is normally a force of nature, and when in love…unstoppable."

"Men can be stupid sometimes," the duchess said with an impish glance toward Penny. "They think they have everything figured out and don't realize we women know so much more than they do. It's our job to make them do as we want without their realizing it is we who put them up to it."

"And suddenly I can't help but feel sorry for His Grace." Penny's teasing made the duchess laugh.

"Yes, poor man. He never knew what happened. You know our story, how I was visiting Lord Newbury and fell helplessly in love with his father. I will tell you something I never told anyone else—I tried so hard for so long to make him change his mind about being too old for me that I finally gave in. I had run out of ideas on how to win him over."

"What happened?"

"It was all it took. That I gave up made him realize how life would be without me around, and he came crawling, practically on his hands and knees, to my father to ask for my hand in marriage."

"He's such a proud man, it must have been hard for him."

The duchess shrugged. "Not really. If it means enough to you, you can do anything as long as you win in the end. Later he told me he didn't mind the crawling or my father teasing him for years. All that mattered in the end was my shining eyes when he told me he couldn't imagine a life without me."

"Is this a subtle way to tell me to not let my own low self-esteem stand in the way of a chance for happiness with Thomas?"

"God, no," the duchess yelped, and clutched her throat dramatically. "You have me all wrong. I'm trying to tell you to not give up on Richard. No, you don't have to say it; I know he insulted you terribly, but I want you to think about what I told you about His Grace. Richard might be a bit stubborn about his bachelor lifestyle, but just because he is doesn't mean he doesn't care for you. He would never have asked you, Penelope de Vere—a highly beloved family friend—to become his mistress if he wasn't desperate for you. And such desperation is born out of strong emotion—like love."

"You never give up, do you?"

"No, which you should know by now; you have known me all your life, after all. In my heart, you two are the perfect match, and the only thing the last few months have done is create another obstacle for me to tear down."

"I agree to see Thomas, and I promise I won't hide without giving him a chance. But I can't give you the same promise about Rake."

"If you promise to be civil, at least, I'm satisfied."

Penny shook her head again and stood up. She put her hand on the duchess's arm as it was offered to her and let the grand lady of the house lead her out of the library.

Strangely enough she felt much better.

It had been an odd conversation indeed, but it had released some of the knots in her soul, and she found herself looking forward to meeting Thomas again. He was a good man and had, during those few months early in the year, become one of her best friends.

She had nothing to lose by meeting him. If his feelings remained the same, she might even consider marrying him even though she knew she had to tell him what had happened at Lord Bolton's before she could accept his proposal.

Did she trust him to keep her secret? She ransacked her heart, and the answer came without doubt—yes, she trusted him. He was a man who not only would keep what she told him to himself but also would be honest enough to let her know if he didn't want to marry her because of it.

The duchess and her little speech about not giving up had helped Penny a lot in her rocky climb back to life, but not in the way it was intended.

The loving mother was gently trying to nudge Penny to open up toward Rake and not let his stubbornness destroy their chance of happiness. But Penny knew the story between herself and Rake would never end happily. It had been an easy thing for Her Grace to follow His Grace around, relentlessly trying to persuade him into admitting he loved her, as he was a man who never would sink to the level of asking her to become his mistress.

The problem for Penny was that Rake had.

And if she followed him around out of a silly hope

it would make him love her, she would sooner or later—probably sooner—end up in his bed. She had no strength against him, and if she happened to get too close to him without an audience he wouldn't let it stop at a mere kiss.

And, as she once had told Charmaine, she knew if he ever did change his mind and marry her, he wouldn't stay satisfied for long. She would soon be lonelier than ever, while he rummaged through the *ton*, once again bedding every woman who looked at him twice.

Rake might be the true love of her life, but it didn't mean she was blind to what he was. The wicked, arrogant libertine was, after all, such a big part of him and, ridiculously, also one of the things she adored about him. Not the libertine part, of course, but his twinkling eyes, the amused voice, and the constant teasing. He had a wonderful way with words, and he had more than once driven his family crazy with his illogical logic.

Rake might be every woman's dream because of his dashing looks and wicked grin, but that was not why she loved him. For her, it was the Rake at Chester Park who had set her heart on fire.

The family man.

She loved the way he respected his father and brothers. She adored how he let his mother nag about this and that without ever cutting her off, how he let her kiss and hug him even though he was his own man.

But most of all it was the Rake who had let two little girls follow him around without ever uttering one word of complaint. Even when he was on the verge of adulthood and they interrupted his flirt with some young woman he didn't get vexed. Instead, he laughed, sent the indignant prospect away, and went swimming in the lake with them.

"James!" The duchess's happy voice cut through Penny's thoughts as they joined the rest of the family in the salon for afternoon tea. "I didn't know you had arrived from London. Did all go well in the end with our happy couple?"

Jamie, Rake's twin brother, hugged his mother close and gave Penny a quick peck on the forehead. "It all ended perfectly. Fanny is disgustingly happy, and the only one who can even come close to her extraordinary happiness is that silly husband of hers."

"How lovely to hear. All's well that ends well."

Penny ignored the pointed look in her direction and went to the tea table. Most of the Darling family had now returned from London and would stay at Chester Park until it was time for next year's Season in April, only leaving occasionally for a visit with friends or extended family.

The only ones missing were Francesca's closest family and Rake. The other five Darling brothers all sat in the salon, chatting and teasing, a normal Darling meal.

"It's lovely weather outside. Would you like to accompany me on the terrace?"

Penny looked up into Jamie's silvery grey eyes, of a much lighter shade than Rake's smoky ones, and she nodded, letting him lead the way. He must have something on his mind, and she knew better than to try to avoid him. The Darling men could be quite obnoxious when set on a mission, and it was better to stay put and pretend to listen than to hide and hope you weren't found.

As she put her hand on his arm, she couldn't help noticing how different Jamie and Rake were, despite being twins. The other pair of twins, Edward and William, one year older than these youngest brothers, were replicas of each other and hard to tell apart.

With Jamie and Rake, on the other hand, it was easy to tell they were brothers, as they both looked much like their father, but where Rake had darker coloring with his dark brown hair and smoky grey eyes, Jamie was much lighter, almost silvery in his coloring.

His too-long hair was tied with a leather strap and hung down his back like a thick silver snake. His dark eyebrows emphasized his light grey eyes in such a way they shone.

Her mother had once said she thought Jamie's eyes were wolf-like, cold and ruthless. But Penny knew better. Jamie was one of the kindest, most thoughtful men of her acquaintance.

It was a beautiful September afternoon, and the sun warmed them as they sat down on the small terrace outside the open French doors. Surrounded by the last roses of summer, it was almost as if they had stepped into a bottle of perfume.

"I haven't seen you for a while, Penny, but I must say I'm glad you look so much better than the last time I saw you. It's almost like having the old you back, only prettier than ever."

"Thank you." She blushed over the unexpected compliment. "I feel better."

"I know we are not to ask you about what happened to you, so you don't have to worry about me pressuring you for answers. But I do want to ask you one thing, and I hope you won't think less of me for doing so."

She looked into his eyes, which seemed much older than his years. Jamie had, together with his uncle Harry and his cousin Lee, joined the army and gone off to deal with that upstart Napoleon. Penny knew he had come home a changed man, a broken man. His refusal to tell anyone what had happened during his time in France had hurt his family deeply, but the one who had been most upset had been Rake, his twin brother.

Once Jamie had been almost as wicked and unstoppable as Rake, but since his return he hardly looked at women and avoided most of his peers as much as he could.

If anyone knew not to ask too much, it was Jamie, and she nodded to let him continue.

"What is it with you and Rake?"

The question took her by surprise, and she stared at him, openmouthed. She had been prepared for any question regarding her night at Lord Bolton's. Now she was completely caught off guard.

"Don't act so surprised, Penny dear. You two have been acting like two fighters since last summer, circling each other with your fists raised."

She didn't know what to say or where to begin. The question might be a single sentence, but the answer was much longer.

"I know my brother," Jamie continued, "and he's not a man to hurt women. Honestly, his problem has always been keeping them off him. But the way you two act around each other... Let's just say I'm not sure what to think anymore. I have tried to talk to Rake, but he just snaps at me to put my nose back where it belongs, and since I have been shutting him out, well, you could say I'm not in a very good position to pressure him for an answer. This is why I come to you, because you are the other side of this, and maybe you could ease my fears a bit."

"What is between me and Rake has nothing to do with anything he has done," Penny assured him, and she could see how his shoulders started to relax a bit. "We have a difference of opinion in a matter close to my heart, and as neither of us wants to give in, I'm afraid it has become quite an obstacle between the two of us."

"This is indeed a mystery. You say there is nothing more than a verbal disagreement between the two of you, and yet he behaves as if he has nothing left to live for. The old Rake used to live life to its full, but this new Rake…Penny, it's like he doesn't care anymore."

Penny wrung the delicate fabric of her skirt between her fingers. "Jamie, I don't think this is about me. The last time I spoke to Rake was in April, before the night when I…when I arrived at your townhouse in such an unorthodox manner."

"Are you sure?"

She nodded. "I am. I have avoided him as much as possible since. Well, not only him. I have avoided most of you."

"Hasn't he tried to talk to you at all? He was constantly nagging the rest of us for months about you and what possibly could have happened to you."

"He tried to talk to me a couple of times in the beginning, but I didn't want to talk to anybody. I wanted only to be left alone."

"You told him that?"

"Of course I did. I said the same to anyone who

tried to corner me."

"But did you tell him to leave you alone?"

"I might have. Honestly, I don't remember. It's such a hazy part of my life."

The frown on Jamie's forehead became deeper. "There is something I'm missing here, something of great importance."

"I wish I could offer you more help." Penny smiled with sincere apology.

Jamie shook his head, frustrated. "This drives me crazy. Really it does. You haven't been to London during the last part of the Season and seen him, so you don't know how outrageously he has been behaving. At first we didn't think much of it. Rake has always been the ladies' man, and seeing him surrounded by eager women has always been a normal picture. But lately…"

Jamie's voice trailed off, and Penny found herself waiting for him to continue, with an uneasy feeling in her whole body. What had Rake done?

"He's always been a gentleman about his women and behaved with discretion. Before, it used to be quite difficult to figure out who his current mistress was, as he never let any special interest show, both because of the need for privacy and to honor the lady in question. Now it's like he doesn't care who he hurts or who knows about his escapades. He has been acting in the worst way, and it's rumored he has been dueling a couple of times, too, because of some angry husbands with tender toes." Jamie sighed deeply, his frustration clear. "The Rake I know and love would never behave like this. Something is terribly wrong with him, and I'm desperate to help him, if I only knew how to."

He gave her a look worthy of a puppy, still hoping

for her to enlighten him.

"I'm sorry," she breathed. "I didn't know, and I can understand your concern. I too know this is not the Rake we all know and…"

She caught herself before she let out the word "love," but Jamie noticed, and a small amused smile flew over his full lips like a memory from the days when his heart wasn't as troubled.

"Anyway," she continued quickly to hide her embarrassment, "I wish I could help you with Rake, I really do, but as I said, I have hardly seen him."

"And yet you two are in full disagreement over something?"

She blushed as he lifted an eyebrow. Jamie had a way of seeing straight through a person and hardly ever missed the right conclusion. "Our disagreement has nothing to do with his behavior, I assure you."

"May I ask what you are disagreeing about?"

She shook her head and blushed, and he chuckled knowingly in response, which made her turn even redder.

"I think you are quite wrong, Penny dear. You two obviously have had a lovers' quarrel, and now he's rebelling because of it."

"It's *not* a lovers' quarrel."

"No?"

She frowned at him, and he gave her another amused smile, obviously not believing her at all.

"There is no love between Rake and me."

"Oh, come on, Penny, I'm Rake's twin brother and we have a very special bond. I don't know what's in his head, but I know what's in his heart, and I can tell you one thing—he wants you badly."

"I know he wants me," she snorted. "He has told me as much."

Jamie stared at her open-mouthed. "He has?"

"Why, yes. He has been quite frank about it, too."

"B-but..." Jamie looked as bewildered as he felt. "Why aren't you two living happily ever after, then? Why are you hiding here at Chester Park, slowly withering away, while he is in London breaking every rule there ever was?"

"Because life isn't like a fairytale, and everything I have been through this past year has shown me more than anything how dreams never come true. Until now I have spent most of my life yearning for the moment when Rake would look at me and really see me. And you know what? When he finally did, he asked me most sincerely to become his mistress. Not wife—mistress."

"I don't believe you."

"It's the truth."

"You are a friend of the family; of course he wouldn't ask you to become his mistress. It would not only be most disrespectful to you but also to the rest of us who care deeply for you. You must have misunderstood."

"I'm sorry, Jamie."

"I can't believe you. I can't."

She put her hand over his where it rested on the bench. "Then don't believe me. I don't mind."

He sighed, a deep heavy sigh from the bottom of his heart. "Of course I believe you. It's just that it's not like Rake to behave like this. Now you have me more worried than before. So he's not trying to ruin his own life only, he has been after yours, as well? It doesn't make sense."

"Everything can't always make sense."

"No, indeed not." Jamie laughed bitterly. "But I'm a practical man, and I have a thing for making things at least seem to make sense. It soothes me."

He stood and took a few steps toward the French doors before he hesitated and looked back down at her where she sat on the bench. "I'm sorry to hear he never asked you to marry him. I would have loved to have you for a sister."

Before she had a chance to reply, he disappeared into the salon, where his family still drank their afternoon tea.

This was indeed a day of revelations.

First the duchess, who had more or less forced her to drag herself up from the hidey-hole she had created. And now there was Jamie, who had emerged from his own cave and revealed his deep concern for Rake. She wouldn't be honest if she said she didn't care, because she did. Her heart was filled with jealousy—mixed with worry over his careless behavior amongst the *ton*.

The mere thought of him cornering another woman with his dark eyes filled with lust made her want to scream. Jamie's words had tortured her, and the lump in her throat threatened to strangle her.

Laughter from inside the castle broke through to her clouded mind, and she shook the thoughts of Rake away. He had made his choice the day he asked her to become his mistress, and what she had left now was to find someone who wouldn't mind marrying a young lady with a possibly bad reputation.

Thomas's image rose before her, and she closed her eyes as the obstruction in her throat slowly vanished. All her life she had only had one wish—to

155

belong to someone who wanted her; someone who needed her.

If Thomas still wanted to marry her after hearing what she had lived through, she would know without a doubt that she had found the right man to fulfill her dreams.

Chapter Twelve

"I've been waiting for you to send for me, and I must admit I am glad you finally did."

Penny blushed as she looked up into Thomas's warm brown eyes. The honest admiration with which he showered her was like manna for her tarnished soul.

"Me too," she admitted shyly.

A playful wind tossed his blond hair, and unconsciously he lifted a bronzed hand and tried to straighten it, but only succeeded in tousling it a bit more.

"Please indulge me. What did you think of your first Season in London, now when you have seen it with your own two eyes?"

"It was quite fascinating at first, I assure you. I found it most entertaining to watch how everyone interacted with each other."

"Really?" he drawled as he opened his eyes as wide as he possible could in feigned surprise. "You found it interesting and entertaining? Do tell me—who are you, and what have you done with Penny?"

She put a hand in front of her mouth to hide the smile which escaped her.

He was such a dear, dear man. He held himself high above everything that was the essence of the social life of the *ton,* and she couldn't admire him more for it, especially now when she'd had her own share of the

Season and found it much less appealing than she had dreamt about when she was younger.

Slowly she crossed the terrace and sat down on the low wall surrounding it. She patted the stone next to her invitingly and, as a gentleman should, he sat down on the offered spot.

"What a lovely day it is today." He lifted his face toward the blue sky and the golden sun. "It's hard to imagine we had early snow at this time last year."

Inside Chester Park, on the other side of the French doors leading out to the terrace, the Duchess of Berkeley fought with her embroidery. She was the best of chaperones, Penny thought, as the understanding lady had chosen a chair on the other side of the salon, as far away from the young couple as possible yet still keeping them in view. There was no mistaking her approval, as she turned her side to them and let them interact without her watching their every move.

Penny blinked away the tears which blurred her vision. The love she felt for that older lady inside was overwhelming, and she knew she would never be able to express the extent of the gratitude she felt for the love and trust bestowed on herself.

"Her Grace is one of the most kindhearted ladies I know," Thomas said softly as he followed her gaze to their not-so-attentive chaperone. "I have always held her very high in esteem and, if you don't mind my honest words, I have to admit I'm quite glad you have such a close relationship with a lady of her heart."

Penny's heart skipped a beat.

There was no mistake in what was going on. Thomas was on the verge of proposing to her. The panic which shivered through her was a surprise—

wasn't this what she wanted? Then why was her first spontaneous thought to run as far away from him as she possibly could?

A few deep breaths later she had managed to calm herself enough to erase the last bit of panic.

She wanted this.

She wanted Thomas.

The sudden fear must have been the last of her silly childhood dreams recognizing this was a road of no regrets—if she chose to accept this proposal, she was never going to fulfill those dreams. But hadn't she already realized that life could be just as good even though one didn't follow one's deepest wish?

Thomas wasn't a substitute for Rake, whom she never would be able to have. He was simply another path in life. And as he gave her a smile filled with true devotion, she knew this was a path she didn't fear to travel.

He made her feel calm, cherished and—as Charmaine had put it—boringly serene. With him, she knew what she had and she knew what life would be like. And after all the horrendous things she had been through, she desperately wanted to know what was next in line for her.

Thomas would never make her feel vulnerable and unsure. So maybe he never would be able to love her the way she had dreamt, for the first seventeen years of her life, that Rake would. He still had the ability to make her perfectly happy. But more importantly, she knew she could make him a content and happy husband.

That was, if he still wanted her when she had told him the truth about her Season and her current home at

Chester Park.

"Penelope, you know how I felt about you six months ago, and I want you to know my feelings still remain the same. My heart, my hands, and everything else I own are yours if you want them."

The seriousness of his voice and the firm directness of his gaze brought new tears to her eyes. What had she ever done to deserve such devotion from this wonderful man?

"I'm honored to admit this is what I had hoped for," she whispered, and his grip on her hands tightened as his smile broadened.

"So you will become my wife?"

"Y-Yes, but there is one thing…"

"Penelope, you have made me the happiest of men!"

He moved an inch closer and she could sense his eagerness to seal their betrothal with a kiss, even though they were not quite alone. His honest reaction made her want to cry with despair over the possibility of maybe destroying this special moment.

But she had no choice. She would never be able to live with herself if she wasn't completely honest with him.

"Thomas, please."

The stress in her voice cut through his happy state of mind, and he hesitated for a second before retreating a little. "What is it, Penelope? Are you regretting your answer already?"

"No, of course not, but I must tell you something which might change your wish to have me as your wife."

He chuckled and leaned forward again. "I will

never change my mind. I have known for a long time that you are the woman I want to spend the rest of my life with."

"Please, just listen to me. I want you to know I will not hold you to your proposal if what I tell you is against everything you feel is right and what you can live with. If you still feel the same, you can ask me again, but I will not accept anything until you have listened to what I have to say."

He frowned at her, unable to imagine what she was talking about, but as her frenzy got through to him he nodded slowly. "I promise to hear you out. But I also promise you I will not change my mind. You are all I want in a wife."

Ignoring his kind words, she stood and began pacing in front of him, not able to look him in the eyes. She didn't want to watch his warm admiration turn into cold loathing. "You know I have been back at Chester Park for quite a while now, and that I didn't spend much more than a week in London before I left. You must have wondered why I returned so quickly and why I have been avoiding you these last months."

He nodded solemnly. Then, before she could change her mind, she blurted out the whole story from beginning to end, not skipping any part of the gruesome tale.

"And that is the reason I now live here at Chester Park. The duke and duchess have opened their arms to me and promised I will always have a home with them. If you choose to not propose to me again, I will understand why. If this ever comes out, my reputation will be destroyed forever. No one will ever believe my innocence, as the truth is I was left without chaperone in a bachelor's home. My father has more or less disowned me even though he is the one to blame, not me. But I can't ignore the fact it will be I—and the man I marry—who will suffer from this, not my father, if it ever becomes common knowledge."

As silence settled between them, she met his unreadable eyes for the first time since beginning her horrifying tale. Nothing in his complexion or his statuesque stance told her what he thought of her experience, and doubt made her shiver.

She couldn't help but think her honesty had destroyed her last chance at happiness. She could see him going through what she had just told him, trying to make sense of it.

All she could do was to wait. Wait for a verdict she was too terrified to hear.

When he finally spoke, he made her heart bolt.

"I'm grateful for your honesty. This must have been hard for you, opening up to me like this, and I want you to know how much I appreciate it."

The finality in his words brought tears to her eyes, and she couldn't do much more than whisper a thank you.

"I've been quite distraught over your refusal to see me, but this explains it all for me, of course. Your father…"

His voice broke off, but it had shaken with anger, and he opened and closed his hands as though desperate to hit something. Or someone.

"Your father is despicable. I can't understand how a man can behave like that to a child in his care. I really don't. I'm so sorry for the grief he has put you through by refusing to let you see your mother and sister. It must be so hurtful for you."

She nodded. The pain over not being able to see her sister and especially her sick mother was hard to live with. All she wanted to do was give her mother one last hug and whisper every word of love she could think of before she lost her forever.

But her father had made it very clear he would never tolerate her presence near any of them. She was *persona non grata* now and must not ever contact them again.

"I wish there were something I could do to lessen your pain." He stood and took her hand, so close to her she had to lean her head back to be able to look into his eyes. "I know you, Lady Penelope de Vere, and I know you are innocent in all of this. Of course I still want to marry you. In fact I can hardly believe you still want me after meeting men as heartless as your father and this Lord Bolton."

He wiped the tears off her cheeks and pulled her into his arms, hugging her close to him in an effort to offer her love and protection. She held on to his jacket as if her life depended upon it, savoring his compassion.

"I do hope finding you two like this means you are about to get married, because if you are not, I'm afraid I will have to force you into holy matrimony without any regard to your feelings and wishes."

Breathlessly they broke apart, and Penny couldn't hold back a happy smile at the duchess, who stood in the doorway, an amused smile on her face.

"Your Grace, I do apologize for my wanton behavior. I usually don't act this way, but as you have guessed, Penelope has accepted my proposal that she become my wife, and I was quite beside myself out of sheer happiness."

"Oh, it's all right, Mr. Bedford. I have known you all your life, and I know you never would openly show such bodily affection, especially in front of others, without great reason. I have always admired your gentlemanly ways and how stoically you hold yourself to your late mother's lessons about how a young country squire should behave. As a mother of young men not as well behaved as you, I admit being quite impressed with your mother's achievement."

Thomas beamed with satisfaction at the duchess's kind words. "I'm pleased to hear this, Your Grace. My mother always spoke highly of you, and I know she would have been proud to hear your words today."

"Did your mother ever tell you we knew each other before either of us married? We were of the same age and debuted together in London all those years ago."

Thomas bobbed his head eagerly. "Yes, Mother told me. She said you two and a couple of the other debutantes were quite close then, and you were the best of friends."

"Oh, yes, indeed." The duchess gave Thomas a radiant smile, but Penny could tell the lady lied; Lady Anna had never been a good liar, which her sons had used all through their childhood days.

"I wonder if you could tell me where to find His Grace? I have something very important to ask him, something a man normally asks a girl's father. But, as you know…"

Thomas voice broke of, and the duchess patted his hand with affection. "Yes, of course. His Grace is in his study. If you go to the foyer, you can ask one of the footmen to show you the way. We will await your return here. Please ask my husband to join you, by my request."

"Thank you, Your Grace."

Thomas bowed his head politely to her before he turned to Penny. "I will return shortly, and hopefully you and I can start planning the rest of our lives together, starting with the wedding."

Penny blushed as he lightly kissed the back of her hand and, with a last lingering look, left her alone with the duchess as he disappeared into the salon. Not until she heard the door close behind him did she turn toward her companion.

"Thank you," she said with all her heart.

"For what?"

"For accepting Thomas as my future husband and for not letting him know his mother wasn't one of your closest friends."

The duchess laughed, a bit embarrassed, caught in a lie. "Bloody bad liar that I am. I don't think he noticed, though. He seemed quite impressed by his mother's connections, and I didn't think there was any need to take that away from him. And regarding my accepting him as your future husband—I must admit I still desperately cling to my wish for you to become my daughter in name, too, not only in heart. But I don't hold it against you, my dear. I too recognize how perfect Mr. Bedford is for you in your current state of mind."

"My current state of mind?"

"Yes, dearest. I don't think you would have been this keen on marrying Mr. Bedford if you weren't too much in need of feeling safe and being able to trust someone. This is your life, and I'm not going to tell you how to live it, but I want you to please indulge me and wait with the wedding until Christmas."

"I won't change my mind."

The duchess smiled sadly. "I know. But the only thing I now can hope for is that Richard will, before it's too late."

"He won't, which I know you are well aware of. He never changes his mind about anything."

Penny bit her lip, unable to continue without bursting into tears. She didn't want to think about Rake right now, especially not at this moment that should be the happiest in her life. But the duchess seemed determined to talk in her son's behalf, and Penny knew there was no way to stop her.

"He might. If you let him."

"If I let him?" Penny scoffed. "What on earth makes you think I would have something to do with his changing his mind? He is a man of his own and with quite an intelligent mind of his own. There is nothing I could say or do that would ever make him rethink."

The duchess looked down at her nails and seemed almost uninterested in the conversation. "You could tell him about the night at Lord Bolton's."

"No!"

"Why not?" The duchess lost her indifferent attitude. "He has every right to hear this too."

"No, he hasn't," Penny snorted, indignant.

"Yes, he does, because he loves you."

"No, he doesn't."

This time it was the duchess who snorted. "Yes, he does, and the only one who is stupid enough not to realize that is you."

Penny snorted again, but not as indignantly as before. Her silly, stupid heart immediately started to do somersaults with joy at the duchess's words, and she let herself float away on a wave of dreams for a moment before reality came back and hit her on the head.

"Lady Anna, please, he doesn't love me. And furthermore, I know he never will."

"Maybe we will always disagree about what he feels for you, but please hear me out when I ask you to tell him about what happened that night."

"Why?"

This time Penny couldn't stop the tears, and soon she sat on the terrace wall again, sobbing because of a pain which would never leave her. The duchess sat down next to her and handed Penny her silken handkerchief.

"Because he needs to hear it. He's not been himself since the night when you crashed into Fanny's bedroom and he could see quite clearly that you had been through something horrendous which had left you a terrified shell of yourself. Your decision to not tell him—or anyone else—about it devastated him. For the first months he kept tormenting us for information. But we had promised you to not talk about it. In the end he gave up and closed us all out, just as we had closed him out."

The duchess's motherly concern was overwhelming, and Penny wanted to give in to her wish. But the mere thought of having to face Rake and tell him the events of that night made her nauseous and more determined than ever to never let him know.

It had been difficult enough telling Thomas about the incident; telling Rake would be like walking through the nightmare again, and she knew she couldn't. Rake wouldn't as lightly brush it away as Thomas had. No, Rake would demand retaliation and wouldn't rest until all the culprits had been caught and punished. Rake was a fighter, a man of revenge. He wasn't a healer.

And she needed time to heal.

She needed a chance to put it all behind and continue on with her life quietly.

Telling Rake would be too much raw emotion and too little redemption. She knew he didn't love her, but she couldn't deny the fact that he did care for her. He had, after all, known her throughout her whole life, and even though he had spent most of the time trying to avoid her, he still had always shown her an absentminded brotherly affection.

The duchess's dejected sigh interrupted Penny's thoughts. "I know I can't force you to do as I want, and you know I will never break my vow of secrecy and tell Richard myself. But I need you to please hear me out for one last time. If you do, I promise to let you live your life as you want. Well, at least as long as Richard doesn't change his mind. If so, I won't be able to stop myself from interfering on his behalf."

Penny smiled teary-eyed over the honest request and knew she couldn't deny her benefactor anything. She cared too much about the duchess. She nodded in response and was rewarded with a smile just as teary-eyed. "Thank you."

The duchess twitched the delicate fabric of her skirt between her fingers, seeming more distressed than Penny had ever seen her.

"I love my son dearly, and I can hardly stand

watching him suffer like this without being able to help him. I know you love him too. Probably more than you ever will admit, especially to him."

The last part came with a very pointed look, and Penny blushed. She could hardly deny her feelings for Rake. They had been her constant companion for the last eighteen years.

"He has changed over the last couple of months," the duchess continued forcefully. "And now he's behaving like a man without sense or sensibility. He's no longer the man I brought up, and James tells me no one can reach through to him."

"Jamie told me as much yesterday," Penny admitted. "He seemed quite worried."

"You know how absentminded and elusive James has been over the last year, burying himself in his bad memories, so that must show you I don't exaggerate how large the problem with Richard is."

"Of course I believe you." Penny sighed over the impossible situation. She felt desperate in her need to help the duchess with her concerns regarding Rake, but she still didn't want to enlighten him.

"Just talk to him. You don't have to tell him anything if you don't want to, but at least he will see you are not avoiding him anymore. I know he will not be too overjoyed about your upcoming engagement, but at least he will know you two are on speaking terms again. He needs you, Penny."

"I-I wouldn't know wh-what to say."

The duchess hugged Penny close. "Don't you fret over this, my dear. You don't need to do much. Just look at him. Talk to him. Laugh with him. Make him believe you are fine again and have overcome your earlier problems."

"What if he doesn't want to talk to me?"

"Why wouldn't he want to talk to you?" The duchess snorted most disrespectfully. "I promise you, all you need to do is smile at him and he'll be rolling at your feet faster than my husband's beloved dogs."

"Really? Smile?" Penny rolled her eyes, effectively taking away the seriousness of the conversation.

The duchess laughed, obviously relieved at Penny's light response. "Yes, smile. You have quite an overwhelming smile, my dear. He won't be able to ignore you."

"Who is ignoring our Penny?"

The duke's booming voice filled the rose-clad terrace, and the two ladies greeted the two gentlemen eagerly. Penny slipped her hand into the crook of Thomas's arm, which he offered her politely as she smiled at the duke.

For being such a mean-looking man, Hannibal Darling had the softest heart she knew of. He was her champion and would turn a mountain into pebbles if it meant saving her.

During these last couple of months, he hadn't once tried to make her open up to him. Instead, he had only hugged her whenever he thought she needed a bit of love and devotion. To a scorned soul, a bearlike hug now and then meant everything.

"So," the duchess purred. "Have the two of you had an interesting conversation?"

"Indeed we have." Thomas beamed. "His Grace has most graciously agreed to my request for Penny's hand in marriage."

"Oh, what fantastic news!" The duchess clapped

her hands with a little too much excitement, and her husband rolled his eyes knowingly. "Now I have a wedding to plan."

When Penny opened her mouth, the duchess wagged warningly with her index finger. "Don't you even try to take this away from me, Lady Penelope de Vere."

"I wasn't." Penny laughed. "As if I ever would dare."

Thomas laughed too and absentmindedly patted Penny's fingers where they rested on his arm, something she found most adorable.

"Penny and I would be honored if you would help us with this affair. I'm currently quite busy with the harvest and haven't got many hours to spare. I would rather spend the few hours I do have enjoying Penny's company instead of planning a wedding."

"How gentlemanly of you, Mr. Bedford," the duchess praised him, and Penny hid a smile when Thomas blushed happily. He was such an easy man to satisfy. She wouldn't have any problems keeping him happy. And a happy Thomas meant a happy Penny.

Married life promised every minute to be better and better.

"Oh, I forgot about it being harvest time." The duchess almost succeeded with looking as distraught as she sounded. "Then I guess an autumn wedding wouldn't be a good thing."

Thomas blinked, distressed. "Your Grace, if you want an autumn wedding, I will of course take the time for it. Marrying Penny is on the top of the list of my chores."

She didn't really like to be called a chore, but

Penny guessed she couldn't be picky. She was, after all, *on* his list.

"Maybe a Christmas wedding sounds better?"

She was the worst of actors, but Thomas didn't notice the duchess's badly hidden satisfaction over the outcome of things.

"A Christmas wedding would be perfect," Thomas breathed, relieved. "By then I will have had plenty of time to take care of the more important tasks and will have all the time in the world for Penny."

For being such an educated man, he was quite miserable with expressing himself, Penny thought with an affectionate smile. Their Graces stared openmouthed at the poor man who had unknowingly insulted his wife-to-be in the worst way, but she didn't care.

"Christmas it is," she agreed and hugged his arm lightly as he smiled just as happily back.

"Only a few more months…"

He didn't finish the sentence, but she knew what he meant and blushed. Only a few more months and she was his.

Memories of the one kiss they had shared in the carriage from Sandhurst made her feel warm and longing for more. It hadn't been as shattering as the kisses Rake had given her in the Darling townhouse, but it had been enough for her.

It had felt nice and comfortable. All her senses had still worked and she hadn't needed time to catch her breath at all.

"Maybe you two would like to take a stroll in the garden?" The duke nodded toward the small stair which led through the rosebushes and down into the maze where Penny had spent many hours as a child.

"What?" His lovely wife gasped, but he ignored her outburst.

"I think you two need a little solitude, and as you now are engaged to be married, I think we should offer you a bit more room to get to know each other."

"Thank you, Your Grace." Thomas immediately moved toward the steps, dragging Penny with him. By the time they reached the bottom, the arguing voices of the married couple on the terrace could no longer be heard. Completely alone, they entered the magnificent maze that generations of Darlings had contributed to, creating these grand walls of mystery.

When Thomas hesitated at the opening, not knowing whether to walk left or right, Penny grabbed his hand and, with an inviting smile, ran to the right. With him close behind her, she didn't stop until they reached the opening in the middle of the maze.

"This is marvelous," Thomas breathed, as he feasted his eyes on the little pond with its small wooden bridge leading to a fanciful gazebo on a man-made island.

"Fanny and I have spent most of our summers as children here, playing and laughing, and I always love coming back. I have been so happy here I can't help but feel good standing here."

"This must have been heaven for two little girls with great imaginations."

"Indeed it was." She laughed, took his hand again, and led him over the bridge to the gazebo.

As soon as they were inside he let go of her hand and instead grabbed her waist, hauling her closer to him.

"Hello, my lovely wife-to-be." He smiled warmly

at Penny, and she put her arms around him, lifting her face up toward his invitingly. Slowly he leaned down and placed his lips gently against hers. She closed her eyes, waiting for more to come.

"The hell you will!"

The menacing roar tore through the comfortable silence of the gazebo, and before either of them had a chance to react they were ripped apart.

As Penny stumbled across the floor, she saw Thomas fall and heard a large thud as his head banged against the hard wood. The air went out of him with a moan as he fell unconscious.

Openmouthed with horror, Penny stared at Rake, who hovered over Thomas looking more like an avenging soldier than a fashionable gentleman of the *ton,* his handsome face twisted with hatred and his hands clenched threatening.

"Are you hurt?"

Not until he turned his head and his dark eyes settled upon her person did she understand it was she he meant.

Speechless, she numbly shook her head, too outraged to find the right words—or any words, for that matter. What on earth was he thinking? Why had he attacked them like he was some sort of savage from the darkest of medieval times?

"I knew he would try something, when I spotted the two of you entering the maze," Rake said through his teeth. "I could see it by the way he followed you so close."

"You hit him," Penny accused, when she finally found her voice again. "You…Hit…Him…"

"Of course I did. You can thank me later, when

you feel better."

"Thank you?" There it was—he had finally lost his mind. "Why on earth would I thank you for hitting Thomas unconscious?"

He arched a perfect eyebrow as he looked down at her. "He was attacking you."

"He was not!"

"Yes, he was. I saw him throwing himself all over you, when I reached the centre of the maze."

She couldn't stop a snort. "He wasn't throwing himself all over me. He was hugging me."

Rake frowned at her as he reached to grab her chin, forcing her to look into his smoky eyes. "Are you sure he didn't hurt you? You sound a bit distraught."

"Of course I'm distraught, you snake. You almost killed him."

"Come on, Penny," Rake grinned as he lost the last of his earlier anger. "You know me—I'm too good a boxer to kill anyone. He's only a bit knocked out. He will be just fine when he wakes up, even though he doesn't deserve it."

He tenderly caressed her chin for a brief moment, and then before she had a chance to react he pulled her into his arms.

"I was so afraid I wouldn't be able to save you this time either," he whispered into her hair. "All I could think about was how you looked in Fanny's room that night, all messy and bruised. I was too late then, but not this time. This time I saved you."

"For goodness' sake," Penny muttered, not really listening to him as she tried to free herself from his too-enticing embrace. He didn't yield. Instead he held her even closer to him, and she was starting to feel lightheaded as she felt his body against hers.

"Please, let me go," she begged, desperate to get away from him and the emotions he awakened in her. Thomas was lying unconscious on the floor, and here she was burning for another man.

What kind of woman was she?

"I will never let you go." His lips touched her neck and she lost her ability to breathe. "You are where you belong—in my arms."

"I don't belong in your arms," she squealed as his lips moved closer to her chin and her lips, creating waves of excitement throughout her body. "I belong in Thomas's."

He lifted his head and gave her an amused grin. "Really, Penny, I thought you had given up that stupid wish by now, about becoming Mrs. Boring Saint Thomas."

"Don't call him that."

"Why not? He is boring. He spends his days farming and his evenings reading and detests anyone who likes to do something more frivolous. How much more boring can a man get?"

"I don't find him boring at all, especially as I too love to read."

Rake shook his head, amused over her stoic siding with Thomas. "You don't have to defend him to me, Penny. He was the one who was molesting you, right?"

"He wasn't molesting me at all," Penny gasped in outrage as she once again tried to rip herself loose from his grip, but he stubbornly refused to let her go.

"Your gasping drives me crazy," he whispered hoarsely. Eyes smoldering, he leaned forward. With a cry of distress she threw herself backwards, away from his full lips that sought hers, to save herself from her traitorous body that wanted to give in to his gentle demand.

She managed to surprise him enough to get loose, and quickly she scooted to the side and ran over to Thomas who still lay unmoving on the floor.

"Oh, my God, Thomas," she moaned as her hands caressed his head in search of any wounds. "Please wake up."

"Penny, don't feel bad about him. He's the one who acted wrongly, not you."

She looked back at Rake over her shoulder and knew he had misunderstood the whole situation when she met his compassionate eyes. He still thought he had saved her.

"No, Rake, you are the one who did wrong. Thomas is the one who did everything right."

Rake snorted. "He has no right to fondle you."

"I beg to differ," she snapped. "He's my fiancé and it was with your father's approval we walked to the maze without a chaperone."

Rake froze and his face lost all color. "Your fiancé?" he echoed with an odd hollow voice, and she nodded, glad the truth finally was out.

"Yes, my fiancé. We are to be married at Christmas. Your mother is quite happily arranging the occasion as we speak."

Penny looked down at Thomas to hide her face and the lie about his mother's happiness. She knew the duchess would plan the event if she had to, but not with pleasure, and definitely not happily.

"Married..."

She almost missed his broken whisper, but as she

caught the one word he never had mentioned between them, bitterness rose inside of her.

Before she had a chance to think twice, she lashed out at him, still without turning around. "Yes, married. Funny thing, you know? Thomas admits to wanting me, too. But he doesn't humiliate me with proposals of hidden houses for as long as he's interested. No, Thomas wants me for the rest of his life."

When Rake didn't answer, she turned around to see how her words had affected him, but to her surprise she found the gazebo empty. Only she and Thomas remained, as Rake silently had left without another word.

She sat down on the floor beside her fiancé and stared out through the empty doorway. A part of her regretted the harsh words, but another felt strangely satisfied over being able to throw back his selfish behavior at him.

She had shed too many tears over Rake in the last year, and for the first time she felt as if she had reached him, that she finally had made him understand how insulted she felt over his unconventional proposal.

Thomas moaned, and she looked down at him, watching him slowly come back to consciousness. This man was her future. Rake was her past. She had to learn to live with both, and maybe now she finally would have a chance.

Rake had been taken quite by surprise when she told him about her engagement to Thomas, and she could only hope this meant he wouldn't persist in chasing after her, relentlessly trying to seduce her. She didn't want to end her visit with her friends at Chester Park out of distress at the possibility of meeting him.

Maybe, in the long run, they could become friends again? She didn't want to lose him forever; she appreciated him too much for that. Could Rake knocking Thomas unconscious turn out to be the best thing that ever happened to her?

Chapter Thirteen

"I can't believe you knocked him out."

Howling with laughter, William raised his glass toward his younger brother, who grinned in response, looking extremely pleased with himself.

"I'm so embarrassed."

No one answered the duchess. She had been moaning all day because of her youngest son's barbaric behavior.

"Only one hit?" the duke asked, clearly impressed. When Rake nodded, he leaned back with a satisfied sigh. "I wish I had been there. It must have been quite a punch."

"Sent him sprawling." Rake oozed with manly satisfaction, and his mother moaned again.

"Oh, lord, how will we ever survive this?"

Charles patted his stepmother's hand reassuringly. "We have survived worse. Remember George when he found Caroline kissing that vicar in the chapel?"

"Oh, my God," the duchess moaned even more dramatically. "The embarrassment. The humiliation!"

"Rake or George?"

The duke put a hand up, effectively stopping Charles from disturbing the duchess in her moment of utter shock. "Please leave your mother alone. As soon as she has come to terms with what happened this morning, she will become her normal obnoxious self again."

"I can't believe you knocked him out!"

All the men laughed and cheered for Rake, the barbarian gentleman. Only the two women in the room stayed quiet, the duchess because she was still too occupied with the scandal of it, and Penny, who felt smaller and smaller every passing minute.

Thomas had been quite furious with Rake for attacking him—which he had every right to be—and had demanded an apology. But as Rake was nowhere to be found, he had slowly calmed down, and in the end he had been quite civil about the whole thing.

"I guess I should at least be grateful he was trying to rescue you, but the throbbing pain in my chin is a bit too much right now for me to be able to forgive him on the spot," Thomas had admitted to Penny before he left, and she had almost cried over such a heroic stance.

The rest of the day she had pondered over what she would say to Rake when she met him later at dinner. The depths of his rage had stunned her, but what had disturbed her the most was his obvious need to rescue her. She had been completely surprised by it.

So maybe he wasn't the knight in shining armor she used to transform him into in her most vivid daydreams. At least he was a knight at heart, even if his armor had become a bit tarnished over the years.

For a moment she had started to doubt her decision to marry Thomas, the very sane and practical decision she'd made out of a desperate need to belong and be close to someone.

She had settled for friendship, but what if love awaited her around the corner? What if a life together with Rake was reachable?

In the end she had come to the same decision as before; life with Thomas would be right for her. But even so she still dissected Rake's every word, trying to make sense of what it all meant.

When she finally joined the Darling family for dinner, she was quite nervous, and she had stopped for a minute outside the massive door to the dining room to calm her pounding heart.

Would Rake be there?

And if he was, would he ignore her, or lash out with all the repressed anger she had sensed in him? She had held her breath as she walked into the room, prepared to her teeth for anything to happen.

But she hadn't prepared herself for the old Rake, the wicked libertine who arrogantly bickered with his family and chuckled, amused, with an arched eyebrow, whenever he felt so obliged.

Gone was the consuming rage.

Gone were the strange sadness and the unusual moodiness. Back was the lighthearted and laughing scoundrel who lived life to its full with a wink and a grin.

After congratulating her on her upcoming marriage, the members of the Darling family had laughed and joked about Rake's outrageous behavior throughout the five-course dinner and were still at it now in the salon where tea was served.

As she sat there with her untouched cup of tea in her lap, Penny felt almost betrayed as she watched how lightly Rake laughed this morning's happenings away. It had been quite world-turning for her, an occasion which had been both enlightening and uplifting.

But to Rake it was only something to joke about.

The duchess, who finally seemed to have gotten over her family's occasional habit of embarrassing her socially, sat next to Penny and patted her hand devotedly.

"I will be in debt to you the rest of my life."

Penny tore her eyes away from the grinning Rake, who was reenacting the knock-Thomas-out scene to his brothers' and father's high amusement.

"I'm sorry?"

"Richard." The duchess waved her hand toward her son. "I don't know what you did or what you said to him, but somehow you managed to bring me back my beautiful son."

Penny took a deep breath. So now it was *her* fault he was behaving oddly? This day became worse by the minute.

All she wanted to do was to rip that indifferent grin off his face. Or even better, knock him out cold, just the way he had knocked Thomas out.

"I think this is a cause for celebration," the duchess said, and clapped her hands happily. "We will have to throw an engagement party for you and Mr. Bedford and invite everyone to celebrate with us."

Oh, no.

Penny shook her head. "Lady Anna, there really is no need for a party. Really. Thomas has too much to do with the harvest, and I'm…I'm not a partying person. I'd much rather just spend the engagement quietly and then just as quietly get married, come Christmas."

"Absolutely not," the duchess cried out distressed—and caught the attention of her family.

"What?"

The duchess waved an upset hand toward Penny.

"She doesn't want an engagement party!"

The duke bit back a smile. "I can relate to that. Why throw a party when you don't have to?"

"Penny needs to be launched into the county society as the future wife of a country squire. As soon as the engagement becomes official, everyone will expect to have a chance to congratulate the happy couple. I will not stand idle and let Penny hide in the library among her books until the wedding."

"A party sounds like a perfect ending to this last year's ups and downs," Charles agreed, and was awarded a thankful smile.

"Why not a masquerade?" the duchess mused. "We could invite everyone we know to a grand ball, and let everyone live out their most secret fantasies, and in the height of the evening we will announce Penny's and Thomas's engagement. It will be perfect!"

"A masquerade at a house party?" Rake chuckled. "Mother, you know you are more or less begging for scandals to happen."

The duchess blushed and mumbled something inaudible, which told them all she was perfectly aware of this.

"Why create the perfect opportunity for scandals?" Jamie frowned at his mother, whose blush deepened.

"So everyone will forget about Penny's strange situation in life, living with us and not her own family. You know as well as I we can't invite the de Vere family, as Lord Nester will never accept such an invitation. But in the midst of scandals happening, no one will think twice about it, and if we announce the engagement as late as possible, they probably won't even notice that Penny's family isn't present."

"Oh."

"Well, when you put it like that, it unfortunately makes perfect sense. A masquerade it is, then." The duke leaned back, resigned, as he too knew Penny needed as good a start in her new married life as possible. She didn't need a touch of scandal.

"I know the perfect outfit for me." The duchess squealed with anticipation. "This is so exciting; I can hardly wait!"

"Do we all have to wear costumes?" Jamie asked cautiously, not too pleased with his mother's grand plans.

"Of course you do. And don't you think I will accept any excuses. You will all participate, even if I have to drag you there myself."

"I hate masquerades."

The duchess patted Jamie's knee. "I know, my dear, you always have. But don't you ever think that's reason enough to not attend."

Unanimous in their distaste for such an event, all the men in the salon sighed, defeated, and Penny almost smiled. Lady Anna was quite petite, but she ruled the large men of her family with a firm albeit loving hand.

Of course they would do as she told them. Not one of them knew how to deny her anything, not even the duke.

"And for you, Penny dear, we are going to come up with the most spectacular outfit, one which will send Mr. Bedford and the rest of our guests crawling for mercy at your feet."

"Mother, I don't think Penny would appreciate that," Rake said, to Penny's surprise. "She's not the flamboyant kind."

"But she needs to be seen."

"I don't want to be seen."

Mother and son didn't acknowledge Penny. Instead they frowned intensely at each other.

"It's a masquerade. No one will know it's her."

"At the unveiling they will. And as they stand there in perfect awe over who this siren is, we are going to announce the engagement and turn the evening into one of the most talked about for years to come."

"I think you exaggerate the importance of the right costume," Rake insisted. "I think Penny would be much more comfortable in something not as overwhelming."

"Fine." The duchess shrugged. "Then you will take care of Penny's outfit. You two can go to the seamstress in Sandhurst. She's quite handy when it comes to masquerade costumes."

So that had been her game all along.

Anna Darling, the Duchess of Berkeley, knew her son too well and had lured him into her trap without even breaking a sweat. Penny couldn't stop a smile as Rake sat back in his chair, staring at his mother.

The duke had once said England could win any war if the War Ministry would only be wise enough to put Anna Darling in charge of the planning.

"You can go for the first visit tomorrow, and I will send a maid with you as chaperone. We don't want to create another scandal this close to the wedding, do we?"

Rake shook his head slowly, an amused grin lighting his features. "No, Mother, of course not. I will take Penny to Mrs. Frazer and have her order something appropriate for the ball."

"With a maid."

"Yes, Mother, I will bring a maid."

"Don't you try to patronize me. I'm your mother, and if anyone is going to patronize someone, it is I who will patronize you. I know of your reputation as a libertine—no need for you to try denying it—and these last couple of months haven't made you any less libertine in the eyes of the *ton*, I must say."

Rake shrugged. "I am what I am because of how you have brought me up. Can't hold your own choices against me now, can you?"

"Richard Darling!"

The duke howled with laughter. "That's my boy. Always look upon the bright side of life and put the blame where it belongs—on your parents."

"Hannibal Darling!"

"What?"

The duchess stared openmouthed at her husband. "Really, Hannibal? Put the blame where it belongs? Whenever have I told Richard to go and behave as badly as he can?"

"I…"

"And have I ever told my son, whom I love most dearly, to turn every little chance of happiness away?"

"No, I…"

"Are you saying I applaud his decision to let the only woman for whom he has ever shown feelings marry another man without even a blink, so he can continue his restless bachelor life of bedding as many women as he can?"

"Mother!"

"Charles, be quiet. This is not for you. This is between me and my husband."

"So please take it upstairs. The rest of us would

rather have a nice cup of tea instead of having to listen to this. It's quite embarrassing, you know."

The duchess shrieked, and Penny bit back another smile. The older woman loved her drama and knew how to use it. The men in the salon stared at the duchess, horror written all over their handsome faces, and not one of them dared to move for fear of provoking her anger.

As the duchess ranted about who was embarrassing and who was not, Penny quietly stepped unnoticed out of the room and left the temporarily not-so-happy family alone.

Rake hadn't looked too pleased with his mother as she mentioned his choices, but it was hard to tell if he disliked her mentioning his feelings or the way she had slaughtered his lifestyle.

Everyone knew Rake had an affection for Penny, even she did, although until recently it had been only a brotherly affection. She had always wished for and dreamt about more from him, as had his family.

But it wasn't Rake's fault he didn't love her as much as she wanted him to. No one probably ever would.

She just wasn't a loveable person, she guessed.

For some reason she always brought out the compassion in people. Love—especially the world-turning kind she had read about and longed for—seemed to elude her.

If she were completely honest with herself, she would have been satisfied with a man loving her just a tenth of how much she usually had dreamt Rake should.

She stopped halfway up the stairs and closed her eyes. A satisfied little smile came crawling as her old friends reappeared inside her head.

She had missed them, the daydreams. They had filled her head most of her life and put a golden frame to her meager life. Yet ever since that precious moment when she had met Rake at the lake she had tried to stop them, in an attempt to force herself to grow up and face reality.

But it wasn't for her. She knew that now.

She would marry Thomas without remorse, as he knew the truth about her and didn't hold it against her. She would take care of him and spoil him with a calm and sated life. And if her head would occasionally fill with dreams about another man and a life which never would be hers—so be it.

Her heart belonged to Rake and always would.

But she wanted more out of life than he had offered her so far. This morning's incident hadn't changed her chosen path at all. She would still go on with her engagement and marriage to Thomas.

But if Rake would come forward…

Maybe Charmaine had been right all along when she had told her not to close out any options? It wouldn't hurt to be open-minded when it came to Rake, as long as it didn't mean becoming his mistress.

If Rake looked at her again as he had this morning, when he still thought he had saved her, she would know it was for real and for life. That look had been honest and emotional and not Rake's normal indifferent amusement.

"Daydreaming about me?"

She woke from her thoughts and turned to look down at Rake, who had come up behind her on the stairs and stopped a few steps farther down.

Her spontaneous reaction was to deny, but then a little imp inside told her to for once open up to him. She had never let him come closer emotionally to her than an arm's length, to save her poor heart from more suffering.

But she was a different woman now.

She had lived through a year which would have knocked most women down forever, yet somehow she had found strength to move on.

Moments ago she had decided not to close down the option of Rake, so why not let him in a little bit. The best, of course, would be to flirt with him, but she didn't know how to do that.

"Actually, yes," she said and forced herself to smile lightly toward him.

"Really?" His smile deepened. "Seeing yourself in my arms, perhaps?"

"Maybe."

She must have succeeded to seem flirtatious, as she could see his eyes widen a bit in surprise at her response.

"Maybe? What a confusing answer to come from your delicious lips." He took two more steps until he stood next to her, giving those just-mentioned lips a smoldering gaze. Without thinking, she nervously bit her lower lip, and he growled as he grabbed her waist and leaned closer to her. "Bloody hell, Penny…"

She gasped as his lips closed in on hers, and again he growled, sounding as barbaric as he had earlier this morning. This was not the fashionable gentleman—this was the savage man inside him responding to her.

Her heart pounded hard as she looked into his eyes and felt the heat. Without a doubt she knew she preferred this Rake to the socializing libertine.

This was her Rake.

She felt his breath wash over her face, and before she had a chance to change her mind she grabbed his neck and helped his lips find their way.

The force of the kiss was amazing.

He was amazing.

The kiss continued on and on as his hands moved over her and hers over him, each exploring the new territory. Afterwards she knew she would have lost her virginity most willingly in the grand stairwell of Chester Park if the butler, Ivanoff, had not interrupted them with a haughty "Hrrrm."

Penny thought her cheeks would explode from the hot blush that flowed into them. She was mortified with embarrassment. Not only was she found in the arms of a man who wasn't her fiancé, she was also most openly kissing him without a thought of who might walk in on them.

Ivanoff obviously had the same thought.

"You can be thankful it was me who found you, Master Richard. Had it been anyone else, Miss Penelope's engagement would have been off and you, sir, would have had to marry her yourself."

Rake opened his mouth to speak, but Penny cut in before he had a chance to say a word. "Thank you, Ivanoff. This will never happen again."

With a lovely smile, one he reserved for only her and Francesca, Ivanoff acknowledged her words.

"Anything for you, Miss Penelope. As for you…" The butler turned to Rake, and this time there was no lovely smile, only a menacing glare. "You deflowering bastard…"

Rake arched an amused eyebrow over the butler's obvious anger. "Deflowering? Ivanoff, really?"

With a wagging finger the butler took a step closer to his young master. "You should be ashamed of yourself. Throwing yourself all over an innocent young miss like that? Where is your self-respect?"

"When it comes to Penny, I seem to have lost it completely."

Ivanoff snorted. "Off you go, you young fool. Off and find some other woman to lose the steam with and let this little girl stay innocent until her wedding day."

And without listening to her halfhearted protests, the butler more or less dragged Penny upstairs and didn't leave until she had closed her bedroom door behind her.

Well inside, she threw herself on the bed with a thud.

What a strange, wonderful day.

She closed her eyes as the memory of Rake's hands touching her body came back to her. It had been pure heaven until Ivanoff had interrupted them. At the moment she had felt a bit annoyed with the kind butler, but now she was only thankful.

She sighed, a bit embarrassed as she thought about Thomas. He was such a kind, good man and not at all deserving of a fiancée who dreamt about another man.

The only thing making the engagement still seem real for her was how they never once had lied and called it love. They were friends, and as friends they planned to enter holy matrimony.

If not Rake…

A deep sigh from the bottom of her heart escaped her as she sat up again, not as giddy anymore. She had to stop hoping Rake would do the honorable thing. When it came to women he wasn't honorable. At least not if it would include more than a few hours of mutual pleasure. And especially not if it meant something more lasting—like marriage.

For a married woman seeking a bit of excitement, he must seem the perfect man. But to an unwed virgin he was nothing more than the devil in the disguise of an eligible bachelor.

She would give him a chance to step forward. It was all she could do. For her to ask him to marry her was out of the question. Besides her disliking the mere thought of being the joke of the next Darling dinner, she wanted—no, *needed*—him to come to her.

He knew what she felt for him.

She had thoughtlessly made that quite clear to him at the Green Park picnic all those months ago. Not that it had gained her anything. He had only tried harder to convince her to become his mistress.

But the past was the past.

Tomorrow they were heading to Sandhurst, and she would make the most out of the little trip. It was only a few months until her wedding, and as soon as she had Thomas's ring on her finger she would never be able to spend time alone with Rake.

It was unheard of—a platonic friendship between a married lady and an unmarried gentleman. Of course they would meet at social occasions at Chester Park over the years. But they would never be able to do more than exchange a few polite words, and never would they find themselves alone together again.

She knew there were many married ladies who got themselves a lover, someone like Rake. Indeed, rumors said *he* had been lover to most of the married ladies of the *ton*. But she could never do such a thing to Thomas. If they married, she would become his forever. And even if her mind and heart might dream of a man who never would be hers, so be it. What Thomas didn't know would never hurt him. And as she wasn't about to tell anyone about her daydreaming, Thomas would live happily ever after, which was all she could wish for.

But until then...

She was still unmarried and free to roam the countryside with the man of her heart—and a maid for chaperone.

Tomorrow they were heading to Sandhurst, and anything could happen.

Chapter Fourteen

"Lady Penelope, you look lovelier than ever."

Penny blushed as Rake bowed over her hand and put small lingering kisses on her fingertips.

"As do you, Lord Richard," she breathed. "As do you."

Rake chuckled softly as he straightened his back again without releasing her hand. "I know. I have tried to look my best for you."

"Must have taken you all night." Jamie ducked as Rake took a swing with his free hand and countered with a pat on his twin's back that could easily have made a smaller man crumble. But Rake was used to his brother's antics and didn't budge.

"James and Richard, behave."

The duchess emerged onto the front stair, where the threesome stood in the warm morning sun, waiting for the carriage that would take them to Sandhurst.

"I thought you had left already and had forgotten the promise you made me yesterday."

Rake lifted an inquiring eyebrow, but before he could speak a young maid came forward, clad in her best clothes.

Penny bit back a smile. So this young and inexperienced maid, with eyes as big as saucers, was their chaperone? Did the duchess want them to do something they shouldn't, so she could get her heart's wish fulfilled without having to continue with the masquerade plans?

"Great." Rake grinned wickedly. "She will fit just perfectly in the other carriage."

"What other carriage?"

Rake gave his frowning mother an innocent look. "Oh, did I forget to mention I was taking my new phaeton for a drive? Testing it, you know. And as you are well aware, a phaeton only holds two people. So I had the town coach ordered forward for the maid to travel in."

"The town coach? For one person? A bit much, don't you think?"

"I'm going, too," Jamie interjected sternly. "I have some errands to do in town, and this arrangement suits me just fine. The maid can share my carriage with me, and I will make sure the phaeton stays close and in sight the whole way."

The last part was directed to his twin, who shook his head with feigned sorrow. "Why does it sound as if everyone thinks I will do something lewd to Penny if we happen to get out of sight?"

"Because you will," his brother and mother said unanimously, and Rake shrugged toward Penny.

"I guess they're right. You're too gorgeous for me to keep my hands off, if we manage to get lost."

"Richard!"

"I said 'if.' "

"You said it as though you were planning to get lost."

"Of course I'm not planning to. But if we were… Let's say I wouldn't mind a little solitude among friends."

"Penny, you can go with Jamie in his carriage, instead. I'm reluctant to admit my son has lost his common sense."

"And here I thought you would love to have a good solid reason to force me into marrying poor Penny."

"So I might be a bit partial when it comes to whom Penny is to marry, but it doesn't mean I will allow you to handle her any way you like. You are a gentleman, even if you seem to forget that a little too often."

Rake rolled his eyes toward Penny. "And she thinks *I* lost my common sense."

The duchess gasped. "I heard that!"

Penny laughed as Rake grinned wickedly toward her behind his mother's back. Oh, how she loved this family. Someone who didn't know them as well as she did would probably be shocked over how outrageously they behaved to each other when not in public.

But not she. She had grown up listening to their constant bickering and their strange discussions, and she knew this was something she would miss immensely if she married Thomas. Neither she nor Thomas had many relatives, and she guessed it would be a bit lonely at family occasions.

"Ah, there are the coaches," the duchess exclaimed, and soon the four of them were seated in the two carriages, with Rake and Penny in the phaeton and Jamie with the maid in the larger, more practical carriage.

As soon as they were beyond the gates of Chester Park, Rake increased the speed and left the others farther and farther behind, but Penny didn't mind. She closed her eyes and enjoyed the warmth of the September morning's sun caressing her face.

Rake hadn't lied when he told his mother the coach was new to him. During most of the ride to Sandhurst he tried out different turns and speeds, ignoring Penny except for informing her of various utterly uninteresting tidbits regarding this fantastic vehicle.

As they arrived in Sandhurst, Penny was relieved to leave the carriage behind and meet up with Jamie and the maid outside Mrs. Frazer's shop.

Jamie was frowning more than ever as he told them to meet him at the inn in a couple of hours, and Rake shook his head, saddened as he watched his twin's back disappear into the crowd.

"There is something bothering him, something which consumes him from inside out. But he just won't tell me."

"Maybe he doesn't know how to."

"I'm his twin. He can tell me anything."

Penny put her hand on Rake's arm. "But maybe he has seen or done something which he feels is so horrendous that he doesn't know how to tell anyone, even you. You know what Raleigh told us when he came back from the frontier—it was worse than hell on earth."

"But I'm his twin…"

She cut a sideways glance at him. Even while frowning he was still one of the most handsome men she had ever met. He wasn't as perfectly beautiful as Francesca's new husband was, but with Rake it was something more than simply good looks. It was something in the air about him. Something with how he held his head, how he moved his hands, how his eyes twinkled when he smiled.

Even now, when the twinkle was gone and an ugly

frown marked his forehead, he still looked special and unique.

"Maybe you two should go somewhere and just talk about what's in both of your hearts."

She caught his attention with that remark.

"Whatever do you mean? Has Jamie said something to you?"

"He's been a bit worried about you lately."

Rake snorted. "Why? There's nothing with me to worry about."

She managed to keep herself from rolling her eyes. He must have the shortest memory in history. Or maybe he never had thought twice about how he had been acting over the last months.

"Maybe not, but still, Jamie was worried."

"What? Did he say something to you?"

"Not much. He said he had tried to talk to you but you hadn't been very approachable."

Rake frowned. "It doesn't sound like me. I'm not the one to refuse to talk to my family, especially not Jamie. That's been more his game lately."

"Exactly his words. And also the reason he felt he couldn't push it with you, as he himself hadn't been sharing much with you or anyone in your family."

"Did he say something about himself?"

Penny shook her head. "No. We agreed we both had our share of secrets we didn't want to talk about, and then we continued to talk about you."

"Much more interesting subject, eh," Rake drawled, and she laughed politely.

"It wasn't a subject that lasted long, though. Not much to talk about there."

"You minx." Rake grinned at her and offered her

his arm. "Come on, let's go find Mrs. Frazer and have her sew the perfect outfit for you. We can continue this conversation later, when we're not surrounded by too many ears."

They strolled through the small town with the maid a few steps behind. Now and then they would meet an acquaintance of Rake's, and he greeted them all lightly, although the ladies always got the grin with the wicked gleam.

Inside Mrs. Frazer's shop, he continued his reckless flirting, and soon he had all the seamstresses giggling and batting their eyelashes. The women competed with each other to find the perfect fabric for the dress to be bought, but not one of them asked Penny, the one who would wear the dress.

No, they were all too busy flirting with the handsome gentleman who promised them everything with his twinkling eyes and fast smiles.

Penny was ushered farther and farther away from Rake until she stood in the back of the shop, desperately trying to hide the jealousy which was eating her. She hated that he had such power over her. It made her feel so small and petty. He was very much the confirmed bachelor and she *was* engaged to another man. He had every right to flirt with other women. But still…

She really didn't like it.

To keep herself occupied with something else and not stand there fuming at Rake's behavior, she went to the table where all the fabrics lay, turning her back to the commotion and letting her fingers play with the delicate materials.

"They're so beautiful." The young maid stood on

the opposite side of the table, staring at the rich materials between them.

"Yes, they are. I don't know how I'll ever be able to choose only one."

The maid let her hand lightly touch the nearest fabric, a thin pink muslin with small white flowers sewn over it. "So beautiful," she whispered in awe, and Penny, who had grown up in a home which lacked funds, knew exactly how the girl felt.

It wasn't envy, it was amazement at the luxury you never would be able to afford.

"What's your name?"

To Penny's surprise the maid froze, as if she had asked her to tell a terrible secret, not just a name.

"Mina."

"Mina? How unusual. Is it a nickname?"

"No. It's just Mina."

Penny recognized the need of secrecy when she saw it and didn't push further. She gave the maid an understanding smile. "Mina it is, then."

The relief in Mina's face was almost laughable, but Penny had no problem holding back a smile as all the women behind her giggled hysterically over something Rake had said.

Instead she muttered something inaudible about men and punching bags before pretending to again look at the fabrics which now had, in her eyes, lost all their earlier glory.

"He never takes his eyes off you."

She met the compassionate eyes of Mina and knew she should set the maid straight: This was not the manner in which to address your superiors.

But something inside held her back. There was

something about this maid that didn't add up, and Penny knew there had to be a story here. The only problem was that Mina was one of the duchess's personal maids, and she knew better than to question that particular lady or anyone she presented.

So she let the slight overstep pass and instead asked the question which burnt on her lips. "He doesn't?"

"Not once. He flirts and laughs with all the women surrounding him, but his eyes never leave your person."

"That's nice."

"Isn't it?"

They shared a secretive smile, two young women in a small world where unspoken boundaries made a friendship impossible. They giggled as they moved into the next room of the shop—and out of Rake's line of sight—where more tables held more colorful fabrics. Mirrors were placed in a corner, surrounding a small podium so fittings could be made in full overview.

"Isn't that your fiancé outside?"

Penny looked through the window to where Mina pointed, and she nodded with a pleased smile. "Yes, that is Thomas. Is there a door there? I would rather not have to go back through the other room."

Mina took a few steps farther into that side of the shop. "Yes, there is another door in the next room, and it leads back into the street."

"Penny!"

Thomas's happiness over unexpectedly meeting her was evident, and it soothed the edginess Rake's outrageous flirting had created in her.

"Are you visiting the seamstress?"

"Yes, Lady Anna has decided to honor us and our

engagement with a masquerade ball, and I needed something to wear."

"A masquerade ball?"

"What is it with men and masquerades?" Penny laughed. "When Lady Anna came up with the idea yesterday, most of the Darling men looked like they had taken a sip of Almack's infamous lemonade."

Thomas blushed. "I didn't mean to sound ungrateful. It's just that…I don't really…" He pulled his fingers through his windswept blond hair and took a deep breath. "Damn it, Penny, it's a bloody masquerade! I sort of detest those."

"Me too," Penny admitted. "I tried to talk her out of it, but she was quite determined, and in the end I couldn't refuse such generosity."

"Thank you, my dearest Penelope," he breathed with relief and put his hand softly against her cheek. "For you I will clench my teeth together and stoically endure such a horrendous evening."

They laughed lightly together, two friends in perfect harmony. Everything with Thomas was easy; they were a match made in a sensible heaven, and their life together would be serene and without surprises.

She thought of the man of her dreams, who currently was spending his time flirting with seven very eager ladies in the shop behind her. Life with Rake would never be dull or lonely, but it wouldn't be a calm road. There would be more bumps than she would ever be able to count, but she knew it would be worth it—if he only loved her.

And there was the sum of everything.

If Rake loved her, she wouldn't let anything or anyone stand in the way of their mutual happiness—as long as it meant his ring on her finger.

But if he didn't… Or if he did but chose not to act upon it… Then she would continue with life as it was, including marrying her friend Thomas and being perfectly and sensibly content.

"Would you like to join me for a cup of tea at the inn? I have most of my errands done and would really like to sit down for a while, and what could be better than having you sitting next to me."

He looked like a small child waiting for a present, and right then she would have given anything to be able to tell him yes, but she had things to do herself, and if Rake would stop flirting with the seamstresses she might even get her errands done.

"Sorry, old chap, but today she's mine."

Thomas stiffened as a cold voice interrupted their conversation, and Penny could tell he hadn't forgiven Rake completely yet for the slight yesterday morning. Slowly he turned and met the dark, inscrutable eyes of his antagonist, who stood surrounded by women excited at the prospect of a fight between two dashing gentlemen.

Penny looked from Thomas's frowning face to Rake's cold and arrogant one and knew she had to do something before they disgraced themselves in front of everyone on the street.

"Thomas, I can't go with you to the inn today. The duchess has ordered Rake to help me with the choice of my dress, and later we are meeting with Jamie for tea. Another time, perhaps?"

Thomas tore his gaze from Rake and looked down into her eyes. She tried wordlessly to convince him to humor her this time. *No more drama, if you please.* For once he seemed uncommonly perceptive, as he gave her a small smile. "I wouldn't dream of intruding on your plans. Perhaps I could come and visit you tomorrow afternoon? Say five o'clock?"

"Please do. I would be honored."

"We all would be deeply honored," Rake drawled behind her, and she could see Thomas tense again. Quickly she put a hand against his cheek, just as he earlier had put his against hers.

"Please," she whispered. "Don't mind him. He's just being a pain in the…you know."

Thomas bent his head until his forehead almost touched hers. "For you, my dearest wife-to-be, anything."

"Enough time wasted," Rake said as he grabbed Penny at the waist and dragged her back toward him and the shop. "Let's get the bloody dress ordered, shall we?"

And without letting Penny tell Thomas farewell, other than a wave and a glance she managed over her shoulder, he barged into the shop again with her in tow, Mina closely following. Penny could do nothing but acquiesce. This time Rake didn't care about flirting with the seamstresses. Instead he sat down on a chair and looked at her pointedly.

"What?" she asked, when she could no longer stand his staring.

"Do you have any preference? Any disguise you find more alluring?"

"Oh." So she was supposed to have ideas, was she? "I don't know. I have never been to a masquerade. I wouldn't know what costume to choose."

Rake leaned his head to the side. "A siren, maybe,

just emerged from the water to seduce men into forever and ever lusting for her."

There was no doubt he spoke of the time at the lake, and Penny blushed. "No," she chided, embarrassed. "That's not a disguise anyone would believe for me."

Rake grinned wickedly. "I would."

"But this is not for you. This is for Thomas and for our future together."

"No, my love. This is for you and you only. I don't care about Boring Saint Thomas and the rest of his life. All I care about is you."

Why did he say things like that?

Her silly heart immediately skipped a few beats, stupidly believing he meant something with the endearing words. But she knew better.

"All you care about is being obnoxious toward your mother, because she wanted me dressed as something too dramatic."

She tried to look as bland as possible so he couldn't see how affected she had been by his words.

For a moment he looked vulnerable, as if her cold cut of his sweet words had hurt him more than she thought possible. But just as quickly the moment was over and the forever wicked libertine leered at her.

"You know me too well."

"A shepherdess, maybe?" Mina's voice was heard behind them, and Rake lifted an amused eyebrow toward her.

"So the maid wants to join the discussion? Please do, but then you would have to come up with something better than a common shepherdess. For all I know, half the women there will be dressed as shepherdesses. Quite boring."

"Oh, I would love to be a shepherdess if it's the most common outfit. I would blend in."

"Penny, for goodness' sake." Rake snorted. "You have to stop hiding behind everyone else. You are such a beautiful woman, but for some reason you are determined to never let anyone know about it."

"I don't hide."

"Yes, you do. You hide behind anyone who takes more place than you."

"I do not. I'm just not as interesting as other young ladies, and that is the sole reason for me not being seen."

Rake shook his head and gave her a knowing look. "You, my love, have always hidden behind others, mostly behind your sister and Fanny. For some reason, you don't seem to think you are worth the interest, and I think you have succeeded so well with persuading yourself of this that you have made everyone else believe it, too."

"Thomas sees me."

"Of course he does. I'm sure you are the living image of the perfect woman to him. How can you not be? You are a beautiful girl with extremely good local connections but without a too-interfering family. You also love to read and, amazingly enough, don't mind listening to him rant about his—in his mind—intellectual tidbits."

"Rake," Penny gasped, outraged over his crude words, and immediately the look in his eyes changed from arrogant contempt to smoldering lust.

"Penny," he breathed, not hiding the passion he felt for her. She wondered if it was only the presence of

Mina and the gaping seamstresses that held him back from kissing her senseless.

With this thought she doubted the trip had been such a good idea after all. Maybe she and Rake needed time apart, to be able to think straight regarding the situation between them. As it was now, both were unable to think about the future when so often interrupted, she by her heart's erratic bouncing and he by his constant lust.

Soon she would be married to Thomas, and then it would be too late for them, too late for love. Unfortunately, Rake didn't seem to realize this. Instead he behaved as though nothing out of the ordinary had happened during the past year, as if life as they had known it would continue into eternity and beyond.

Mina, who must have sensed Penny's desperation, took a step forward. "Lady Penelope, if you go dressed as a shepherdess, maybe Mr. Bedford could go dressed as a shepherd?"

"What a wonderful idea." Penny clapped her hands together. "I will send Thomas a note about it as soon as possible."

Rake wandered to the table and rummaged through the delicate fabrics, to the seamstresses' distraction. "I think going as a sheep would suit him better."

"Rake!"

He sent her a grin over his shoulder, and she shook her head, defeated. "You just can't help yourself, can you? You must slander poor Thomas through the gutter even if you know he is better than that."

"Maybe. Or maybe I only tend to be a bit selfish regarding my belongings and don't like him thinking he can strut in and take whatever he wants without my consent."

Oh. So now she was one of his belongings, was she? She shook her head again, but this time she wisely let the subject be. He was, as always, too logically illogical for her to ever be able to make him see her side.

"Ah!" he finally exclaimed, and held up a thin white fabric which almost seemed fluffy. "This will be perfect."

Penny frowned at the frilly fabric. "Really? For what? Not a shepherdess, I presume?"

He laughed at her. "Of course not. You are not a simple shepherdess, my love, you are my angel. And as such you will be clad at the upcoming masquerade."

"An angel?" She stared at him, astonished over his choice of costume.

"Yes, my love. An angel. It will be perfect. Boring Saint Thomas can still go as a sheep if he likes, or he can dress up as the saint we all think him."

"He will not go as a sheep."

"I'm sorry to hear that. It would have meant no need for a costume at all, and I think he would have appreciated that."

The seamstresses giggled as they rushed over and saved the delicate fluff from Rake's large hands. The next hour was later only a blur in Penny's memory, as orders and ideas flew around her like bees around a jar of honey.

Without once asking for her opinion, Rake decided how the dress should be made, and after measuring Penny, Mrs. Frazer and her girls said they would come to Chester Park with the almost-finished dress in a week's time for the final fitting.

"Mother plans to hold the ball in about a month, so your dress will be ready in good time," Rake said as they walked down the street again toward the inn, closely followed by Mina. "I must admit I feel quite satisfied with the result. You will look divine."

"I hope so," she agreed, a bit uncertain. "It was a lovely fabric, and Mrs. Frazer seems quite competent."

"You will be perfect." Rake chuckled. "Beautiful enough to be awe-inspiring, but not a knockout as was mother's wish."

"Thank you for stopping her. I saw this vision of me walking in dressed like a rosebush just to satisfy her need to shock her guests."

He laughed loudly at her joke. "That would have done it, I'm sure. Please do tell me if you change your mind and choose to honor my mother's wishes, because I wouldn't want to miss you dressed as a rose."

"Bush," she clarified with a feigned haughty voice. "A rose*bush*, if you please."

"Ah."

He grabbed her hand and squeezed it lightly before placing it in the crook of his arm, and she felt an overwhelming urge to press herself closer to his side and lean her head against his arm. It was amazing how easily he made her feel her place was here at his side. She belonged there with her hand on his arm. She only wished he would realize it too, before it was too late.

"There you are. Finally."

Jamie didn't look pleased with life when they came up to him outside the inn. He stared sourly at them from under his hat and ushered them, without proper greeting, through the door, almost knocking poor Mina to the ground.

"Bloody hell, Jamie, what's your problem?" Rake said as he was pushed down into a chair that, fortunately, happened to be empty.

"Nothing. I just want my tea. You!" He waved to Mina and gave her one of the most condescending looks Penny had ever seen. "You can go and make sure there will be some tea and sandwiches brought here as soon as possible."

Mina's eyes widened, but she didn't say anything, simply shaking her head in Penny's direction before doing as asked.

"I like that girl," Rake mused as he watched the maid scurry away between the tables.

Without warning Jamie stood and reached across the table to grab Rake by his cravat. "Don't you ever, *ever* touch that girl. She's off limits."

If she hadn't been so shocked over Jamie's brutish behavior, Penny would have laughed out loud over the ridiculous expression of astonishment gracing Rake's handsome face. But the obvious anger which seemed to ooze out through every pore in Jamie's body kept her serious.

"Bloody hell, brother, what's your problem?" Rake grunted as he ripped his once perfectly folded cravat out of his twin's hands. Jamie took a confused breath and sat down again.

"Oh, God, Rake, I'm sorry. I-I just haven't been myself lately, and I-I wasn't…"

"Thinking?"

Jamie sighed. "No. I just…"

"Thought I was going to make love to the girl here on the table?"

"No!"

Rake arched an eyebrow, and the air went out of Jamie.

"No. Of course not. It's just that she… She's a bit special, and I just want…need…to protect her."

"From me?"

Jamie nodded, looking more ashamed than Penny had ever seen him before, and she decided to cut in, to stop Rake from overhauling his poor brother in public.

"I would too," she said with feigned compassion, patting Jamie's hand. "We all know what Rake's like."

Jamie looked up at her and blinked once before he caught her game. Then his eyes started to twinkle. "Yes, we sure do."

"But she's safe now. I don't think even Rake will have the guts to try to seduce Mina now, after having his best cravat destroyed."

"I don't know," Rake mused while rubbing his cheek. "She's quite pretty. She might be worth losing a brother. I have so many, and I don't think I would notice if one was gone."

Jamie's laugh seemed a bit forced, but Mina, who had just returned, looked relieved as she sank down on a chair behind Penny. Minutes later, the servants of the inn brought a large tray with tea and delicious-looking sandwiches.

Afterwards, they walked out into the sunlight again, and Rake pointed with his cane toward his phaeton. "Come on, my love, it's time to go back to Chester Park before Mother sends out a search party."

"She can go with us in my carriage," Jamie offered kindly, but Rake shook his head.

"She's with me."

And without another word he grabbed Penny by

the waist and threw her in a most unladylike fashion onto the high seat of the shiny carriage and jumped up after her. Before Jamie and Mina had a chance to get inside their carriage, the phaeton raced down the main street and soon left Sandhurst behind in a cloud of dust.

They drove fast for a while, until they were alone in the middle of the forest, where he decreased the speed until the carriage stopped completely. The sunbeams working their way through the leaves of the trees made his dark hair glisten as he removed his hat before turning to Penny with a lustful gleam in his smoky eyes.

"Oh, no, you don't," she started, but to no avail. With a soft chuckle, he put his hands against her cheeks and forced her mouth closer to his so he could claim her soft lips.

The kiss was different from all their earlier kisses, warm and tender, and Penny was lost. All thoughts of Thomas blew away, and all that was left in the world was only Rake.

Always Rake.

She put her arms around his neck and pressed her body closer to his, and he moaned into her mouth with pleasure. One of his hands moved downwards and found the hem of her skirt and the leg it hid. Slowly his fingers travelled up along the soft skin of her calf, to her knee and then her thigh, until she whimpered with an unknown need for something more.

"You taste so good," he whispered in her ear as he moved his lips to nibble on her earlobe. "I don't want to stop before I have tasted all of you."

She mumbled something inaudible in full agreement; she didn't want him to stop either. But neither of them could ignore the unmistakable sound of wheels coming closer: the carriage with Jamie and their chaperone Mina in it.

Rake draw back with a painful sigh. "That brother of mine. His timing is the worst."

"You knew he was coming."

"I know. I just hoped he would do the honorable thing and try to drive as slowly as possible."

Penny giggled as she straightened her hair. "The honorable thing would have been forcing me into the carriage with him and Mina."

"Then I guess I have to be thankful he's not so honorable after all." Rake grinned, and she found herself staring at him with awe at how handsome he was when he let his guard down. He lost his smile as he met her eyes most seriously.

"I wish you would change your mind about marrying Thomas Bedford before it's too late." His smooth voice vibrated with restrained emotions. "You know I want you more than anything in the whole world, and I know without doubt that you feel the same way for me. Why continue with this farce? Why not end it now, before mother announces the engagement to the whole world?"

She had longed for them to have this conversation, but now as he finally brought up the subject he still didn't mention love, and he still didn't mention marrying her himself.

"Give me a reason," she whispered, her voice full of the love she couldn't hide. He put his hand against her cheek just as Thomas had done earlier and gave her an odd, sad smile.

"What more reason do you need? I haven't got

more than myself to offer, but I hoped it would be enough for you."

"I need more," she whispered and tears started to fill her eyes.

"You love me."

She nodded. "Forever."

"So let him go."

"I need to belong to someone."

"You already belong to someone, you belong with me. Your life is with me."

She wiped away the tears streaming down her cheeks. "Then give me a reason to throw away the only future I have. Give me a reason to be with you."

He let go of her and drew back slightly, his jaw clenched hard. "I don't know how to live without you. What more reason do you need?"

As the other carriage pulled to a stop beside them, Penny shook her head sadly. "More."

"Rake, you bastard. Don't you ever try such a prank again. Mother trusted me to keep your hands off Penny, and the first thing you do is get a little…"

Jamie's voice trailed off as he noticed the dark-faced Rake and the teary-eyed Penny. It was obvious something was going on here, and it had nothing to do with saving Penny's virginity and good name.

"Why don't we take the lead home," Jamie suggested softly, and when Rake nodded solemnly, he drove off with a last lingering look at his brother's stern face.

As the phaeton started to move, Rake chuckled softly and Penny turned toward him, surprised at his sudden humor.

"Look at us. This is such a lovely day, and we're

here together alone—or almost, if you don't consider my obnoxious brother in front of us—but instead of happy faces you would think doomsday is awaiting us around the corner."

"Maybe it feels like doomsday is closing in."

"Well, then I guess it's up to you to change the course you are traveling. It's easy. You just have to learn to stand on your own two feet instead of insisting on hiding behind someone else."

"I told you, I don't hide behind anyone, not Charmaine and not Fanny."

"And yet here you are, desperately trying to hide behind Bedford."

The frustration she had carried inside her for so long grew even larger, and before she could stop herself she had clenched her fist and struck him on the arm. Hard.

"Ouch!"

"Oh, my."

He stared at her as if she had completely lost her mind. "You hit me!"

"It felt so good." Her evident astonishment matched his.

"You…Hit…Me…"

She looked at him with dazed eyes. "I know. I did, didn't I? And it was wonderful. Thank you."

He frowned at her. "You're welcome. I think. Don't do it again, though."

She put her hand in front of her mouth to stifle the laughter which threatened to erupt. "Oh, I can't promise you that. It felt too good."

"Humpf," he said, pretending to be eternally humiliated, but he couldn't hide the telling twinkle in his eyes.

"You are such a snake," she laughed, and he chuckled with her.

"And you, my love, are a minx."

"I thought I was a siren."

"That too."

Passing Harveyfield, Penny lost her mirth as she glanced at the house where she had grown up. It looked unwelcoming and cold, as if it too had thrown her out of its life.

"Do you want to stop?"

"No." She shook her head slowly. "I would rather return to Chester Park, if you would be so kind."

"What happened, Penny?"

"I don't want to talk about it."

He took her chin and forced her to look into his dark eyes filled with what she would have thought was love and understanding if she hadn't known better. "Please enlighten me. I can't see you suffer like this without knowing why."

"Rake. Don't."

He let go of her with a harsh grunt. "All right, it's your choice to not tell anyone. I guess the only good thing is you haven't told Boring Saint Thomas, either."

When she didn't answer, he stared at her in disbelief of the truth which was written all over her guilt-stricken face.

"You have told Thomas Bedford what happened to you that night?"

"Yes."

"Why him?" he whispered as his voice cracked. "Why not me?"

"I couldn't accept his marriage proposal without

telling him the truth about me, the full truth."

Rake didn't answer, and she was grateful for the respite. She knew she had hurt him more than he deserved when she refused to tell him about the night she arrived drenched and bruised. But she couldn't stand to see his respect and warm feelings turn ice cold.

She could live with Thomas loathing her, but she would die if she knew Rake despised her even the tiniest bit.

As they stopped in front of Chester Park's magnificent entrance, he jumped to the ground and without another word stood still and stared at her angrily, slowly clenching and unclenching his fists, before he turned and walked away with an angry stride.

"Whatever it is, he will get over it."

Penny looked down at Jamie, who gave her a reassuring nod. She shook her head sadly.

"Not until it's too late, I'm afraid."

"Are you sure?"

She nodded without answering, and he sighed deeply.

"I'm sad to hear it. After seeing you two today, I hoped you finally had come to the conclusion you are meant to be together."

"We did, but unfortunately, as ever, without any lasting ties. I can't live like that, so I don't have many choices left."

"It saddens me to hear this, Penny. You two belong together."

She watched Rake disappear around the corner of the castle and unconsciously wiped a tear from her cheek.

"I know," she whispered. "I know."

Chapter Fifteen

The grand ballroom of Chester Park glistened in the flickering light of thousands of candles as Penny slowly descended the curved stairs.

The room was filled to the brim with people dressed in the most fantastic creations. There were soldiers from different times, Romans and Greeks, and—she noticed with a wry smile—quite a lot of shepherdesses.

She herself felt more beautiful than ever, but it was all because of the elegant angel dress Rake had ordered for her. The thin white fabric floated around her and enhanced the gracefulness of every step she took.

The Chester Park carpenter had been most helpful and had created a fragile cast made of bendy willow branches. Then Mina had with deft fingers fastened hundreds of white chicken feathers and now Penny proudly could boast having the most beautiful angel's wings on her back, completing the costume.

Her hair hung thick down her back, diamonds fastened all over the wavy mass, glistening in the candle light as she moved. Her face was covered in a beautiful white mask which also was decorated with white chicken feathers.

All in all—she looked marvelous.

Had everything been all right between her and Rake, she would have felt marvelous, too. But ever since the trip to the seamstress he had avoided her as much as possible. When they did meet, he hardly said a word to her, just nodded curtly in greeting and then ignored her.

So his feelings were hurt. It was understandable, she supposed. She had opened her heart to Thomas and not to him. But he had to get over it—the sooner the better—because in a few hours' time the duchess would announce the engagement between Penny and Thomas, and then there was no way back.

When it was official, it would be final for her, even though the marriage itself would not take place until Christmas. To repay Thomas's kind heart for his gentle acceptance of her not-too-clean background, she knew she had to show him that much respect.

But if Rake would come to his senses before the announcement was made... Well, then she wouldn't have any problems breaking an engagement nobody knew about.

As she moved through the crowd, she tried to spot Rake's tall frame, but as far as she could tell he was nowhere to be found.

The duchess wasn't so hard to find though, dressed in a stunning pink creation she swore was meant to be a sunset. Penny had a feeling the duchess didn't care what she was meant to represent, as long as she wore that particular dress.

Behind the duchess stood a group of men in normal evening clothes and hidden only by simple black masks, and Penny bit back a smile as she recognized Hannibal and his sons.

"We don't like masquerades," Jamie grunted, and she nodded compassionately.

"I can see that."

The duke took a step closer to her, after making sure his duchess wasn't close enough to overhear. "Can you please ask my wife to let us leave?"

Penny looked at the duchess, who was having the time of her life, and shook her head. "I don't dare. She's having so much fun she'd probably kill anyone who tries to destroy it for her."

"We know," the men sighed unanimously behind her as she continued through the crowd.

When she found Thomas, she couldn't stifle an appreciative laugh as he, bless his wonderful humor, was dressed as a saint and so turned the joke back on the backstabbers.

"An angel and a saint." He let his admiring eyes take in her outfit. "What a pair we make. Couldn't be a better fit, could it?"

"It's a match made in heaven," Penny joked, and Thomas laughed heartily.

"Indeed it is," he agreed warmly. "Do you think a boring saint like me could have the honor of a dance with the most beautiful angel I've ever seen?"

"I think a dance with you would be pure heaven." Penny blushed, not used to being flirtatious. But Thomas beamed with pleasure over her choice of words. He was such an easy man to please, and not as difficult to read as Rake.

As Thomas led their way to the dance floor with a firm grip of her hand, a sense of panic surged through her. For the first time she realized that in a few hours she would be this man's property for the rest of her life. This was how she would live the rest of her life, following his gentle tug in any direction he chose.

Rake, her heart cried out in a desperate plea, *where are you, my love? Please come and save me before it's too late for us, too late for a life together!*

But his dark head was nowhere to be seen.

The duchess had decided to live life dangerously and had, in the heat of the moment, ordered the dance of the evening to be the new dance not yet introduced at Almack's but on everyone's lips—the waltz.

It felt strange to move so close together with another person, and especially a man. Thomas wasn't a keen dancer, and to have her so close apparently made him even more nervous, because he trampled her feet many times before Napoleon Bonaparte, with a bow, cut in to save her toes from falling off.

Thomas's relieved face was the last thing Penny saw before the warlord twirled her away in the opposite direction. Soon another man cut in, and then another. Again and again a new man bowed to her and put his hand on her waist, until she was so confused she almost missed Rake when he cut in.

He came dressed as the devil, the opposite of her outfit, and she could have cried for the unspoken message he sent her.

"So, my lovely angel, are you having the time of your life?"

"Yes," she lied, and offered him her most cheeky smile in an effort to hide how painful she found the ball and the reason why it was held.

"Of course you are," he sneered. "There's probably not a woman on this earth who wouldn't love to look like you and be as popular as you have been. Hate the dress, by the way. It doesn't suit you at all."

She frowned at him. Something was off. He was

behaving strangely, not his usual elegant self. And then it hit her. "You are drunk!"

"Nah," he drawled. "Not drunk. Just a little bit tipsy. Just enough to take me through this bloody evening."

"You don't have to be here."

"On the contrary, my love. My mother made a vow that she will personally castrate me if I would choose to not show up. And as you love to point out, my only mission in life is to bed as many women as possible. And without my…" He swaggered and bumped into another man, who turned around and stared angrily at him.

But Rake didn't care. He just dragged Penny close again and tried to waltz. After bumping into three more men, Penny gave up and, with a little nudging, got Rake to move toward the edge of the dance floor.

"You shouldn't be dancing." She frowned at him.

"I have to. If I don't, all those men will have their dirty hands all over you, and I can't stand it. I just can't."

"Have you been watching me?"

"Of course I have." He snorted. "I've been watching you since you arrived, and did it with a strengthening glass of brandy in my hand to keep myself from killing that smug fiancé of yours."

"Thomas isn't smug."

"Oh, yes, he is. He is the smuggest of the smuggest. You should see how he looks at you when you don't notice. The man can hardly wait to rip that dress off you. Heck, who am I to blame him? I hardly can keep my own hands from tearing it off you right now."

She closed her eyes in frustration. A sober Rake was hard to handle, but a drunken Rake was impossible. She looked around to see if any of his brothers were nearby, but even in their ordinary clothing it was hard to find them in the colorful crowd.

"I think I'm going to throw up," Rake groaned behind her, and she took a deep breath to strengthen herself. She had to get him out of here before he did something that would mark this evening forever.

"Come," she said and pulled his arm. "Let's go and find some place more quiet."

"You and me?"

His face lit up with a wicked smile, and she shook her head. "You never change, do you?"

"I change all the time, but not as much as I have since I met you."

"You have known me since I was a little girl, so of course you have changed since you met me. You were a mere boy then, and now you are a grown, experienced man."

"To no good," he muttered, as they entered the hall. Servants were scurrying back and forth, and there was not a seat to be seen.

"Come, let's take you to your mother's salon. There you can lie down on the sofa and sleep this off."

He stumbled into the salon, and she followed to make sure he didn't hurt himself, but she made sure the door stayed open behind her. She didn't need a scandal on the evening of her engagement ball, at least not a scandal of her own.

Moonlight filled the room with cold white light, and she went to the large windows and pulled the curtains closed so no passersby would see Rake asleep on the sofa.

When she turned, she immediately noticed two things. Rake had moved and was now standing behind her with a lecherous smile on his handsome face, and the door to the salon was firmly closed.

"Are you out of your mind?" she gasped and started toward the door.

"Forget it, my love. I've locked it."

"You have *what*?"

He took a step closer to her, and the smile he gave her was so filled with promises her heart began to pound. "Locked the door. Please feel free to try to find the key. I have it somewhere on my person. I can give you a hint—it's in my trousers."

This was not good.

This was extremely not good. She was locked into a room with a drunken Rake who appeared determined to have his way with her, and she knew it would be just a matter of time before he succeeded. Drunken or not, it didn't matter. Her body was already responding to his lustful glances.

"Oh, God," she moaned, not knowing what to do.

"Quite the opposite, my love," Rake purred as he stepped the last bit of distance between them. "Quite the opposite, I assure you."

"Rake, please let me go."

"I can't. God knows I have tried, but it's impossible. You are impossible."

He grabbed her waist and pressed her body to his, and she almost fainted from the heat of him. With a groan he ripped the angel wings from her back and threw them into a corner before he scooped her up and laid her on the sofa and covered her body with his. His mouth found hers, kissing her until she didn't care about anything but his hard body, his roaming hands, and his demanding lips.

His fingers were everywhere on her skin, creating paths of sensation wherever they touched. She pulled her own fingers through his dark, silken hair and held on tight as he deepened the kiss until she couldn't think anymore.

Not until an uncomfortable pain between her legs surprised her did she wake from the passionate bubble he had created around them, but then it was too late. With a growl he pushed hard into her, faster and faster, until his body stiffened convulsively and he collapsed onto her.

A strange throbbing soreness brought tears to her eyes, and only the heaviness of his body made it impossible for her to sob hysterically. She tried to make him move, but he was out cold, and in the end she had to push him off her. He landed on the floor with an "Ouf" without waking up.

She sat up and put her legs together, frantically stroking the delicate and now wrinkled fabric of her skirt as the truth of the moment hit her.

She wasn't a virgin anymore. The man of her heart had finally succeeded with the mission he had started over a year ago—he had turned her into a disgraced woman. And what made it even worse was the fact that she had been almost frantic in her need to let him.

As she looked down on him where he lay sprawled by her feet, an odd mixture of panic and relief went through her. Now she couldn't marry Thomas. No matter what happened between her and Rake in the future, she could never let her kindhearted fiancé save her, knowingly or unknowingly.

She would have to end the engagement immediately, before the duchess made her big announcement. No one knew yet about the wedding plans, so there would be no whispers and no gossip.

He could continue with his life, not too hurt, she hoped, and unaware of how close he had come to marrying a woman who had lost both her heart and virginity to another man.

And she would have to find a new path in life. The only thing she knew was that she would never become Rake's mistress. She couldn't leave the only caring people she had left in her life for a short time of bliss in his arms in a large bed in a conveniently placed house somewhere in London.

With shaking hands she bent down to his unmoving body and searched his clothes until she found the key exactly where he had said it was, in his trousers. She stumbled to her feet and made her way toward the door, not stopping until she caught sight of her own reflection in the enormous ancient mirror decorating one of the walls of the salon.

She looked like a mess, her hair all tousled, her face still flushed, and her shimmering dress disheveled. With a deep sigh she tried to straighten as much as possible with her numb fingers.

When she was satisfied with the effects of her straightening, she stopped for a second and looked at Rake where he lay on the floor, unmoving. Not knowing what to think or what to say, she took a deep breath to strengthen herself before unlocking the door.

As soon as the hallway was empty, she slipped out and locked the door behind her again, then pushed the key back under the door. At least no one would happen to find Rake before he woke from his stupor.

It wasn't until she slipped into the lively ballroom she realized her wings still lay forgotten in the corner of the salon, where Rake had thrown them. But now it was too late. There was no way to get into the salon before Rake unlocked the door, and all she could do was hope no one would notice them missing before she had found Thomas and then the duchess.

"Penelope." Thomas looked down at her with a warm and slightly relieved smile when she joined him. "Please tell me it's time for the duchess to announce our engagement. I can hardly hold back the very eager women surrounding me. They are like vultures, searching for dance partners and not accepting 'no' as an answer."

"Could we go somewhere private? I need to talk to you." Penny's grave voice effectively removed the tender smile from Thomas's face, and without another word he led her to the terrace.

Politely he helped her to sit down on a bench, which afforded a perfect view of the ballroom, and she couldn't help but think how Rake would have chosen the one farthest away, in an attempt to be as alone with her as possible. Thomas, who still thought she was his fiancée, showed no such urge. He had no wish to be alone with her, and again she couldn't help being amazed at her own relief that she would never become this man's wife.

He was a good friend. But finally she had understood that she was too in love with Rake to ever be able to live with herself as Thomas's wife. Of course both Charmaine and the duchess had told her this, and embarrassingly enough even Rake had. Thomas, however, had never noticed her lack of true emotions, for he had never asked for any.

But she would have known.

She was Rake's woman, whether he wanted her or not. And even though she probably would have to face a life without him, she would at least not have to pretend to be happy with someone else.

"I can't marry you."

Thomas blinked at her bluntness. "Eh... You can't?"

"No. It wouldn't be the honest or the right thing for any of us."

"What...? Why...?"

He shook his head, confused, not knowing what to think, and she grasped this window of opportunity. "We don't love each other, and I think we both deserve love in our lives. Especially you, because you are the kindest and nicest man I know, and you should have a wife who wants you."

"Of course I love you," he snapped, as his head finally started to work again. "Otherwise I would never have asked you to become my wife in the first place."

"You love me as a friend, Thomas, which is exactly my point. I too love you dearly, but again—only as a friend."

Thomas threw out his hands in despair. "So what's the problem, then? We both agree to loving each other."

"But you need someone who loves you as a man. Someone who is so desperate to be with you that a few hours apart is too much. Not someone who would find it nice that you now and then happen to join her at the dinner table."

He shook his head, as if he couldn't grasp the truth of her words, and she put her hand on his where it rested on the bench between them. "You deserve more than me."

With a snarl, he removed his hand from hers and stood up. "I guess I should be thankful for your timing, as it would have been quite a big mess if the duchess had announced the happiness I thought we shared."

"Thomas…"

"Don't. You have already said enough."

Without looking at her again, he turned and ran down the stairs, disappearing into the darkness of the garden still dressed as a saint with his shiny halo firmly in place. She felt terrible for him, knowing she had crushed his belief in love.

Crushed by an angel who lost her wings.

She took a deep breath, a bit confused over the sadness which filled her heart. She would have thought she'd be more relieved than this, now, when the engagement was over. But instead, she felt lonelier and more left out than ever, even though this was her choice.

For the hundredth time, she wished she could see her mother, to confide in her and be comforted by her soft embrace.

"There you are!" The duchess's voice cut through Penny's sadness.

"Lady Anna. I was just about to—"

"What a lovely night for a declaration of love," the duchess interrupted, too caught up in what she thought was about to happen to notice how rudely she behaved. "I still think Richard should show up and do something about it, but as he seems determined to stay truly unhappy for the rest of his sad life, I guess there is no other way than for me to announce the happy couple. Do you happen to know where the man of the evening is? I haven't seen Thomas for a while, not since he maneuvered an escape from the evil clutches of Miranda Walsh."

"Thomas is not here. He has…"

"I can see that, dear. I might be old, but my eyes still work for me, and I too can see you are quite alone out here, something I must confess I'm not too happy about, by the way."

"Lady Anna…"

"Oh! Where can he be? I thought he would be as giddy as I am about announcing the engagement. When I met him earlier, he made perfectly sure that he wouldn't mind if I made my speech earlier than we planned."

"Lady Anna…"

"Oh, this vexes me. Where can that young beau of yours be? And where is Richard? I most definitely thought he would have done something or other to end this farce, and yet here we stand, on the edge of ruining your life forever."

"Lady Anna…"

The duchess threw out her hands in despair. "I can't believe he will let you go through with this. I never thought I would actually have to make that darned announcement."

That was news, indeed. Penny almost smiled over the duchess's intrigues, but the seriousness of the situation took away all humor for her.

"Then you will be glad to hear there will be no announcement for you to make."

"What?" The duchess stared at her, mouth agape. "Has Richard finally stepped in? Oh, I would love to make *that* announcement!"

"There will be no announcements at all, unfortunately. I have told Thomas I don't want to marry him, and that's all there is to it."

"Oh."

"And here I thought you would be happy." Penny couldn't stop herself from teasing the duchess a little. "You have been berating me about not marrying him, and now as I finally do as you have asked, you don't seem happy about it."

"Well, I..." For once, the duchess didn't know what to say. She sat down on the bench, on the very spot Thomas had left only minutes before. "I must admit I wasn't too happy about you marrying that boring young man, but in the end it's your happiness it's all about, not mine. And if you have lost your opportunity for a happy life just because I desperately want you for my daughter-in-law..."

"I could always marry Jamie."

The duchess lightened up for a second before she caught the sarcasm in Penny's words and sank back into her misery again. "No, that's not an option. It would be marrying Mr. Bedford all over again. No, you belong with Richard. I only wish he would understand that too."

Penny bit her lip nervously. Should she tell the duchess about what had happened in the salon? No, she had to fight that battle herself. She knew now it was Rake and only Rake she wanted, as it always had been.

But she didn't want a forced Rake. She wanted him to know with all his heart that he wanted her too.

She was too tired now, and her head was spinning from everything that had happened this evening. But time was on her side, and tomorrow was a better day to attack the problem with Rake.

She needed her sleep. She needed time to think.

Tomorrow was just as good as this evening. Rake was probably still out cold, and she wouldn't be able to have a decent conversation with him anyway.

She bid the grieving duchess good night before running with light steps up the stairs to her room.

Tomorrow would be a new day.

Chapter Sixteen

"I guess there is no turning back now."

Penny looked up from the book she had been reading and hid her amused smile as Rake slowly walked, or rather stumbled, into the library, grimacing against the radiant sunbeams which drowned the room with light.

"I beg your pardon?"

He squinted at her where she sat on her favorite windowsill. "Lose the act, my love. You know what I'm talking about."

She didn't know how to respond to that and decided to stay quiet and, for once, let him do the talking. She wanted this man with every part of her being and could so easily grab the lead and drag him into marriage. But yesterday she had made a solemn promise to herself to marry him only if he felt the same way, which meant he actually needed to tell her so.

Wringing water from a stone would probably be an easier mission, but she was determined to be either devastatingly unhappy without him or absurdly happy with him. She wouldn't settle for something between, whether it was marrying Thomas or marrying a Rake who thought he had no other choice.

"How can you stand the light? My eyes hurt like hell. Do you think we could go somewhere else to talk?"

She nodded, jumped gracefully down from the sill, and motioned for him to follow her into the small windowless room in which the duke stored all the family's oldest books.

"Ah, better." Rake let out a sigh filled with contentment as he sank down onto the comfortable sofa, the only piece of furniture in the room besides the book-filled shelves covering all four walls.

Penny stopped in the doorway, all too aware of what had happened between them the last time they were alone in a confined space. This was not the time to let him try to seduce her again—which he probably would, the scoundrel, if she let him any closer to her than an arm's length.

"You can come inside. I promise I won't bite."

He looked at her with an amused arch of his eyebrow, and she felt her cheeks heat as she shook her head without answering him.

"No?"

"I'm fine here, thank you."

"It's a very comfortable sofa."

"I know."

Again he lashed his unreadable grin at her, and again she felt her cheeks burn. This was Rake the wicked libertine, and it was surprisingly good to see him. It was almost as in the old days, before everything went bad. Before she went to London for her first Season.

"Can you at least close the door, please? I think we need some privacy for this conversation."

"No."

"No? Why not? I won't throw myself all over you as soon as you…" His voice trailed off, and his grin came back. "Oh."

He chuckled, crossing his legs in a leisurely manner, clearly enjoying this situation a lot more than she did. It wasn't too hard for her to guess why, though. He thought he had her in his hand, that he finally had won the struggle between them that had lasted over a year.

Little did he know she wasn't ready to give in just yet. She almost chuckled wickedly herself, but managed to stop in time. No, her beloved scoundrel, who sat there with a victorious gleam in his smoky eyes, would soon be aware he wouldn't win so easily.

"I have to admit I don't remember much from yesterday's ball. I have a distant memory of you and me dancing, but then it's kind of a blur until I woke up locked inside my mother's salon, with my trousers loose and falling to my ankles."

He looked at her as if he expected her to respond in some way, and she forced herself to stand still, to show as little emotion as possible.

With a slightly irritated frown, he continued, "At first I didn't understand what had happened, but considering the status of my trousers and... Anyway, I rather understood what had happened then, but it wasn't until I found your wings in the corner I realized it was with you."

Again he stared hard at her, as if mentally trying to force her response, and she dug her nails deep into the palms of her hands in her effort to not give away any emotion or reply in any way. She must have an evil core inside her, she knew, as his obvious frustration with her silence pleased her immensely.

Let him suffer a bit. Let him feel as confused as

she had felt over the last months. It would only do him—and her—well. At least she hoped it would.

"Are you all right?" He stood up and walked over to her, not stopping until he stood so close she had to lean her head backwards to be able to look into his narrowed eyes.

"I'm fine, thank you." She gave him a small smile which was meant to calm him, but instead his frown deepened.

"No, you are not. You can't be. You just had quite an experience last night, and even though I know I never would do you any harm, not even when drunker than I've ever been before, I might not have been as gentle with you last night as I would have otherwise."

"I'm fine. Truly, I am."

"Penny, my love, you can be honest with me. I can take the truth. If I scared or hurt you in any way, I need to know. Please indulge me."

"Truly, I'm fine. No need for you to be this anxious about it."

"Well, then, was I any good?"

She stared at him openmouthed. "What?"

"I have never been that drunk while making love, and I just wondered if I'm as good a lover drunk as when I'm sober. Good to know, you know."

"You..." She couldn't believe her ears. The snake. The selfish, awful snake. How could he even think that...

It was the smug smile he couldn't hide that told her he had only been teasing to finally get a reaction from her, and she cursed silently as she clamped her mouth shut, but too late.

His victorious sneer told her as much.

Damn. Bloody double damn.

"Shall we start this all over again?" He leaned closer to her, and she caught her breath as his mouth came closer to hers, and not until she felt the door bump into her backside did she realize he had only been reaching for the door to close it firmly behind her.

Again she was caught in a room alone with him, but this time he was sober—almost—and had a determined look upon his handsome face. Quickly she slipped under his arm and rushed to the sofa to put it between them as a barrier.

"I could easily jump the sofa, you know." He leaned against the now-closed door and crossed his arms with an amused grin. The snake was obviously enjoying the situation a bit more than she did.

"I know," she admitted through her teeth. "I might be ignorant of much, but I'm not stupid."

"I never called you stupid or ignorant. Simpleminded, I might have said, though, now and then."

She snorted but decided wisely against replying. She would never win a battle of words with him and knew it was better to get to the core of this conversation as soon as possible, before he kissed her senseless, as his smoldering eyes hotly promised.

"I *am* fine. You don't have to worry. I was a bit distraught last night, I admit, but now I can handle it."

He nodded, accepting the truth in her words with a relieved little sigh. "All right, then. Let's not spend any more time going over what happened yesterday, which we have all the time in the world to talk about later. Let us instead talk about something more important now: our future."

She liked his words "our future" a bit too much, she realized, and hardened her soft heart against him. He still hadn't mentioned loving her, and she had made her vow: for her it was all or nothing. She didn't want anything in between, and all she had to do now was to see it through.

"For starters, you have to tell Thomas you can't marry him," he continued, a gruesome note in his voice. "I know it's a bit much to ask of you, especially considering my mother's big announcement yesterday, but it's not fair of you to keep him to his promise."

"How low is your opinion of me?" She growled at him. "Of course I broke off the engagement before your mother had a chance to announce anything. Thomas is too good to ever be lied to in any way."

"The engagement is off?"

His obvious astonishment irritated her. Why was it so hard for him to believe that she already had told Thomas it was off? She wasn't an ogre, like him, to keep others dangling without caring.

Thomas deserved the truth.

"Yes, I spoke with Thomas as soon as I could after, after, you know…"

"No, I don't know. After what?"

She couldn't resist sticking out her tongue toward him, the snake. He was such a tease, never able to resist an opportunity to bicker. Life with him would have its ups and downs, but if she only knew he loved her with all his heart it would be worth it.

If only he would tell her.

"So let us talk about *our* future then." She ignored his amusement over her childish action.

He raised an eyebrow. "Let us, indeed."

When he didn't continue, she sighed, frustrated. So she would have to drag it out of him? Why couldn't he just act the perfect gentleman and tell her what she needed to hear? Then everything would finally come to its perfect fairytale end: happily ever after.

"So where do we go from here?" She was unable to withhold her irritation any longer.

"To the closest bedroom?"

"Rake!"

"Ah, woman, I love it when you gasp. Are you sure you don't want to meet me on the sofa instead of hiding behind it?"

She sighed. He didn't make it easy for her. "Please, can't we just talk about the future? This is not the time to tease the subject away."

He gave her his most wicked grin. "How can I talk about the future when I can't remember the past? If you could help me remember last night a bit, I might feel much more obliged to talk about more boring things than kissing that lovely spot under your ear."

This time her sigh was defeated. "You almost make me regret ending my engagement with Thomas. *He* wouldn't have been too afraid to talk to me about something more serious than kissing."

"No, he would have discussed the political climate in Scotland rather than anyone's emotions. Don't forget my dear, I know Thomas too. He hasn't got a romantic bone in his boring saintly body, and you would have suffocated as his wife." Slowly he started toward her, mesmerizing her with the lustful promises in his eyes.

"Now you're being rude," she rushed to say, to put some mental distance between them. "Thomas might not be the most passionate of men, in your eyes, but that doesn't mean he can't enjoy a private moment as much as the next man."

Rake stopped on the other side of the sofa, his eyes losing their warmth. "And how do you know this? By experience?"

Oh, Lord, save me from simpleminded men.

She shook her head slowly. "I give up. Obviously you are not interested in what I find important, as all you can think about is, as you put it, kissing. Let us just part here and now and go on with our lives as they are. I'm too tired to let you bounce me around like this. I need peace and quiet, and you offer me neither."

"I think you are overreacting a bit, my love. I'm merely teasing you..."

Angrily she walked to his side of the sofa and shoved him hard in the chest, forcing him to stumble back slightly. "Overreacting? *I'm* overreacting? That's quite rude of you to say, since you don't react at all. For all I know, you don't care a bit about me or what happened between us yesterday. And honestly, right now I don't either. So let it be. Let *me* be." With a last snarl, she walked right past him, yanked the door open, and stomped through the empty library and out into the hallway.

She met the duchess on the stairs to the first floor, and the poor woman paled as Penny sent her a don't-you-even-dare-to-ask look as she passed her. Not until she was securely inside her bedroom door did she breathe again, deep, shaky breaths which tore through her body.

So be it. She would have to continue with her life devastatingly unhappy, but at least it was by her own choice. She would die an old maid—almost—but at least she would know she had lived her life fair and square.

So what if she would spend every day and night longing for him and for what could have been—it didn't matter. Not in the long run.

She couldn't face a life that resembled the almost-conversation she'd just had with him, with her constantly on her toes trying to get him to show her any emotion at all, and him trying to seduce her instead, unable or unwilling to let her come behind the walls he raised around his heart.

A soft knock on her door interrupted her erratic thoughts, and at first she decided not to answer. It didn't matter who it was standing on the other side of the door, she wasn't ready to talk about what had happened. Or rather, what hadn't happened.

But as the knocking stubbornly continued, she gave in and went to the door, where she leaned her cheek against the hard wood. "Yes?"

Rake's voice was sharp. "Open."

"No."

"Don't do this, Penny. Don't do this to us."

"I just tried to talk to you, to reach out to you," she cried out, and she heard him lean against the door heavily.

"I know."

"But you didn't let me."

"I know."

She almost rolled her eyes, but something in his voice stopped her. "Why?"

"It's not easy for me. Why can't we just kiss and agree that everything is good between us again? Why do you so stubbornly have to talk about it?"

"Because *I* need to."

She heard him chuckle, but there was no amusement in the dead, almost defeated sound. "I don't. I only need you."

By now, tears were streaming down her cheeks, but she wiped them away angrily. "*Why* do you need me?"

"What kind of daft question is that? Why do you think I need you? Because I want you."

"But *why* do you want me?"

He was silent for so long she almost thought he had left. Just as she had decided against her better judgment to open the door to see if he still was there, he spoke again. "I need you, Penny. I need you in my arms, in my life. But that is all there is. I can't give you what more it is you want, because you refuse to let me know what it is. I have shown you every card I've got, and if that's not enough for you…"

His voice trailed off, and she heard him breathe as deeply and shakily as she just had, before he continued, "If that's not enough for you, I'll do as you ask and leave you alone."

This time she didn't care about the tears which clouded her eyesight. Instead, she closed her eyes and put her hand against the door, pretending it was his beloved face she touched.

"I need more."

"Then I'm not the man for you."

She heard him move away from the door, leaving her alone as he'd said he would. With a groan she grabbed the handle.

What was she doing?

She had everything she'd ever wanted within her reach, but because of her stupid pride and a wish to be loved she was about to throw it all away.

But she was too late.

As she lunged out into the corridor, she saw him dashing down the stairs to disappear to the ground floor, and she knew there was not a chance for her to catch up with him now. She rushed back into her bedroom and to the window, where she could see him striding across the courtyard toward the stables, in a desperate hurry to leave Chester Park.

To leave her.

She spent the rest of the day in the foyer, waiting for Rake to return and biting the head off everyone who dared to ask what she was doing there. But when it was time for dinner, he still hadn't shown his face, and she sighed.

What was she to do?

She desperately needed to talk to someone, but she didn't know whom. The duchess was too much involved to be able to help her sort her confused thoughts, and she didn't feel comfortable approaching any of the Darling men about her emotions and Rake's reactions.

There was only one person who could give her what she needed right now, other than Rake himself. Only one person who would listen to her without judging her or putting her own feelings in front of Penny's.

Her mother.

She went to the window next to the front door and looked down the dusky road which led to her childhood home, her heart crying for Lady Nester.

She needed her mother. She needed to hide in her loving embrace and listen to her steady heartbeat while spilling out all about her confused state of mind.

This wasn't right. Why was she standing here like a fisherman's wife, staring longingly toward the horizon, eagerly waiting for her loved one to return, without knowing if he actually would?

She was done with being a thoughtless doll. She had to act. No, she needed desperately to act.

She had to do something about it and not just stand here waiting for him, day in and day out. She knew she had somewhere during the last year chosen the wrong path. Or, to be honest, she had probably done that more than once.

When it came to Rake, she didn't seem able to think straight. She had her dream of him, which she had nursed with care for as long as she could remember. A dream of a perfect man in a perfect life.

But Rake wasn't perfect. And the last couple of months had showed her she wasn't either. So why chase the perfect love? She already had Rake. What else did she need? A child's dream of a life that wasn't real?

No, she needed the real Rake, her Rake: the laughing family man who would spend the rest of his life driving her crazy with his teasing and his hot kisses.

So what if he wasn't the knight in shining armor she had been looking forward to? She didn't want that boring, unflawed man. Hadn't her whole relationship with Thomas Bedford shown her as much?

With a determined breath she rushed out through the door and dived into the dark evening, ignoring the chill her thin shawl couldn't hold back. She didn't care if she wasn't wanted or if her father was going to throw her all the way back to Chester Park.

She was going to her mother.

Chapter Seventeen

"Don't you think the drivers will be a bit upset over you emptying their stash of good liquor?"

Rake squinted up at his father, who stood hovering over him where he slumped in a pile of hay in the darkest part of the Chester Park stables.

"I thought no one knew I was here."

"Penny doesn't, if that's what you mean. The rest of us are well aware of your whereabouts, as we all know the two things you prefer to do when you're upset."

Rake lifted the bottle of wine and let the red liquor fill his mouth. He didn't need this harassment. Not now. Not ever.

All he wanted was some privacy, so he could drink himself into a stupor he would hopefully never wake up from. If it meant he would have to stay drunk the rest of his life, so be it. Just as long as he didn't have to face the pain of reality.

The pain of loving Penny.

That woman could drive a saint crazy, and for all he knew she probably already had, considering poor Thomas Bedford.

Maybe he should seek Thomas out. They could drink together, and maul with words the wicked witch named Lady Penelope de Vere, who thoughtlessly walked over every man's heart, not once thinking about their feelings.

Or not. If he came any closer to Thomas than a mile, he would probably thrash the poor man who had kissed Penny not only once but twice. Put his ugly lips against her lush ones and pressed his tongue gently against hers, tasted her sweet mouth…

This time he emptied the bottle in one final gulp before he threw it away in the same direction he had thrown the first bottles. The clanking noise when the bottle landed with its friends made his father arch an eyebrow against him.

"Feeling a bit thirsty?"

"A bit."

"Water would be a better choice."

"No, it wouldn't. Go away."

Hannibal, as the understanding and loving father he was, ignored his son's harsh words and instead sat down by him and, without a word, reached for the next bottle, which he opened and offered his son.

"Here, don't let me stop you."

Rake grabbed the bottle, but instead of putting it to his mouth, he looked at the swirling wine inside. It felt good to have his father beside him in his hour of need. If his family was the solidness of his life, Hannibal was his guiding star.

Even though they were as different as night and day, he had always tried to live up to his father's standard.

Hannibal Darling, the Duke of Berkeley, was the most honest and caring man he knew of. Without remorse or embarrassment, the duke showered his sons with love, not once caring who saw how soft he was when it came to his boys. So what if Hannibal didn't want to leave Chester Park? When he was home at the ancestral castle, Rake knew he had his father's full attention whenever he wanted it.

And occasionally when he didn't want it.

"This has gone too far." His father spoke softly, as if he didn't want to scare the moment away. "You and Penny have to work this out somehow. You are both suffering immensely from it, and besides that, it drives the rest of us crazy."

Rake snorted. "Don't you think I have tried to? But it's like talking to a mule: she refuses to listen to me. It doesn't matter what I do or what I say, it's just not enough for her."

"So what is it she wants?"

"I don't know! She refuses to tell me."

Rake felt Hannibal's probing eyes and knew he sounded lunatic. But the whole Penny situation was crazy from beginning to end. He didn't know what to do, and the fact that she didn't seem to know either didn't make it any easier. It was a never-ending story, destined to run in circles forever and ever.

"I-I'm not a man of words, not when it comes to emotions," he continued, too tired to care whether he was revealing too much. It was his father, after all. If he was going to open up to anyone, who better than the man who loved him without boundaries? "I have tried in every way I can think of to show her how much she means to me, but it's never enough for her. There is nothing more I can tell her that I haven't already shown her in a thousand ways. And yet she stubbornly persists…"

He broke off and shook his head in desperation. It was too much for him, all those feelings, and the frustration over not being able to get past one obstacle on his way to eternal happiness: Penny herself.

"I don't know what's going on in that beautiful little head of hers," he continued. "Every time I try to talk to her, I seem to end up just as angry and frustrated as I feel now. Somehow it feels like she doesn't want to listen to what I have to say but instead hears only a word or two before she gets all upset over them."

"Don't you think you are overreacting a bit now?" Hannibal stood and began in a very Darling-like way to walk to and fro in front of his youngest son, obviously caught up in finding a solution to the situation which rendered Rake this unhappy. "Penny is a smart girl, although she tends to live with her head in the clouds a bit too much sometimes. But more importantly, she loves you with all her heart. Always has and always will. If you just try again, maybe you two could find a way to meet in the middle."

Rake couldn't stop the hysterical laughter which erupted from his chest. "Don't you think I have tried? Oh, Lord, how I have tried."

The emotions were too much for him, and he flew up too, ignoring the spinning inside his head, and walked to and fro beside his father. "It's like the first time I talked to her about us joining our futures, having a house of our own. I asked her where she would like to live. I thought it was obvious, considering the lack of tactfulness from the rest of you Darlings…"

"What?" Hannibal gasped outraged. "We are not untactful. Of course we would stay out of the way for you and your new bride."

"Of course you would," Rake sneered, "For an hour or two."

Hannibal snorted, but even he couldn't deny the truth in Rake's words. He too knew, just as Rake did, that the Darling family was a bit over-intrusive when it came to other members of the family, and not one of them would have thought twice about the newlyweds wanting some privacy.

"All I wanted was to be alone with her during the first months of our marriage, so we could have time to adjust to our new life together and get to know each other, body and soul. But Penny, my lovely little dove, missed the part of me hiding in a house with her as her husband and thought I was telling her I wanted to put her in a house as my mistress."

"What?" Hannibal hooted with laughter. His large shoulders shook so much his wavy white hair bounced upon his head. "That's hilarious. My God, how I would like to have heard that conversation. You—my wicked libertine son—giving up your bachelor lifestyle for this slip of a girl, while she accuses you of wanting to turn her into your mistress. Truly hilarious."

Rake stopped his pacing and shook his head over his father's obvious delight. "Your compassion overwhelms me."

"Oh, come on, Richard." Hannibal gave Rake a whack on the back that would have sent a smaller man flying. But Rake had inherited his father's large frame and was used to his constant whacking, and so held his stance.

"Really, Father, it's not as funny when you're in the middle of it."

"No, of course not." Hannibal cleared his throat in an attempt to regain his composure. "Please, continue. What happened after Penny thought you were trying to turn her into one of your mistresses?"

Rake glared at his father. "Why does everyone think I have hoards of mistresses everywhere? Penny does, too, and the jealous little minx wouldn't listen to a word I had to say after misunderstanding me."

"Don't you?"

"Don't I what?"

"Have a couple of mistresses waiting around for you?"

"Of course not."

Rake could see his father had trouble believing him and, frankly, he couldn't hold it against him. He had been a bit infamous when he was younger and had let his manly lusts lead his way for a couple of amorous years.

But when Devlin left for the military, Rake had more or less left that part of his life behind and instead spent most of his time helping his father and the rest of his family with the financial side of the estate, increasing the already enormous Berkeley riches.

He was a man with certain needs, of course, and he had not been without female company for more than a few weeks, over the past six years, and for a while he had even had a mistress tucked away in a house for him to visit when he felt so obliged. To his credit, he had never been with more than one woman at a time, never with unmarried ladies, and never, ever, had his heart in it.

And from the moment he laid eyes on Penny at the lake last August, he hadn't even looked at another woman, much less bedded one. His body burned with need, but it was a fire only Penny could ease. Something he knew from experience, embarrassingly enough.

After Penny had tumbled into Francesca's bedroom that night a year ago and then refused to talk to him about it, he had behaved in the most destructive way. Something had happened to her, something so awful it had turned her into a shadow of herself, and he was kept outside of it. By her choice.

He knew he had acted the reverse of what he should have, but in a desperate need to have revenge against Penny for shutting him out, he had flirted outrageously with every woman he met, not once caring about who she was as long as she could be a possible bedmate and for a short moment of time erase the image of the drenched and bruised Penny on the floor that night.

But in vain. It never went farther than him arriving at the woman's bedroom and making a humiliated escape from it in a couple of minutes. Not because he wasn't able to perform. No, it was simply because he felt like an ogre, thinking of being unfaithful to Penny, and he never got over that enough to be able to stay.

After a while he gave up his foolish quest for bodily satisfaction and let the truth sink in. Everyone always joked about how a reformed libertine made the best husband, and he guessed he was the living evidence of that.

Not that he knew what kind of husband he would be—probably suffocating poor Penny with his silly need of being near her, touching her, looking at her, loving her—but it was obvious he had no need for anyone other than her, *his* woman.

"Why don't you just explain to her how wrongly she thinks of you?"

Rake scowled at his father. "Why? Because you all keep joking about me being the lover of all time, something you always have done, and probably always will. Is it so strange that she, who has heard about this her whole life, believes it to be the truth?"

"No," his father admitted, looking a bit embarrassed. "I've never thought twice about it. We all have our place in the family, and I'm sorry to say that you, dear son, have always been the wicked libertine."

"I might have been in my early twenties, but not for years, now. But to her that is all that counts."

The memory of Penny's words, that his mouth had kissed every woman of the *ton*, rang in his head, and he sighed heavily. He had a sinking feeling that he had tried to fight a cause already lost. Penny loved him, something he had no doubt about, but for her that apparently wasn't enough.

Telling her he wasn't the man for her hadn't been a complete lie, because he knew if she just opened her eyes and saw him for what he really was, and not what she had been told all her life, she would know too that they were meant to be together. But if she couldn't get past the image of him that his family's constant teasing had given her, he knew he had to let her go.

He would probably die a little every lonely day without her, but at least he wouldn't live this strange half-life waiting for her to come around.

"Why don't you just go to the foyer and talk to Penny? She's been sitting there for hours, waiting for you to come back home."

"She has?"

His father rolled his eyes dramatically. "You don't have to look so happy over that. The poor girl is probably boiling mad right now, after sitting there in that drafty room all day. Last time I spoke to her she practically bit my head off. She's not in the best of moods, I dare say."

Rake felt a hope build in his chest as he heard his father's words. So she had been sitting there all day, waiting for him to return, while he had been drinking in the stable across the courtyard? How nice.

"Oh, that smile I know." His father chuckled and whacked him again on the shoulder. "Go on, get your girl. Become as ridiculously happy as you deserve, my son."

Rake took a few steps toward the castle, but something in the back of his head kept nagging him. It didn't feel right. Something inside him didn't want him to go to the castle and take Penny in his arms and live happily ever after.

He hesitated at the large stable door. He had always followed the voice inside him, and it had not once failed him. Now it told him to wait.

Or, to be honest, he had to admit it practically screamed to him that this wasn't the time for him to erase everything in the past and throw himself into a happy life without remorse.

There were too many things that still bothered him when it came to Penny. Would he ever be able to let bygones be bygones?

Aside from everything else, he wanted her to know she had been wrong about him. Bloody hell, he needed her to know who he *truly* was before he could marry her. If she didn't know the real him, how could they ever be completely happy?

How could *he* ever be completely happy?

And if she never told him what had happened that night six months ago, how could he ever completely trust her? He needed her to trust him. He needed her to feel she could confide in him, tell him anything that was on her mind, without restraint.

Like she had told Thomas…

The pain he'd felt when she admitted that had almost knocked him off his feet. His darling girl, his love, had confided the truth to that outsider, to that unimportant man she didn't even love, and still she refused to tell him—the man she *did* love.

"What's wrong?"

His father's voice broke through his confused, wine-dazed thoughts, and he took a step back from the door, shaking his head slowly but nevertheless determined. "I can't."

"You can't what?" Hannibal frowned. "Open the door? I can help you with that."

Rake snorted. That joke was too bad even for his father. "No. I can't go to her. Not yet, at least. I need to clear my head first and to think things through before I do anything else."

Hannibal's grey eyes, so much like Rake's, looked up toward the castle and he sighed deeply in defeat. "Of course you have to. Why don't you go out the other way and sneak up the back stairs? I'll talk to Penny and tell her you'll speak with her tomorrow—say, noon in the library?"

Rake nodded. It sounded fine to him. This would give him a respite, and he could gather his thoughts enough to be able to make a plan on how to solve the problem with Penny.

"Well, I can't say I like it, but at least this shows

me you are serious about the girl."

His father put his hand on Rake's shoulder and gave him a smile filled with love and encouragement, and for a second Rake put his own hand on top of his father's, letting the old man know without words how much he appreciated him.

"Off you go," his father grunted, obviously touched by the moment, and with a last smile, which felt more like a grimace, Rake left the stable and went to his room without being seen.

Not caring about how dirty he was, he stripped his clothes off and lay down on his bed, closing his eyes with a contented sigh as the soft sheets embraced his body. Before he had a chance to think things through, his head became empty and he fell promptly asleep, not waking up until shouting voices in the corridor roused him.

Just as he opened his drowsy eyes, the door to his bedroom flew open and his twin Jamie barged in, looking quite a mess.

"She's gone."

"Who's gone?" Rake shook his head in an effort to force his sleepy brain to start work again.

"Penny. He took her."

What? Rake sat up in bed, suddenly wide awake. "Who took Penny?"

"Lord Nester."

"Her father came here?"

Jamie shook his head. "No, she went to him."

Rake stood and reached for his trousers in one single movement. What on earth had possessed Penny to go to Lord Nester? As far as he knew, she didn't even want to talk about her father, let alone see him, and Rake had long ago guessed her tragedy had something to do with him. It didn't make sense.

"Come, the others await us in the parlor."

They rushed through the dark corridor, and when they passed a large clock, it told Rake the time was just past midnight. In the duchess's parlor his whole family had gathered by one of the sofas—their faces worried.

When he came closer, he saw his mother on the sofa hugging Charmaine, who looked beautiful despite her disheveled appearance and her obvious need to throw up.

As his mother saw him, she put a finger against her lips, ensuring that he would stay quiet and not disturb the girl.

"There, there," the duchess soothed, and with a deep breath Charmaine managed to compose herself again.

"I'm so sorry," she whispered. "It's just been too much, and I didn't know what to do."

"You did the right thing to come here. Now, please tell us what happened when Penny arrived at Harveyfield."

Rake watched Charmaine wring a soiled handkerchief between her slender fingers and wanted to throw himself upon her and shake her hard to force her to start talking. As if she felt his urgency, she looked up and met his eyes.

"Why couldn't you just have married her?" she accused him hoarsely. "It would have made everything so much easier, and she would have been safe."

Rake could feel his family's probing eyes on his person as if they wondered the same thing. Instead of answering her question, he asked her one back.

"Where is Penny?"

"I-I don't know. He took her with him."

"Who took her? Your father?"

Charmaine nodded, and her delicately beautiful cheeks paled even more. "H-he caught her when she tried to sneak into Mother's bedroom. I think she thought he was at his usual weekly card game, as he always used to be before. She couldn't possibly know that he stopped going to them when he ran out of…"

Her voice trailed off, but there was no need for her to continue, as every last person in the room knew about Lord Nester's extensive gambling and the pile of debts he collected wherever he went.

"What happened when Penny and Lord Nester met?"

"When I woke up because of the raised voices outside my room, father was already carrying her down the stairs, bellowing for the carriage. I-I ran as fast as I could, but I was too late. The carriage was already moving by the time I got outside, and I had no means to stop it."

The duchess patted Charmaine's blond hair soothingly. "Did he say anything about where he was taking her?"

Charmaine shook her head slowly. "No. But it's not so hard to guess."

To Rake's frustration, the duchess only nodded, obviously knowing what Charmaine meant, and he couldn't stay silent any longer. "*Where* exactly did he take her?"

Charmaine glanced at the duchess, who sighed. "There is no way I can continue to honor Penny's wish for us to stay quiet about it. He took her to London."

"To London? Why? What's in London?"

"Not what—who. The man to whom Lord Nester gave Penny and from whom she managed to escape."

Rake had to sit down. His head was spinning so fast he couldn't think straight. What was his mother talking about? Had Lord Nester given Penny away? But that was unheard of. A father didn't give a daughter away, at least not without a ring on her precious little finger.

"He's been pestering Father with letters demanding Penny's immediate return, and Father has been so frustrated at not being able to fulfill the request. Finding Penny alone in the house must have seemed as manna from heaven to him."

"That man is pure evil." Hannibal's voice was full of hate, and Rake felt something build up inside, as well, something so ugly and dark that he felt it would consume him.

"Who?"

Nobody answered his clipped question. Tired of all the secrecy he had lived with for the last year, he strode to Charmaine and, without caring whether he frightened her, leaned forward until his nose almost touched hers.

"*Who?*"

She started to shiver compulsively, but he didn't care. He ignored his mother, who begged him to step back, and he grabbed Charmaine's chin and forced her to look at him. He didn't have to ask his question again, as her weak voice whispered the only thing he wanted to know.

"Lord Bolton."

When he let go of her chin, she fell backwards with a sigh, fainting into his mother's embrace, but he didn't stop. Hatred filled his heart and his soul, and the only thing he could think of was to get to London. Without a word, he snatched the jacket Ivanoff held out to him and went straight to the stables, where he grabbed the closest horse.

As he fastened the saddle, he saw the youngest three of his brothers had gathered and were also saddling horses, and he closed his eyes briefly, thankful they would be going with him. He needed someone to be with Penny while he slowly killed the two men who had hurt her—Lord Nester and Lord Bolton.

It didn't take the four Darling brothers more than a couple of hours to reach London, horseback being a quicker mode of travel than a carriage, and soon he stood outside a large stately townhouse, one he had passed many times without knowing what horrors Penny must have endured under its roof. Lord Nester's carriage stood outside, and the driver, who recognized the determined four, pointed at the house without uttering a word.

Afterwards, Rake couldn't remember what had happened inside Lord Bolton's house or what he had done to the vile man. All he knew was that his knuckles were sorer than they had ever been before and that he had a whimpering Penny in his arms when the hackney he'd found came to a halt at the Darling townhouse at Berkeley Square.

He ignored the helpful footmen and carried her himself up the staircase and into her room, where he carefully laid her down on the bed. He practically growled at the maids who rushed into the room to assist him, and his ferocious manner sent them running.

He couldn't leave her. Not like this.

She stared silently out into the air, her unseeing eyes filled to the brim with tears which never fell. Silently he helped her undress while he desperately tried to ignore the shivers which went through her body every time he happened to touch her.

She still hadn't said a word about what had happened during the two hours she had been in Lord Bolton's house. Lord Nester's driver, who wasn't overly impressed by his employer and was therefore quite talkative, had been the only source of information they had.

Lord Bolton and Lord Nester had been sitting in the study, lightly sharing some jokes over a glass of port, when the Darlings rushed through the door. When Rake looked into Lord Bolton's gloating eyes, his mind went blank and his fist had landed firmly on the man's aristocratically straight nose and forever changed its appearance.

After that satisfaction, he couldn't really remember what he had done, not until he stood over the bed where Penny lay outstretched, her arms and legs tied to the bedposts in preparation for the evil man to have his way with her.

When Rake entered the room, she turned her head away and refused to look at him, which he was thankful for at the time, as he cried the whole time he was unfastening the ropes around her hands and feet.

His brothers had been just as angry as him, although their anger seemed to end as soon as they left the Bolton townhouse behind them with Penny secure in Rake's arms.

But Rake couldn't stop the anger which raged through him. As he stood by Penny's bed in the Darling townhouse and looked at her stiff back under the covers, all that was visible of her now that she was tucked in, he could hardly breathe because his chest hurt so much.

Seething anger was eating him up from inside out, and he knew he soon wouldn't be able to control it. The anger he felt toward her selfish father and that bastard Lord Bolton was nothing to the anger he felt toward Penny for denying him the truth.

What her father had done to her was beyond him. How could anyone so coldly and without remorse give away his daughter to a man as cruel and vicious as Lord Bolton? Those two, he was told, had known each other since their childhood days, and Lord Nester must have been aware of—or at least had an idea of—what Penny would live through when he had given her to his friend.

That men like Lord Bolton existed was no news to Rake. He had heard rumors about satanic men who could perform sexually only if there was pain involved. But he had never heard Lord Bolton's name mentioned. As a matter of fact, he had never met the man before, which also was kind of strange, as Rake always had spent the months of the Season socializing as much as possible.

"Go away." Her fragile voice broke through his thoughts, even though it was only a shadow of a whisper.

"I will."

But he didn't do as he said. Instead he stayed, not able to move because of all the answers he desperately needed and only she could give.

"Please, Rake, just go away."

He heard the tears in her voice, and for a second

his heart softened toward her, but the rage inside him quickly hardened his heart again. This was not the time to leave her alone, not the time for her to deal alone with what had happened. He had done that once before, and it had been six months in hell for both of them.

"Why didn't you tell me?"

He saw her back stiffen more over his harsh question, but she stayed quiet, as if she thought he would go away if she refused to oblige him. It didn't matter, though, as he could wait the whole night for her to come clean with him if he had to.

This time he was going to get her to speak the truth, no matter what.

"*Why* didn't you tell *me*?" he repeated his question, and the anger he felt was clearly audible in his clipped voice.

"I can't deal with this right now," she cried and curled her body into a small ball as if trying to save herself from him. "Please, just leave me alone."

"I will leave you for as long as you like, but not until you have told me everything I want to know. Everything I deserve to know."

Finally he got some response from her, as she suddenly sat up in the bed and turned to stare at him with tears and confusion in her violet eyes.

"You think you deserve to know everything about me? Why?"

"Because I do."

"It's not for you to know about. I chose not to talk about what happened because it hurt me too much every time I did, as I had to relive it over and over again. I didn't want to tell you then, and I definitely don't want to talk about it with you now."

"You told Thomas Bedford."

She snorted angrily, as the weepy martyr faded away and the stubborn young woman started to return. "I see. Thomas. He's what this is all about. Why on earth shouldn't I have told Thomas what I had been through? He proposed to me, remember? How could I accept him without letting him know why I was living at Chester Park and why I was alienated from my parents?"

"You are mine."

"I'm not!"

"Yes, you are. You love me, remember?"

She leaned back into the bed with her arms crossed over her chest. "Of course I remember, but that has nothing to do with this. Nothing!"

"It has everything to do with this. You say you love me, but how can I believe you when you don't trust me at all?"

"What are you talking about? Of course I trust you. I always have and always will."

He shook his head with a wry smile. "No, you don't. You don't trust me, and you certainly don't believe in me."

"Rake…"

Her voice trailed off, and she hid her face against her knees. He sat on the bed beside her and softened his voice as much as he could.

"Why didn't you tell me?"

At first he thought she wasn't going to answer, but just as he was going to force her to look at him, her head moved and he met her sad eyes.

"Because I was so embarrassed."

Of all the answers he had thought she could

possibly give him, this had not been on his list.

"Embarrassed?" His voice cracked with the strain of the emotional storm building inside him.

"H-how could I tell you how unwanted I-I was? My father gave me away, Rake. He left me in the hands of a man who wanted nothing more than to hurt me. How could I tell you that? How could I let you know how unwanted I really am?"

"All I wanted was the truth." He closed his eyes to hold back the tears which threatened to burst forward again, and he felt her hand lightly—almost hesitantly— touch his arm.

"All I wanted was you."

She leaned her forehead against his shoulder as she whispered her confession on a ragged breath. The rage inside him wasn't mellowing. Instead it increased with every word she uttered, and he knew he had to get away from her if he was ever going to be able to face her again.

Not caring about her gentle touch, he stood up and ignored her shivering confusion. "This can't go on, Penny. We can't continue like this. I'm leaving now. I can't handle this anymore. Not like this."

And without another word or glance in her direction he walked out, ignoring the crowd of Darlings standing outside the open door to overhear every heartbreaking word.

"Rake…" Jamie put a hand on his arm as he passed, but he only shrugged it off. He didn't need his twin brother right now. Jamie too kept secrets from him, secrets about what he had endured during his time in France, and Rake had had it with half-truths and self-destructive silence.

Downstairs, he sent for his phaeton and after grabbing a jacket from the closet he walked out through the front door.

As soon as the carriage arrived, he jumped up into it and, without looking back, he left his home and everyone he loved.

Chapter Eighteen

"Don't you think it's time for you to admit you have been handling the whole Rake situation quite badly?"

Penny looked up from the charming baby she held in her arms and frowned at Francesca.

"I have not."

"Come on, Penny. You have been nothing but against him ever since he finally woke up and realized you had turned into a beautiful woman and no longer saw you as an annoying little sister."

"I have not!"

"Oh, yes, you have," Devlin commented.

Francesca glared at her interfering husband. "If we want your opinion we will ask for it. Now, please give me my daughter before you leave."

Devlin ignored his wife and looked down at their lovely little child resting sweetly in his arms, and the smile on his face was filled with fatherly love and pride.

"Isn't she pretty?"

Penny laughed and nodded in full agreement. "Immensely so. I never thought a man could look so silly in love with a newborn girl."

"I heard that."

"Please ignore him. I do."

The little one Penny held whimpered lightly and

she rocked her arms slowly until the little sweetheart slept again. Penny hid her nose in the baby's hair, thoroughly enjoying that special smell only babies had.

"I can hardly believe I'm a mother now," Francesca said softly, and Penny looked up at her friend, who stared down with awe at the third of the triplets she held. "These three little girls are only three weeks old, and I can hardly believe how much I have come to love them during this short period. It's such an amazing feeling, Penny, I can hardly explain it. Nothing matters more than Iris, Lily, and Rose. Nothing."

"I'm devastated," Devlin drawled. "Truly devastated."

Penny felt a prick of envy as she watched the new parents share a look which told her all about how much they loved each other and how the three little girls—the masterpiece of their love—had brought them even closer together.

This was what she had longed for her whole life, this family life her beloved friend shared with her husband and their babies in their magnificent home. Again she put her nose to Iris's hair to hide the tears which threatened to fill her eyes.

"He will come."

Penny sighed. For being a worn-out mother of three, Francesca still didn't miss much. "Of course he will come. His favorite niece and his best friend have had three daughters. Rake wouldn't miss it for the world."

"And that's when the mere presence of you will make him realize what he's been hiding from, and he will wake up from whatever stupid thoughts he has been having over the last months."

"You're such a romantic, Fanny." Penny couldn't help but laugh over her friend's innocence. "It will never happen. He told me he was through with me, remember?"

"I'm sure you misunderstood him. You have been quite good at that, you know."

Penny sighed, recognizing the truth in her friend's words. "I know. I haven't been very good at listening to him, I'm afraid. But then he hasn't really been understanding of me, either. I have more or less begged him to admit to me that he loves me, but it's been useless. And now I've lost him."

"I wouldn't say you have lost him," Devlin said with a wink, ignoring his wife's frustrated sigh over his interference. Again. "You do know exactly where he is, so you could seek him out if you wanted to."

"Is he still staying at Gentleman Jackson's, pounding away on whoever dares to face him in the boxing ring?" Francesca asked her husband, and he nodded.

"Yes. Still staying with John and mauling whoever feels obliged to accommodate him. I don't know what's bothering him, but Jamie said Rake was angrier than he's ever known him and had so many bruises his skin was almost blue. He refused to talk to his twin, whom he usually shares everything with, and in the end Jamie had to knock him down to be able to make him listen to his news about our babies."

"But he did promise to come?"

"Yes, he did. He just had some things to do first, so Jamie had no choice but to leave him behind, as he wanted to come here to Pendragon as fast as possible."

"It's been two months now since he rescued you.

Why is he still acting like an avenging idiot?" Francesca glared at Penny, who rolled her eyes over her friend's inability to let a subject go.

"I have told you at least twenty times since we arrived last week that I don't know. He wasn't interested in enlightening me regarding his feelings. All he wanted was to know was why I kept him on the outside regarding my first encounter with Lord Bolton."

"And you told him?"

"As I have told you before, yes, I did. And then he left me."

"What did he say when he left?"

Before Penny had a chance to reply, Devlin sighed loudly enough that little Lily in his arms opened her golden eyes and stared up into her father's face. "We have heard poor Auntie Penny repeat those words a hundred times by now. Yes, we have. And we think she doesn't need to recite them to you again. No, she doesn't."

Francesca's smile toward her husband was a strange mixture of exasperation and adoration, and Penny couldn't hold back a giggle. Who would have thought the untouchable Duke of Hereford would turn into such a softhearted father?

Clearly not Francesca. She had admitted to Penny he drove her crazy sometimes, as he was constantly hovering around the girls, watching with hawk eyes everyone who came too close to them.

"I am glad he loves them as much as he does, but honestly, sometimes I wish he would spend a little more time with the supervisor of Pendragon, Mr. Brown, as he used to do before the girls were born. With three small babies, I need some peace and quiet, and having a lovesick father standing in the way as soon as any one of them makes a sound can get a bit frustrating," she had whined when the two friends were alone, and Penny had fought hard not to let Francesca know how hilarious she found her.

"Time for the young ones to get their daily bath," Nell said as she stepped into the room, followed by her two assisting maids.

Reluctantly Penny gave little Iris to one of the maids and watched them all disappear out through the door again with the babies.

"I think I'll have to make sure they find their way to the nursery," Devlin mumbled with a worried frown, and before Francesca or Penny had a chance to react he had left the two friends alone.

"It's just three doors down," his lovely wife called after him before she stood with a groan and went to close door behind him. "And now we are alone. Finally. I thought he would never leave."

"How are you?"

"A bit sore yet, thank you, but giving birth to three babies in a row does that to a woman. Next time I hope it will be only one."

"Next time?" Penny asked, amused.

Francesca shrugged in her dainty way. "Give me a month or two, and then I think I'm ready to get pregnant again. Unfortunately, I have quite some work ahead of me to convince Devlin to ever touch me in that way again, as the girls' birth made him swear an oath to everyone he met that he would never give in to his manly needs again. As if he ever could withstand me…"

They giggled together in perfect harmony as they

had done so many times before, and Penny felt a sudden sadness over how everything had changed during the last year. Last Christmas they had spent together in Berkshire, dreaming about their upcoming Season and, more importantly, the men of their dreams they were about to meet.

Francesca had had her dream come true, after a few bumps in the road, and was now married to the man she had dreamt about her whole life. For Penny it seemed the story would end differently, as the man she had been in love with for as long as she could remember refused to face her, and she didn't know how she ever would be able to reach him.

Where had it all gone wrong? She didn't know, but she regretted every harsh word she had told him. If he loved her as much as she hoped for, he must have had the worst time of his life the last couple of months. She had practically walked all over him while waiting for him to stand up and be that special someone she'd always dreamt him to be.

Why had it never dawned on her that he already was the man of her dreams? *He* was the one she had fallen in love with, including all his good and bad sides, not the strange version of him she had always met in her vivid daydreams.

He wasn't a chaste, poetry-reciting knight in shining armor who declared himself dying because he loved her so much. He was a man of flesh and blood who grinned through life in amusement, flirted outrageously with every woman he met, and who never, ever, would back down if someone he held dear needed him.

When he left her after his rescuing act at Lord

Bolton's, she had been more humiliated than ever. She had asked herself over and over again why she had admitted how ashamed she was for what had happened, and not until a week later did she realize he hadn't laughed at her at all, as she had assumed he would.

The only thing he had asked for was the truth.

Thinking about it, she realized he had never asked her for much at all over the last year. All he had wanted was to be near her, to kiss her, to touch her, to be with her.

It was she who had been desperate for more.

"Tell me why you want me."

Why? Why had she been so hard on him? The poor man had done everything he could think off to show her how much she meant to him, and all she had done was to wag her finger at him and demand him to answer her, without actually asking a question.

He wasn't the one to blame for all this.

She was.

No wonder he spent his days boxing. She would have wanted to hurt someone too, if he had behaved as she had.

"I still hope you will become my aunt," Francesca said, and Penny laughed.

"You do, do you?"

"Better you being my aunt by marriage than your sister being my sister by marriage. I still can't believe Sin has married Charmaine. It's beyond me whatever possessed him to throw himself onto her in her bed, of all places. Of course he had to marry her when Mother and Father walked in on them."

"It's not like Charmaine, either. I didn't even know she fancied Sin. She has never mentioned him much at all, other than dancing with him now and then."

"What a night that must have been," Francesca said slowly. "You being abducted by your father and then rescued by Rake. Only to later be abandoned by him in front of most of our family in quite a harsh way. And then my poor parents, who sent Sin up with your sister, who was fatigued from having to save you, only to find him fondling her in her bed."

Penny shook her head. Francesca was right about it. There was something strange about the whole Sin-and-Charmaine situation. Both that it had happened and how oddly they behaved toward each other now, after his parents insisted they marry, with a special license.

"It's like they hate each other, wouldn't you say? She can hardly look upon him, and he sneers as soon as she opens her mouth, which has rendered her a silent shadow of her former glorious self. I actually find myself feeling sorry for her, and you know how much I have disliked her through the years."

"I know. But poor Charmaine never had a chance against you."

Francesca grinned sheepishly. "I guess you're right. I'll have to try to reach out to her. She must feel a bit lonely here at Pendragon. Sin dragged her with him against her will, and everyone else has been avoiding her as much as possible."

"I think she would like to have a friend."

"Has she spoken to you yet?"

Penny sighed. "No, she hasn't. The strange thing is that I can see she wants to, but it's like she doesn't know where to begin. I'm her sister, for goodness' sake. It shouldn't be so bloody hard for her to talk to me, should it?"

Francesca did a little grimace as she shook her head. "No, it shouldn't. I must say I'm most curious about what happened. I have tried to talk to Sin, but he just growls at me if I mention her name or the word 'wife.' "

They sighed deeply, in chorus, before bursting out in giggles, as they had often done all through their lives.

A little later, Penny sneaked out the door after her friend had fallen asleep in a much-needed nap. She felt much more content and levelheaded than she had for a long time. To have finally admitted her faults made her feel surprisingly strong, and she knew she couldn't let Rake destroy their chance of happiness. Pondering the problem ahead, she went to her place of sanctuary, the glorious and dust-free Pendragon library. There she slowly let her finger move over the books on the shelves, but her mind was elsewhere.

A sudden memory of another time in another library came to her. Last Christmas she had celebrated with the Darling family at Chester Park, and she had, as always, denied Rake every chance to get closer to her. But that last day, before she left for Harveyfield again, they had happened to meet in the library, where she was reading a travel journal about Gretna Green, and Rake had made her promise never to elope there.

Or—what was it he had said?

Hadn't he made her promise to never elope to Gretna Green *without telling him*, so he could save her by marrying her himself?

A little smile started to grow on her lips and she couldn't hold back a giddy laugh. Her head was already spinning with plans, because now she knew what she should do. Now she knew how to get his attention.

She was going to elope.

And, as the thoughtful person she was, she would fulfill the promise she'd made him and inform him. He was an intelligent man and he would get the hidden message.

Whether he would choose to act upon it was another thing. Maybe she had dallied too long and lost him forever. She didn't know, but she had to try.

Determined, she dashed up the stairs and had a maid show her what room her sister stayed in.

Charmaine's eyes were unusually puffy when she opened the door at Penny's knock, but there was no time to care about that now. She needed someone to escort her to Gretna Green. Preferably someone married, so her journey wouldn't brew a scandal, and who better than her very married—although unhappily so—sister?

"Pack your things, we are going to Scotland."

"W-what?" Charmaine stared at her blankly.

"You, sister dear," Penny said, and poked Charmaine in the chest, "you are going to help me make my dream come true."

"I-I don't understand."

"We are eloping!"

"You and I?"

"Yes. Or no. Or…" Penny sighed, frustrated. "We are going to Gretna Green, which will force Rake to finally stop his fighting and decide what to do about me."

"But we can't go by ourselves."

"Of course we can. You are a married lady now, and as such you can escort your poor unmarried sister wherever you, or I, want to go."

"Oh. I didn't think about that. I keep forgetting that I'm married, that Si-'"—she took a deep breath—"that Sin is now my husband."

"Why did you marry him?"

Charmaine sighed deeply. "I had no choice."

"Of course you had. You could have told him to leave your room, before he had a chance to get in bed with you."

The blush which crept over Charmaine's peachy cheeks was quite telling, and Penny frowned with distress. "Or was it you who…"

As her sister turned even redder, Penny had her answer. "Bloody hell, Charmaine! It was you who forced this marriage, not he. Why? What on earth possessed you to do such a thing? And why Sin? Of all people in the world, why did you have to choose Sin? No wonder he keeps looking at you like something the cat dragged in. He must think you are the worst person possible."

"I had no choice."

"Everyone has a choice."

Charmaine shook her head. "I didn't."

"Well, I haven't time for this conversation right now, but as soon as we sit in that carriage heading north, you are going to tell me every little detail."

Charmaine nodded in defeat. There was no way for her to escape. "When are we leaving?"

Before Penny had a chance to answer, a cold voice was heard from the doorway. "You are not going anywhere."

The two sisters whirled to meet the eyes of a furious Sinclair Darling.

Charmaine stiffened, and Penny couldn't help but

feel sad for the situation her sister had put herself in.

"Please, Sin." Penny took a step closer to him in an effort to catch his attention, but his eyes, just as smoky grey as Rake's, never left Charmaine's face. "I need to go to Scotland and have asked Charmaine to accompany me. I can't go by myself, but she can take me."

"No. She's staying right here."

Penny went to him and put her hand on his arm, forcing him gently to turn his gaze from his wife and instead focus on her. For a second she hesitated, as she had never met this Sin before. Normally he was nothing unordinary at all, a well-built, well-behaved man, as handsome as the next one and burdened by the responsibilities of his heritage.

But the Sin who looked down at her was not ordinary at all. He oozed manly anger and she could sense he was indeed an attractive man, someone for any woman to fall in love with.

"Please," Penny repeated. "I *have* to go."

She saw the coldness in his eyes fade away, and his face seemed less carved in stone as he softened toward her. He had always been like an older brother to her, and she knew he held her in quite high esteem, something she was going to use now. She had to, for her own happiness' sake.

"I can't ask anyone else, because I don't want it commonly known why I'm going. But Charmaine is my sister, my confidante, and I need her. Please."

"Why Scotland?"

"Because that's where Gretna Green is located."

Sin chuckled, amused against his will. "Are you eloping all by yourself?"

"Yes. As a matter of fact I am."

"Why?"

She gave him an impatient look. "It's not necessary for you to know why. Just give me your approval to bring my sister with me as my chaperone."

The coldness came back into Sin's eyes as he glanced toward his wife, who stood beside her bed, head bent and face hidden. "I wouldn't trust her as a chaperone if I were you. She's without scruples and wouldn't think twice about using you if she had to."

"She's my sister."

"She's my bloody wife," Sin sneered, unable to hold back his contempt.

Penny didn't know what to say. She had never seen the usually levelheaded Sin this angry. He was practically seething with rage, and it was all directed toward Charmaine.

The memory of another man, who had stared at her with the same kind of rage, came to her. Rake too had been furious with her, but in her heart she knew it came out of love. He would never have been so angry with her if he hadn't cared for her, and she couldn't help but wonder if this was true for Sin, too.

So maybe Charmaine had snared him into marrying her. It still shouldn't have brought out this kind of anger from him. It wasn't as if he had been engaged to another woman. He had been a quite confirmed bachelor, only interested in the caretaking of the family estate, being the heir to the dukedom as he was.

In a couple of years he would undoubtedly have been searching for a wife anyway, as Sin was a good son who knew his duties. Instead, he found himself forced by his own parents to marry this incomparable queen of the *ton*, the woman of every other man's dreams, without having anything to say about it. Penny knew he had always had a good eye to her sister, something he had admitted to her more than once, preferably in front of Francesca, as it always vexed her a bit. Francesca had never been particularly impressed by Charmaine.

So what had Charmaine done to make him loathe her like this?

"Is it important to you?" Sin interrupted her thoughts, and she nodded solemnly.

"Yes."

"Has it to do with Uncle Rake?"

"Yes."

Sin sighed. "All right, then. But I'm going with you. I don't trust her to do rightly for you, especially not if you get caught in some situation she doesn't know how to solve."

"Sinclair Darling!" Charmaine gasped, flustered. "Penny is my sister, and I would never do anything to harm her. Here I have spent most of my life trying to save her, so why should I do anything to harm her now, when she is almost safe?"

Penny frowned toward her sister. Whatever did Charmaine mean? Saving her? It made no sense, as Charmaine had not been around Penny much at all, always too busy with herself, surrounded by their parents and any available servants.

Charmaine must have realized she had said too much, and she clamped her mouth shut, ignoring Sin's probing gaze and Penny's confusion.

"Well, then," Sin said, with one last glance toward his wife, "why don't we all go and pack our things, so we can leave first thing in the morning. I'll go talk to Fanny, and hopefully she won't be too upset about it. It is, after all, for the greater good."

"Greater good?" Penny laughed at his choice of words. "Am I now a charity, of sorts?"

"Not at all. But it will bring the whole family to peace if you and Uncle Rake finally make up and do what you have been supposed to do from the beginning—live happily ever after."

Penny felt almost lighthearted as she left her sister's bedroom. She could hardly believe she would have closure at last on the whole Rake affair. Soon she would know if he loved her as much as she thought he did, and then they would, as Sin with such extraordinary insight had just said, live happily ever after.

She had never had a dream come true, but if everything worked out as she wished, soon she would have.

Chapter Nineteen

"I dare say every eligible bachelor of south Scotland is present tonight," Miss Lydia Woodley exclaimed with as much happiness as a well-behaved daughter of a local country squire dared to express in the company of others as she stared starry-eyed into the fashionable crowd surrounding them.

The Assembly Rooms in Gretna Green were filled to the brim with ladies and gentlemen who had come to socialize with their peers, to dance, to laugh, and to flirt at the annual January Ball.

"I think I have to agree with you," Penny said as she looked around, somewhat amazed at how many people were present. "I thought the weekly Tuesday dance was well attended, but this is entirely something else. There must be a couple of hundred here, instead of the normal fifty or so."

After spending almost a month in the little town, Penny had started to recognize some of the faces who attended the same functions she was invited to, but tonight those faces had disappeared in the teeming, colorful crowd.

"Oh, look," Lydia breathed happily, as she nodded toward a stylish and handsome man who stood causally by the entrance door looking out on the crowd with the most perfect bored expression. "Lord Elmsley has arrived! Oh, I can hardly believe he's actually here. He is the most handsome man I know, and I have dreamt about this ever since I met him for the first time."

Penny nodded, trying to look as impressed as Lydia seemed to want, but she found the man of Lydia's dreams to look just like any other gentleman she met: nothing out of the ordinary. No amused smoky eyes, no patronizingly arched eyebrow, and no wicked grin.

Poor Lord Elmsley. Here he was, the most sought-after bachelor of this part of the country, and she didn't find him the least attractive. But, fortunately for him, Lydia did.

That kind young woman, whom Penny had met during her first week in Gretna Green, had immediately taken her under her wing and introduced her to the life and the people of her little rural town.

Charmaine, who found the effervescent Lydia a bit tiresome but not as tiresome as spending time alone with Penny, was more than happy to act the role of companion on different outings. Lydia declared frequently that for her it was heaven on earth to suddenly have a new friend who came with the perfect chaperone for daily trips, and she seemed to have a never-ending list of must-see places and must-visit people.

All in all, the days and the weeks had passed quite quickly and Penny had not had too much time to think about Rake during the daytime. But in the solitude of the night, when she lay alone in her bed, she couldn't think about anything but him, and even her dreams were filled with him.

"You are the most understanding friend I have, when it comes to Lord Elmsley," Lydia had admitted earlier while waiting for his arrival. "Everyone else thinks I'm daft to dream about him, even my sisters do, as they find me quite uninteresting compared to the other unmarried ladies. But you don't, which makes me think you too know how it is to love someone who is quite unapproachable."

"I too have a man of my dreams," Penny had said, not able to keep the emotion out of her shaking voice. "I spend every day, every hour, and every minute longing for him, wishing for him to come here and fulfill my heart's boldest wish."

Lydia had given her a radiant you-and-I smile, and Penny had hugged her new friend tightly. In some strange way it felt good to have someone who was going through the same thing and who understood how she felt. Charmaine was trying hard to be understanding and supportive, but she had her sudden marriage with the brooding Sin to handle, which drained the energy out of her.

As if on cue, her sister, beautiful as ever in a vivid blue dress, joined them with three glasses of a suspect greenish liquid and handed Penny and Lydia one each.

"Are you sure it's lemon?" Penny asked with a grimace and took a sip of the vile fluid, the only thing being served during the evening.

Charmaine frowned down into her glass. "I think so. I'm sure I tasted a hint of lemon last Tuesday when I had a glass."

"If I'm going to come here one more Tuesday to have one more glass of this, I'm going to turn into a prune or something else as wrinkly. Lord, it's vile."

Lydia, who must have felt the need to defend her hometown's refreshments, took a big sip.

"It's not so bad," she declared through her pursed

lips. "It's actually quite refreshing."

Charmaine couldn't help but laugh, and immediately the surrounding men took a step closer to them. Even Lord Elmsley's gaze stopped roaming for a second, taking in the radiant beauty, and an appreciative little smile started to play on his lips.

"Oh, he's coming here!" Lydia seemed close to fainting, and she took deep breaths to calm herself. Penny patted her hands.

"I told you Charmaine is like a jar of honey to a bear: men can't withstand her, and they come running."

"I beg your pardon?" Charmaine said, profoundly offended, but Penny ignored her sister's outburst.

"It's even better now she's married, because she's off the maybe-wife list, and instead you will stand next in line to be courted."

"Or you." Lydia breathed, as Lord Elmsley closed in on them. "You are much prettier than I am. If he has to choose between the two of us, he will most certainly choose you. I know I would."

"Then we will make sure he chooses you."

Charmaine rolled her eyes at them before she turned toward the man who stopped in front of her with an elegant bow. "Lady Chilton."

"Lord Elmsley. How nice to meet you again. Let me introduce my sister, Lady Penelope de Vere, and her friend, Miss Lydia Woodley."

Lord Elmsley nodded coldly to Lydia before he bent his head over Penny's hand and gave it a peck that came served with a lecherous glance from his blue eyes.

Oh, he was a libertine, all right, and if she hadn't been too caught up in Rake's web, her heart might have fluttered just a little in response. But as it was now, she only gave him an indifferent half-smile which made him frown a bit at her. He obviously wasn't used to being met this coldly by a young miss.

"Lady Chilton, would you mind if I borrowed your sister for the next dance? It would be an honor for me."

"Oh, the honor would be hers, I guarantee you," Charmaine soothed him. "But unfortunately my sister will have to decline, as she has already promised my husband this dance."

"I'm sad to hear this. Then maybe you would do me the honor?"

Charmaine declined most elegantly. "I already promised this one to our host. But Lydia here is, amazingly enough, still available."

Lord Elmsley's smile faded as he shot a fast look at the blushing maiden, and it wasn't too hard to see he had no difficulty understanding why she wasn't spoken for. As the gentleman he was, he couldn't deny Charmaine her offer, and with a forced smile he held out his hand toward Lydia, who breathlessly let him lead her out onto the dance floor.

"We have to find Sin," Charmaine said as the couple disappeared into the crowd. "He will have to remove himself from the gambling tables long enough to dance with you."

"I can sit this one out."

"No. You. Will. Not."

Knowing too well there was no point in trying to revolt against Charmaine when she used that particular tone, Penny let her sister take the lead in the hunt for her unaware dance partner.

Sin left the gambling tables with a disappointed sigh. "I guess I have no say in this?"

"None." Charmaine's voice was cold as ice. "Penny needs you to dance with her."

"For Penny I'll do anything." Sin said, just as icily, and Penny sighed. Those two were never going to have their happy ending if they didn't get over their differences soon. So Charmaine had in some way lured Sin into marrying her. So what?

It wasn't as if he had married a complete scarecrow, after all. Charmaine was every man's dream. Unfortunately, it seemed she was the dream of every *other* man but Sin.

Penny could only hope the two of them would find a way out of this coldness between them, and as soon as Charmaine couldn't hear them she told him so.

"You could be a bit nicer to her."

"Why?" Sin snorted. "She's not worth it."

"You don't know that."

"I know exactly what she is like, so let us leave it at that."

She shook her head sadly. "After the first week here I thought the two of you were warming up to each other, you seemed almost happy together for a while. But lately you have been behaving as if you were deadly enemies. What happened?"

"Nothing."

"Nothing?"

He sighed. "Please, Penny. Leave it be."

She couldn't continue when he so directly asked her not to, and she nodded, resigned. "All right. But just think of one thing—your marriage is for the rest of your lives. Is this hatred between the two of you what you want to live with?"

"It's not hatred. It's more disappointment, I would

say. And no, this is not what I want in my marriage. But your sister is quite a handful, and not so easy to get through to sometimes."

"Tell me about it." Penny sighed, and Sin chuckled.

"I guess you should know, my dearest little sister by marriage."

They shared a loving smile, feeling the bond of sibling-hood between them, even though they were not blood relatives. But she had practically grown up beside him, and the bond was still there and had only become stronger by his marriage to her sister.

"I'm sorry to be the one saying this, but we can't stay on much longer. Duty calls, you know."

"I know." She sighed, defeated, unable to hide the overwhelming sadness filling her heart. "We have been here for a month now, and he still hasn't shown. I guess I must soon admit the truth—he doesn't want me."

"Maybe he never got the message?"

"Of course he did. He would never stay away from Pendragon knowing his best friend and his niece had their first babies, and Fanny promised to make sure he got the hint about me going to Gretna Green, so he could save me, even if she would have to spell it out to him."

"It's strange, though, him not showing up yet. We all know how much he cares for you, and to not come here for you… It doesn't make sense."

Penny wished she had the same confidence regarding Rake's feelings toward her. But the more time passed, the more her sureness faltered, and now she was beginning to believe he would never love her.

She sighed heavily as the dance ended, and Sin

laughed as he grabbed her hand. "You are pathetic."

"I know I am, and I apologize. But do you know what? I think you'd better get used to it, because soon you will have to see me get more and more pathetic every day, for the rest of my pathetic life."

"Are you trying to prepare yourself for a life as a spinster?"

She giggled as he gave her a look of exaggerated shock, and she whacked him on the shoulder in a sisterly fashion. "Behave, you vile monster. You should ease up on the laughter and instead consider how dark life will seem for you from now on."

"Oh, really?" Sin laughed. "You can't scare me. There's no way you, my dear little Penny, could make my life into bloody hell."

"Don't tempt me," she said between her teeth, together with her best version of an angry glare.

"You keep forgetting I'm not so easily scared," Sin said as he halted at an empty sofa in the corner of the ballroom, where Charmaine's maid stood, looking extremely uncomfortable. "I'm married to your sister, remember."

"Are you now?" Penny tried her best to look just as wickedly amused as Rake in his best days. "And yet you seem to have no problem with her being surrounded by lecherous men, who all want her to admit to being lonely and to let them entertain her while her husband does his best to ignore her."

Sin's eyes darkened as he turned around and looked at his wife who, as Penny had said, was outrageously outnumbered by men who each wanted nothing more than to become her latest lover.

When he hesitated, she rolled her eyes toward his

back. "You have to choose, Sin. Either you care or you don't care. What you can't do is stand at the side and watch your chance for marital happiness walk out the door on another man's arm. I know Charmaine, and she's pretty upset with you and feels quite abandoned. I'm a bit afraid she soon will do something drastic to catch your attention, and as she's not as smart as I am she will probably put herself in a situation she can't control."

Without looking back, Sin barged across the dance floor, and Penny giggled as he without mercy grabbed his wife's hand and hauled her away out through the front door. Charmaine's expression was a funny mix of surprise and expectation, and Penny wished them all the luck possible. They were both too good to be avoiding each other as they did.

"Your sister is a happy woman," Lydia said as she sank down in the sofa beside Penny. "It must be wonderful to have someone who loves you as much as her husband obviously does."

"You think?" Penny lit up.

"Of course he does." Lydia snorted. "Even a child can see he is crazy in love with her."

What an uplifting thought, if it were true. Sin in love with Charmaine made it possible for a much better ending for that married couple than Penny had hoped for earlier.

"If only Lord Elmsley would look at me with a fraction of that love, I would die happy." Lydia sighed. "But I'm afraid he's stubbornly refusing to see my potential as a possible wife. He practically threw me toward you before scurrying away in the opposite direction."

"One day, perhaps?"

Lydia sighed again. "Perhaps. But to be completely honest with you, it will probably never happen. He just doesn't seem to understand we are made for each other."

Her smile was filled with self-humor, and Penny couldn't help wishing Lydia would get her heart's desire and end up as Lady Elmsley. She was such a wonderful friend and deserved to be happy.

"But then again, I wouldn't mind not becoming Lady Elmsley if *that* man became mine."

Lydia sounded almost breathless and without second thought Penny turned and looked in the same direction her friend was staring—and forget to breathe too.

There, in the middle of the ballroom, looking more fashionably handsome than ever, stood Rake in perfect splendor.

With an amused arched eyebrow, he took in the gaping crowd with his usual wicked smile, searching the awed faces for one special one: hers.

"Who is that?" Lydia whispered beside her.

Penny took a deep, shaky breath. "That is the man of *my* dreams."

"Oh, goodness me. I must admit I do understand you wanting him. Lord Elmsley is nothing compared to him. Nothing."

Penny couldn't agree more, and as she stood up she knew no one was anything compared to the man who stood there silently searching for her. That wonderful, sarcastic, loving libertine was one of a kind, and what was even more perfect was that he was all hers.

With a whimper that came from the depths of her

soul, she started toward him. As if he could feel her presence, he tensed slightly before turning toward her and nailing her with his dark eyes.

The crowd, which seemed to sense something extraordinary was happening, moved back and let Penny pass without obstacles, and in the end she couldn't contain herself. Without caring about her outrageous behavior, she ran and threw herself into Rake's waiting arms, flinging her arms around his neck and burying her face deep into the crook of his neck.

His arms moved around her waist and hugged her closely to him. She could feel his hands shaking as they stroked her back hesitantly, as if he hardly could believe she finally was there, where she belonged, in his arms. She tightened her grip around his neck and heard him chuckle in response.

"Penny, my love, I want to live a long and prosperous life with you, so could you please let me breathe a little. Otherwise this happiness will have a fast and sad ending right here on the ballroom floor."

She loosened her grip slightly but still refused to let him go. She knew she was acting scandalously, but she didn't care.

Rake had come, and nothing else mattered.

Without another word, he scooped her up into his arms and carried her through the still-gaping crowd, not stopping until he'd found an empty room where they could be alone, without an audience.

"I might be a bit presumptuous," he said, as he put her feet on the floor again, "but I do get the distinct feeling you are a bit happy to see me."

His amused voice, trembling with emotion, brought tears to her eyes, and she was unable to hold them back.

Her heart felt ready to explode out of sheer happiness.

"I am," she whispered into his neck.

"Are you *crying*?"

"No."

He laughed and forced her head back so he could look into her teary eyes. "Oh, yes, you are."

"A little, maybe."

He smiled into her eyes with all the love in his heart and without the usual wickedness, and she felt wrapped in a soft blanket of happiness, as her tears continued to flow.

"You know, a man with less confidence than I have would start to wonder by now if you really are happy or sad to see me."

She giggled and loosened her hold on him. "Let us be thankful, then, for you being such a confident man."

"I still have to admit I do wonder."

His admittance of how insecure he felt made her heart ache. Had she really been such an ogre toward him, acting selfishly and without regard to his feelings?

She wiped the last tears away and looked up into his smoky eyes as she put a hand gently against his cheek.

"I love you."

"I know."

She rolled her eyes. "Why do you ask if I'm happy to see you, then?"

He let go of her and went to a small window, turning his back to her before he answered her. "Because it has never been enough for you before."

She frowned at him. "What has never been enough?"

"Love."

Lord, what had she done to this proud man in her silly hunt for confirmation? She felt almost nauseous as she looked at his stiff back where he stood by the window, hiding his face from her.

"I just want you."

"Are you sure?"

"That's all I ever wanted."

He turned around and looked at her directly with his dark eyes filled with the insecure emotions he couldn't control, and for the first time she noticed how tired he looked, how dark the smudges were under his eyes.

"Is it really? Because that's not the impression I've gotten during the last year and a half."

"I'm so sorry," she whispered and took a hesitant step toward him. She stopped as she noticed how he stiffened even more. He wasn't ready to let bygones be bygones yet, but she knew she should be grateful he seemed finally willing to talk to her.

The funny thing was that now, when he was obliging her, all she wanted was for him to shut up and kiss her. She wanted, no *needed*, him to tell her with his mouth and his roaming hands exactly how much he loved her. Unfortunately, he had tried that for a year and a half and she hadn't listened to him once, had only been looking for verbal confirmation.

She looked at the closed door and the key in the keyhole, and an idea came to her from nowhere. She hid a smile from him as she slowly moved toward the door.

"Bloody hell, Penny, you can't leave me now!"

She ignored his frustrated outburst, and when she reached the door she locked it tightly before starting to unbutton her dress. She turned slowly and met his dark eyes, filled with pain and confusion.

With a secretive little smile she moved back toward him, with every step trying to show him how much she wanted him, and she saw him lose his breath for a moment.

"Penny…"

"Rake," she purred as she let the dress slip down her shoulders and end up on the floor in a cloud of expensive fabric. Clad only in her thin chemise and silky stockings, she stopped in front of him and lifted her hands to her hair. She removed all the pins, and the honey-colored mass tumbled down her back.

He staggered backwards.

"You don't know what you're doing."

"I don't?"

She let a finger follow the row of buttons in his jacket and felt his chest tremble as he took a shaky breath.

"No. You can't possibly understand what you are doing to me. Please stop, Penny, before I do something both you and I will regret later."

"Why will we regret it?"

He pushed her hand aside as it reached his chin, and she laughed huskily. He trembled even more.

"Because you want to talk, and if you don't stop this I can't do anything else but kiss you."

She moved forward until her mouth was only a breath away from his. "So why don't you shut up and kiss me?"

Her soft whisper slowly found its way into his head, and she watched his insecurity fade away as the smoldering heat returned to his eyes.

"Are you sure?" he asked hoarsely, still not believing what he had in front of him. Tired of waiting for him to get it right, she put her hands at the back of his neck and forced him to lean forward so she could press her soft lips against his and do what she had longed for every night and every day since they last met: she kissed him.

With a groan, he let his hands find their way over her body, and willingly she pressed herself against his palms, showing him without words how much she wanted him. Without ending their kiss, he removed his clothes piece by piece before hauling her closer to him and laying her down on the floor in the pile of delicate apparel.

"I love you so much," he whispered as he let his mouth leave hers and travel to her neck and the very spot he had talked about so long ago below her ear. "Promise to never let me go again."

"Never," she moaned, as his teeth gently bit her earlobe. "Never in this lifetime or the next."

With a tender kiss, he thrust deep into her, and she lost all ability to think or talk. All she could do was follow his steady pace, which in the end took them all the way to heaven and back.

"Shut up and kiss me?"

She looked up into his laughing eyes and stretched with a satisfied smile, feeling too content to care about his teasing. He shook his head and moved away from her slightly, lying next to her on the floor with his arms around her, pressing her body close to his as if afraid she would disappear if he let her go for even the tiniest of moments.

"I'm glad I came," he said softly against her ear,

and she couldn't stop another satisfied smile.

"Me too."

"I almost didn't."

Surprised, she turned her head and looked at his serious face. "Why not?"

"Because you made me feel inadequate."

She pressed her hand against his cheek gently as tears filled her eyes. "I'm so sorry for being so stupid."

"Not stupid." He smiled. "Only a bit simple-minded."

"Just a bit?"

"I'm trying to be nice here, so don't push me."

"I love you, Rake."

"I know."

A rustle at the door broke them apart as someone tried to get in, and they hurried to get dressed. There was no need to make the scandal worse than it was already.

As Rake opened the door, an angry footman burst into the room, yelling about their inconsideration, and laughingly they dashed from the Assembly Rooms and out into the street. Without a word, Rake immediately started toward the closest church, and Penny followed him closely with light steps.

Their wedding ceremony was simple and unemotional, but Penny cried all the way through. When the yawning priest finally blessed the newlyweds before leaving them alone, Rake sighed, relieved. She looked at him with a question in her eyes, and he grinned wickedly toward her.

"Well, I wasn't really sure this ever would happen, so please let me have a moment here rejoicing."

"Why didn't you just ask me?"

He raised an elegant eyebrow. "Ask you? I have practically begged you to marry me, and you haven't accepted me once."

"You have never asked me to marry you," she snorted, and when he looked at her in amazement she repeated her words. "You have never asked me."

"I have too."

"Not once. Not even today."

"I have told you more times than I can remember how much I want you."

"Yes, you have, but that's not the same thing as asking someone to marry you."

He chuckled as the truth hit him. "You mean you just wanted me to ask you to marry me?"

She nodded haughtily, not really caring anymore, although something inside of her still wanted him to understand what had led to all their misunderstandings.

"Leave it to a woman to complicate things."

"So asking me to marry you is to complicate things?"

He frowned slightly. "Well, when you put it like that…"

Suddenly he took her hands into his and looked down into her eyes with all the love he felt for her clearly visible.

"Lady Penelope de Vere, would you please do me the honor to become my wife, and by so turn me into the happiest man alive?"

She shook her head, and he grinned at her.

"No?"

"I'm sorry, I can't. I'm unfortunately already married to the love of my life."

"Thank God for that." He groaned as he hugged

her close and kissed her with all the heat in his heart, ignoring the fact that they still stood inside the church.

Penny didn't mind, though, as he soon lifted her and carried her outside, out into the dark street and into the dream that finally had come true.

Epilogue

It was said that a reformed libertine made the best of husbands and, as it turned out, that was perfectly true. Not one day had passed since that somewhat chaotic wedding day when Penny had felt any less loved or wanted.

Every day Rake without words showed her exactly how much he needed her in his life, and every day she told him in all the words she could think of how happy he made her.

"You two make me sick," Jamie groaned when he found them kissing on the terrace. "She's practically giving birth to your firstborn, and you still can't keep your lusty hands off her."

Rake grinned wickedly and, with a sorrowful sigh, let his hands leave Penny's breasts. "I can't help it. She was made for loving."

"In a bedroom, please, and preferably when she's not in labor."

"I asked him to make me think of something else," Penny admitted, to save her husband from his twin brother's teasing. "And he did."

"You are a lucky man, Rake. I can't think of any other woman who wants to make love while her body is torn apart by excruciating pain."

Rake paled considerably, and Penny glared at Jamie. "I finally made him calm down, and you had to make him all flustered again?"

Jamie blushed, as the truth hit him. "Sorry about that."

"Just go away."

With one last embarrassed look, Jamie left the married couple alone, and as Penny looked up into Rake's worried face she swore between her teeth, which effectively made him lose his breath.

"Are you in pain?"

"Not so badly," she lied.

"You are lying."

"Yes."

"Don't lie to me."

"I always lie to you."

"No, you don't. You are the most honest person I know, and you never lie."

She closed her eyes as a wave of pain tore through her body, and she could tell by his shaking hands trying to caress her gently that he was panicking.

"I have lied to you."

"Oh, really? Whenever could that have been?"

She opened her eyes, as the pain faded away again, and smiled. "When I said I was happy to find out I was carrying your baby."

He laughed softly at her joke, relieved that the pain was over for this time.

"I'm sorry."

She raised an eyebrow toward him. "For what?"

"For not being able to keep my hands off you."

"You wouldn't dare keep your hands off me, Lord Richard Darling."

He chuckled and put a chaste kiss on her forehead. "I can't, so you have nothing to worry about, my love."

When another contraction made her whimper with pain, he lifted her and carried her up to their bedroom, where he carefully put her down on the prepared bed.

As she lay there with her body working hard to get the product of their love out into the world, she couldn't help being thankful for the love he bestowed on her and for his making her feel she was the perfect woman, and between two contractions she told him so.

"Thank you for what?" he asked.

"For making my dream come true."

A word about the author...

Jennifer Wenn has been a great lover of romantic books since she read her first historical romance at a tender age. When not enjoying life with her husband and their four children, she spends every last precious minute writing.

You can read more about Jennifer at:
www.jenniferwenn.com